Praise for *The Secrets You Keep*

"True to form, Kate White's *The Secrets You Keep* kept me up way past my bedtime, anxiously turning the pages. Taut, tense, and utterly gripping, I could not go to sleep until I found out whodunit."

—Jessica Knoll, *New York Times* bestselling author of *Luckiest Girl Alive*

"Suspenseful, twisty, and sharply observed, Kate White's clever psychological thriller lures us into the life of vulnerable narrator Bryn whose marriage is not what she thought it was. The uncertainty develops as the stakes ramp up ever higher, and I was holding my breath as I turned the last few pages."

—Gilly Macmillan, *New York Times* bestselling author of *What She Knew*

Praise for *Eyes on You*

"Sharp as a stiletto!"

—Lisa Gardner, *New York Times* bestselling author

"I couldn't put it down."

—Lisa Scottoline, *New York Times* bestselling author

Such a Perfect Wife

ALSO BY KATE WHITE

FICTION

Even If It Kills Her

The Secrets You Keep

The Wrong Man

Eyes on You

So Pretty It Hurts

The Sixes

Hush

Lethally Blond

Over Her Dead Body

'Til Death Do Us Part

A Body to Die For

If Looks Could Kill

NONFICTION

The Gutsy Girl Handbook: Your Manifesto for Success

I Shouldn't Be Telling You This: How to Ask for the Money, Snag the Promotion, and Create the Career You Deserve

Why Good Girls Don't Get Ahead but Gutsy Girls Do

such a perfect wife

a novel

KATE WHITE

HARPER

An Imprint of HarperCollins*Publishers*

SUCH A PERFECT WIFE. Copyright © 2019 by Kate White. All rights reserved. Printed in the United States of America. No part of this book may be used or reproduced in any manner whatsoever without written permission except in the case of brief quotations embodied in critical articles and reviews. For information, address HarperCollins Publishers, 195 Broadway, New York, NY 10007.

HarperCollins books may be purchased for educational, business, or sales promotional use. For information, please email the Special Markets Department at SPsales@harpercollins.com.

FIRST EDITION

Designed by Jamie Lynn Kerner

Library of Congress Cataloging-in-Publication Data has been applied for.

ISBN 978-0-06-288626-2 (library edition)
ISBN 978-0-06-274749-5 (pbk.)

19 20 21 22 23 LSC 10 9 8 7 6 5 4 3 2 1

Such a Perfect Wife

PROLOGUE

S HE SENSES DANGER EVEN BEFORE SHE HEARS THE SOUND.
It's a gorgeous morning, cloudless and just cool
enough, perfect for a run. She left the house eager to be on
the road, especially after skipping the day before.

But it seems weirdly quiet to her, quieter than it should
be. The few houses she passes sit forlornly, their windows dark,
and so far she hasn't encountered a single car or cyclist. Just
up ahead there are woods on each side, and though the wind
is moving through the tree leaves—she can *see* it—she can't
hear the rustling. It's as if someone has turned off all the sound
today, except that of her footfalls on the blacktop. And her
breathing.

Her body feels off, too. She's been jogging for a mile, her
white T-shirt already damp with sweat, and it's usually by
this point that the endorphins have kicked in, or whatever
it is that creates that floating, free-form sense of calm and
elation she always runs to meet.

But elation hasn't happened. Rather, she feels a low-grade

unease, almost like a hum. An unexplainable instinct that she shouldn't be here on this road—this usually serene, peaceful place—at this exact moment in time.

I should turn back, she thinks. She's only done that once before, when she couldn't massage away a cramp in her calf muscle. She'd hobbled home, annoyed at herself for not having stretched enough beforehand, and held an ice pack to her leg. Within minutes the cramp had vanished and she'd deliberated going out again, but it seemed as if her chance had come and gone.

Yes, go home, she tells herself. Trust your gut. She'll run later, when people are home from work and out in their yards.

It's then that she hears the car come up behind her. She sidesteps to the left a little, still running, waiting for it to pass. But it doesn't. Instead, the car slows, as if *following* her. An image flashes in her mind of a mountain lion, stalking its prey, closing in on its kill from the rear.

The driver's just worried about hitting me, she tells herself. She turns her head to see. But already her heart is pounding in fear.

CHAPTER 1

THE PHOTO OF SHANNON BLAINE I'D COME ACROSS ON the website for her area newspaper reminded me of a woman I used to see running on my block in Chelsea, on her way to the west side jogging path: slim and fit and pretty, with long butter-colored hair, and—if appearances could be believed—totally at ease in her own skin.

On a warmish Monday morning in late September, Shannon had apparently set off for a jog along a series of roads near her home in Lake George, New York, a small town thirteen miles from Glens Falls and roughly two hundred miles north of New York City. Running was something she did most days, her me-time, I supposed, after dropping off her two kids at school.

Except, on this day, she never returned.

Here's what else I knew from the reading I'd done about the case: The first time anyone realized the thirty-four-year-old mother had vanished was at three o'clock, when she failed to collect her kids from school. The assistant principal, assuming that the parents simply had their wires crossed about who was handling pickup that day, alerted the husband, Cody Blaine, thirty-seven. No mix-up, Cody told her. Though he said he hadn't spoken to Shannon since breakfast, he knew she planned to be there. After reportedly trying and failing to reach his wife himself, he arranged for his sister-in-law to head to the school as he raced home from his office. The front door was locked, Shannon's car was in the driveway, and though her cell phone was missing, her purse lay on the kitchen counter. There was not a single clue to indicate her whereabouts.

Along with two friends, Cody searched the roads within a roughly ten-mile radius of his home—this was later verified by the two male friends. Failing to find Shannon, Cody alerted the sheriff's department. Shortly afterward, an official search was initiated, which as of today, Wednesday, involved dozens of law enforcement members, hundreds of volunteers, police choppers, and canines.

I'd covered several other cases in which a woman had gone missing, so I knew law enforcement was not only busting their butts searching for Shannon but also questioning registered sex offenders in the area. Sexual predators were known to patrol areas in cars for hours, hunting for an opportunity to strike, and one such predator could have spotted Shannon on the road while she was jogging and snatched her before she barely knew what was happening.

And surely they were also checking out Cody. Was he a womanizer? Had he recently doubled Shannon's life insurance policy? Was there a history of domestic troubles or abuse?

Cody, according to the paper, had only a partial alibi for Monday morning. After dropping off some paperwork with his assistant at his office, he supposedly drove about thirty minutes south to inspect a plot of land he was thinking of purchasing for his business. No one saw him on that site, but his assistant reported that he had called her twice from the road to touch base about work issues and had sounded "perfectly normal."

It's true what you've heard, by the way. That the husband is almost always a person of interest in a wife's disappearance and/or homicide, even if the cops don't announce it. Maybe Cody had a temper or was having an affair with someone he'd managed to find even more tantalizing than Shannon and he knew that divorce would cost him a bundle or end up restricting access to his kids. Or a divorce might have even required that he step down from his position as president of Baker Beverage Distributors, which Shannon's deceased father had founded and designated his son-in-law to run. There was a decent chance Cody had blood on his hands.

Or at the very least, blood in the trunk of his car.

I'd been handed the chance to cover the story on Tuesday night by a new online publication called *Crime Beat*. It was owned and run by a cocksure former journalist named Dodson Crowe, who'd inherited a bundle from his father and was using the cash to call his own shots now. I was impressed with the un-cheesy tone and quality of the site, and when Crowe had approached me, I'd eagerly agreed to freelance for him if the right story presented itself.

It had taken me about two seconds to say yes to this one.

"If we're lucky, it'll have a few nice layers," Crowe had said on the phone. "Maybe not as crazy as *Gone Girl*, but there might be something weird or kinky going on. Especially with the husband."

Yes, maybe, I thought. But I never believed in letting my imagination off the leash too soon on a story. Better to dig, listen, and see where all the threads led me to instead.

I'd spent a few hours that night scanning upstate media coverage of the case, much of it in the area newspaper, the *Glens Falls Post Star*, by a reporter named Alice Hatfield, though the Albany-area TV stations were in on the action as well and had posted updates on their websites. I also watched a video of the press conference the county sheriff had conducted earlier that day, and searched for whatever I could find out about Cody Blaine, which turned out to be very little. He was originally from Texas and had served with the army in Afghanistan.

Finally, I searched to see if there'd been any other incidents of missing women in the area. Nothing noteworthy surfaced. About ten years ago, two twenty-year-old females had disappeared from a campground on the east side of Lake George, but the police never found any evidence of a crime and eventually concluded that they'd likely taken off for parts unknown in search of their next big adventure.

I left my apartment in Manhattan early Wednesday morning after espressos and bagels with Beau Regan, the man I'd been living with—mostly high on the blissful scale—for the past couple of years. (At thirty-six, I felt kind of goofy calling him my "boyfriend.") Beau was also leaving the city later that day, bound for Bogotá, Colombia, to make a documentary about several contemporary Colombian painters. I was going to miss him, and I welcomed the distraction of my assignment upstate. We kissed each other goodbye and hugged tightly before I left, promising to text each other when we'd both arrived at our destinations.

The drive north in my Jeep Cherokee, mostly along the New York State Thruway, took roughly four hours, and I found myself growing more pumped up with each mile. My first job after college, fourteen years ago, had actually been as a junior reporter for the *Albany Times Union*, an hour south of where I was headed. I'd been assigned to the police beat, covering everything from drug busts to hit-and-runs to homicides. From that time on, true crime became my genre of choice. I've never understood exactly why, but I'm drawn to tales of the dark things people do, fascinated by how needs turn twisted and monstrous and end up wreaking such havoc. And the puzzles of those stories captivate me, too—figuring out the who and the where and the how and the why. I have an insatiable desire to know, even if the answers sometimes chill my blood a few degrees.

After a stint in newspapers, I moved to Manhattan and began writing for magazines, but with print publications in free fall these days, I'd turned to writing true-crime books, most recently *A Model Murder*, based on one of the cases I'd covered. Though reporting for *Crime Beat* called for temporarily ditching the research for my next book, it also meant covering a story in real time again, something I hadn't done much of lately. As the scenery whipped by my window, I realized just how much I'd missed it. The game was afoot, and it felt good to be in the mix.

What I didn't love was the fact that I'd be arriving two full days after Shannon had disappeared, but I had every intention of catching up fast. And with any luck, the story would feature the kind of riveting layers Dodson was itching for.

A big chunk of the route north was fairly monotonous, but about twenty minutes from the end, I took a curve in the road and the Adirondack Mountains suddenly slid into view, these blue-green giants that made me catch my breath. During my stint in Albany I'd never managed to make it this far north, which I could see now was a shame. Since it was only late September, the trees hadn't changed colors yet, but many of the leaves were tipped with yellow and rust, and some of the tangled brush below was already vivid shades of burgundy and lipstick red.

As I neared the village of Lake George, I finally caught a glimpse of the lake, the lapis-blue water sparkling in the sun. But I probably wasn't going to see much of it today. My immediate destination was the hastily organized volunteer command center, a.k.a. Dot's soft-serve ice cream shop, which apparently had closed for business after Labor Day. I abandoned the highway at exit twenty-one and continued north on Route 9N.

It was noon when I finally pulled into the parking lot at Dot's, and I was lucky to find a spot—the place was packed with cars, vans, SUVs, and pickup trucks. Even with my window up I could hear the insistent buzz of a helicopter circling in the sky above. Instantly I felt a double dopamine rush from simply being there. I was smack in the middle of a missing-person case that was packed with not only known unknowns but hopefully some tantalizing *unknown* unknowns as well.

Before stepping out of my Jeep, I stole a couple of minutes to suss out the scene at the far end of the lot. Volunteer centers for missing-person searches, at least from my experience, were generally set up in church basements, hotels, or volunteer fire-houses, any space big enough to handle the swarm of people coming and going. A soft-serve ice cream shop was a pretty surreal choice—I mean, there was a giant chocolate-dipped cone with two eyes and a smile greeting everyone from above the door. Considering what was going on, it seemed like a smiley face above the gates of hell. But the place reportedly had been offered by a friend of Shannon's family.

I counted a half-dozen people inside the shop, and about thirty more milling around near the front of the building, under an overhang with cedar picnic tables arranged beneath it. They were dressed in jeans and sturdy-looking shoes, and for the most part their expressions were grim. Searchers, I assumed, who would be covering a broader area than had first been examined by authorities.

Of course that assumed Shannon actually *had* gone running Monday. At the press conference yesterday, the sheriff explained that Shannon's oldest child, an eight-year-old boy named Noah, told authorities that when his mother dropped him and his six-year-old sister, Lilly, at school, she'd been wearing a white T-shirt, dark shorts, and running shoes, and Cody Blaine had reported that those items weren't in her dresser. But so far the authorities had failed to locate a single person who'd noticed Shannon on the road that morning. According to the owner of the Lake Shore Motel, who was interviewed by the *Post Star*, Shannon Blaine crossed the road in front of his establishment every day—but not this past Monday. He claimed to have turned over security camera footage to the police that backed up his statement.

Had Shannon changed her route for some reason? Had she been abducted before making it as far as the motel? Or had she never actually left her house for a run that day?

I squinted through my windshield, searching for anyone I might recognize from photos I'd viewed online. Cody Blaine didn't appear to be here. Nor was Shannon's mother. But I was pretty sure that a woman beneath the overhang was her older sister, Kelly Claiborne, who, I'd learned, worked as a reading specialist. As I watched, she yanked a handful of sheets of paper from a cardboard box and began to distribute them. I realized that the people gathered around weren't searchers after all but rather volunteers who would soon be tacking up or handing out flyers about Shannon.

It was time to get my ass in gear and cover as much ground as possible before the next press conference, scheduled for five o'clock.

When I swung open the door of my Jeep, I found that the air, laden with the scent of resin from the pine trees all around me, seemed about ten degrees cooler than it had been in Manhattan, a bigger change than I'd anticipated. I felt suddenly stupid in my pink cashmere tee, tan skirt, and suede mules. But I certainly wasn't going to take the time to drive to my motel to check in and change.

I grabbed a jean jacket from the back seat and made my way toward Kelly. She had long hair like her sister, though hers was brown, and pulled back today in a ponytail. She was tall—at least five ten—and fairly slim, dressed in jeans, running shoes, and a zipped navy sweater. From a distance, her stance and decisive-looking gestures gave her the look of someone organizing a political rally, but as I drew closer, I could see from her pinched expression how distressed she was.

"Who wants to head up to Ticonderoga?" she called out, waving a fresh stack of flyers. Next to her was a box loaded with thumbtacks.

"I can take that area if you want," a middle-aged guy volunteered. "You want me to just tack these to trees and stuff?"

"Trees, utility poles. But even better is getting them into shops and restaurants. That's where the real traffic is."

"Gotcha."

"Talk to the manager or owner, engage them. Tell them about Shannon if they don't know already. Encourage them to call if they've seen anyone remotely fitting her description."

She had a real no-nonsense style and a precise way with her words, perhaps reflecting how she worked with her reading students.

I hung back, waiting for Kelly to go through the procedure with a couple dozen people. After the last one departed, she let out a tense sigh and I stepped forward.

"Kelly, hi, my name is Bailey Weggins."

She ran her gaze over me, somewhat distractedly.

"Great, thanks for coming," she said. "But do you have any other shoes? Those are gonna be a bitch to canvass in."

"I'm actually a reporter. With *Crime Beat*. I was hoping you had a few minutes to talk."

"Is that a TV show?"

"No, an online publication. We want to cover the story, of course, but we're interested in getting the word out about Shannon as well."

She scrunched up her mouth and nodded at the same time, one gesture almost contradicting the other. I assumed she had mixed feelings about doing interviews. They took up time she could be using to corral and organize volunteers, but she was also eager for Shannon's image to be displayed as widely as possible.

"Give me a couple of minutes. I need to check in with a few people inside, and then we can talk."

I thanked her, and as she hurried into the building, I plucked a flyer from the box. The word *Missing* ran boldly in red above two color photos of Shannon, both solo, which captured her gorgeous blond hair and grass-green eyes. At the very bottom was a promise of a reward—$15,000 for any information leading to her whereabouts—as well as the tip-line phone number and email address.

"Well, well," I heard a sly male voice announce behind me. "Look who's in town."

I spun around to discover Matt Wong, an obnoxious reporter who was now doing his own stint at the *Albany Times Union*. He'd recently taken a gig there after years of freelancing in New York City, where we'd sometimes crossed paths. I should have known he'd turn up here.

"Hi, Matt. How you doing?"

"Really, really well . . . Shannon's not a friend of Kim's, is she?"

"Kim?" I asked, having no clue what he was talking about.

"*Kardashian*. I thought you only reported crime stories when there was a celebrity hook."

He just couldn't resist making a dig, could he? It was as natural to him as swallowing.

"Oh, come on, Matt. You know I don't work for *Buzz* anymore."

A few years back I'd covered celebrity crimes for one of those weekly tabloid magazines, the kind that features heart-stopping headlines like "JLo Suffers Spray Tan Tragedy." I know, what the hell was I thinking? But I needed the paycheck.

Wong gave a playful shrug.

"That's right, thanks for the correction. You're an *author* now. Thinking of turning this little story into your next book?"

"I'd tell you," I said. "But then I'd have to kill you. How's your new job going?"

"Great, they love me there."

"Good to know. Anything you can tell me about the situation here?"

"You mean, do I think the husband did it? Probably. But you're getting a little bit of a late start on the story, aren't you, Bailey?"

"Oh, you know what they say, Matt. It's not where you start, it's where you finish."

Jeez, I was on a roll with the comebacks, wasn't I? If crime writing fell through, I might be able to find work as a mug writer. At that moment, thankfully, Kelly slipped out of the building and cocked her chin in a gesture that indicated she was ready for me.

"Oops," I said. "Gotta run. Talk to you later."

"Just remember, sometimes even the sweetest-looking sisters hate each other's guts."

With Matt, it was always hard to tell if a comment like that was a friendly tip from one reporter to another or a red herring meant to throw you off the real scent. I ignored him and hurried toward Dot's.

As I reached the building, the small bunch of people who'd been inside began to file out. The last, a middle-aged, barrel-chested man with shiny black hair, held the door for us.

"I'm gonna grab a sandwich," he told Kelly. "Be back in about twenty."

"Thanks, Hank." She motioned for me to enter ahead of her.

"I didn't mean for you to have to chase everyone out," I told her. "But I appreciate the chance to talk."

"I actually have no clue what anyone besides Hank is doing hanging in here," she said, quickly tugging the elastic from her ponytail. She smoothed her hair tightly in place and then wound the elastic back around it. "They're supposed to be finding Shannon, not gossiping like a bunch of ninth graders. Sit wherever you want, okay?"

At first glance, Dot's looked to me like it'd been designed during the JFK administration and not touched since. As

Kelly and I both slid into seats at a metal table strewn with flyers and used cardboard coffee cups, I took a better look at her. She was a fairly attractive woman, sharing some key features with Shannon—the green eyes, strong straight nose, and high cheekbones—but they hadn't come together in the same stunning way. It made me think of shots I'd seen in *Buzz* of celebrity brothers and sisters who bore a strong resemblance to their famous siblings but had not been tapped by the remarkable-beauty fairy themselves.

"I know the police have an intense search going on," I began. "Anything turn up today?"

She quickly shook her head. "Not yet, no. And that's why we need to get the word out further. So that if anyone spots Shannon, they'll call the tip line. You can run the number in your story, correct?"

"Of course. When was the last time you spoke to Shannon?"

"I called her Sunday night, around seven o'clock."

"Did the two of you talk about anything in particular?"

"I was just asking her to drop off dinner for our mother the next day. It's usually my turn on Mondays, but my husband was out of town, so I was the only one who could go to my daughter's soccer game that afternoon."

I couldn't help but pick up on the odd flatness to Kelly's tone. Maybe staying detached was helping her cope with her sister's disappearance. Maybe stress and fear had bled all the emotion out of her voice. Or maybe I was seeing a hint of what Matt Wong had alluded to.

"And there's still no sign of Shannon's phone, right?"

"No. And they can't get a signal because it's off or out of power."

"I read there was at least one call on Monday morning but the police haven't been able to contact the woman."

"That would be J. J. Rimes. Shannon's cell phone records show Shannon spoke to her that morning, but apparently J.J. left later in the day for a camping trip in the Adirondacks and no one's been able to reach her."

"Does that seem like an odd coincidence?" It sure did to me. "Both of them gone the same day?"

"Not necessarily. J.J.'s ex-husband says she told him about the trip a while ago because she needed him to take the kids. . . . Here's what my family and I think—that Shannon's probably injured. That she might have fallen when she was running and hit her head and she's now walking around in some kind of fugue state."

That was a possibility, of course, though it seemed like a really slim one.

"If that's the case, let's hope the searchers find her soon," I said, nodding sympathetically. "Shifting gears a little, had Shannon mentioned any concerns to you lately? About someone watching her or following her?"

"Definitely not. Stuff like that doesn't happen in a place like this."

"Being a mom can be stressful. Is there any chance that things became overwhelming for her? That she needed to escape for a while?"

The question clearly annoyed Kelly—I could read it in her eyes—but she took a breath, tamping down her irritation.

"I know you're just doing your job asking that," she said, "but it's totally off the mark. Shannon loves her kids and would never abandon them, even for a short time."

"She's a stay-at-home mom?"

"Basically, yes. She stopped working full-time when the kids were born. She wanted to take them to school, make unicorn-colored cupcakes for their birthday parties. That sort of thing."

I wasn't sure why exactly, but something about the cupcakes comment came off like a tiny dig to me.

"And her marriage—how's that?"

"It seems fine. Cody runs our family company, and my father—Stan—left it in brilliant shape. They have a nice life."

Hardly a ringing endorsement of her brother-in-law.

"Do—"

"Like I said, we think Shannon could be injured and re- quiring immediate medical help. She loves the outdoors, but that doesn't mean she can cope if she's broken a leg. Fortu- nately, I've been able to take off work to help, but my family needs as many people as we can get to assist with the search."

"Speaking of your family, it would be great if I could speak with your mother."

That elicited another hard shake of the head.

"She's not up to speaking to anyone at the moment."

I sensed I was starting to press my luck with Kelly and decided to back off for now. After all, I'd want the chance to circle back to her later.

"I'll let you return to your work here, but before we fin- ish, what's the best way for people to help?"

"They can check the sheriff's website each day, or stop by here to see where the searchers are meeting. If searching outside is too strenuous for them, they can pick up flyers here to distribute to restaurants and businesses. They can reach out to me or Hank Coulter, who's running our volunteer operation. He's the former chief of police here in town."

"Great, I'll definitely include that information in my article. And if anything else occurs to you, I'd love to hear from you." I reached in my shoulder bag for a business card, and as I slid it across the table to her, I heard the front door swing open with a whoosh.

Cody Blaine had just entered the building.

He was as handsome as his photos suggested, about five ten and well built. His hair and eyes were dark brown, but his skin was extremely fair, creating an intriguing contrast. He wore his beard and mustache close-cropped, and despite how ragged he looked today, there was a worldly air about him. Maybe that came from serving time in Afghanistan.

I turned back to Kelly and saw her shoulders tensing before my eyes.

"Hi," she said bluntly. "What's up?"

"I just wanted to check in before I join the next search," Cody said. "They're organizing something closer to the lake, starting in about fifteen minutes."

"Why *there*?" Kelly demanded. "Do they have a reason?"

"No, simply a next step." If Kelly's tone irked him, he wasn't letting on.

"Where are the kids right now?"

"With your in-laws."

I'd risen by this point and taken a few steps toward Cody.

"Cody, hello, I'm Bailey Weggins with *Crime Beat*," I said, offering him a business card as well. "Can I grab a few minutes with you before you leave? We're planning to do whatever we can to spread the word."

"Sorry," he said. "I'll be part of a search line, and I need to leave at the same time as everyone else."

"How about later today?"

He sighed wearily. "Okay."

"I'm staying at the Breezy Point, so it would be easy enough to drop by your house."

"No, I'll swing by here after the search is over, sometime around dusk." His expression darkened. I had the feeling he was going to add a comment like "Unless we hear news," but decided to skip it.

"Thanks, I'll wait for you here. And best of luck with the search."

This was good. I would be able to include quotes from Cody in the post I filed later today. And I'd also be able to work with whatever the sheriff coughed up at the press conference later in the afternoon. Anything else would be gravy.

After the door closed behind him, I pivoted back to Kelly. Her face was a blank, but I could almost feel hostility coming off her, like heat from a stove. I opened my mouth to bid her goodbye when the door opened again and a sandy-haired, fortysomething guy—a volunteer, I assumed—strode in. He immediately fixed his gaze on me.

"Are you about finished?" he asked.

"Excuse me?" I said.

"I'm Dr. Claiborne, Kelly's husband, and I think she's done enough press for today."

"Doug, please, it's fine," Kelly said.

"Not a problem," I said. No point in rocking the boat. As I took him in, I saw that he was nice-looking enough, but nowhere in the same league as his brother-in-law. He had what to me was a Ken-doll blandness, but hey, some women dug that kind of thing. Clearly Barbie did, right? "Thanks for your time, Kelly."

There were still a few hours until the press conference, so I made a quick trip to the Breezy Point Motel, which I'd booked online last night and was only two miles north of Dot's. My room had been done in classic Adirondack style—rough-hewn wood furniture, birch-bark lampshades, and mounted deer antlers over the door, a kitschy but refreshing change from the mauve-and-green color schemes and Naugahyde chairs I'm used to in the motels and hotels I usually bunk down in for work. There were even some cute toiletries in the bathroom.

I changed into jeans and wolfed down a sandwich I'd packed in a small cooler. I considered making a fast trip to the local elementary school to see if I could talk to any moms who were there for pickup and might know Shannon, but it seemed smarter to save that for tomorrow morning and instead keep an eye on the action at the volunteer center.

Upon my return, I saw that Hank was back in the building, thumbing through papers on one of the tables. I headed over and introduced myself, handing him a card. As I did, I realized that his jet-black hair, which was either defying age on its own or with some help from Grecian Formula, had led me to assume he was younger than he was. He had to be close to sixty, though overall in good shape.

"You come all the way up here from the city?" he asked.

"That's right."

"Well, I bet the networks aren't far behind, are they?"

"You're probably right. Do you have any theories about what might have happened to Shannon?"

He smiled but not the kind that fell into the super-friendly department. "I'd like to help you, Ms. Weggins, but I'm just here to supervise volunteers. That's really a question for the sheriff. Why don't you ask him at the press conference?"

"Fair enough. Kelly mentioned you're a retired cop. Has anything remotely similar happened here in recent memory?"

"I haven't been on the force in five years, so as I said, it's best to direct those kinds of questions to the sheriff." His phone buzzed, and he checked the screen. "Sorry, but I'm gonna have to take this. Hank Coulter."

Okay, so *that* was a bust. I left him to his phone call and set up shop on the hood of my Jeep. As volunteers came and went, collecting flyers or reporting to Kelly or Coulter, I managed to snag a few dozen of them for comments. They seemed to be a mix of stay-at-home moms, retirees, and employees from Baker Beverage whom Cody had given the day off to help in the search. Almost everyone seemed eager to offer their two cents, but no one I encountered claimed to know Shannon more than casually, though many pointed out that she seemed "perfectly lovely." It was pretty clear that the situation had most of them seriously alarmed, particularly the women.

Just after four, the action began to heat up, clearly in anticipation of the press conference. Several Albany-area network TV vans rumbled into the parking lot and reporters spilled out, smoothing their clothes and fluffing their hair. Matt Wong resurfaced, too.

I snaked my way through the crowd of press, lingering volunteers, and what appeared to be good old-fashioned rubberneckers, and grabbed a spot close to the front. I was surprised to see that the sheriff's department hadn't yet set up a podium, so there was no place for the TV and radio crews to position their microphones. In fact, there was no sign of *anyone* from the sheriff's office.

At two minutes to five we found out why. A sole member of the sheriff's team, a female deputy, arrived and announced to the crowd that the press conference was being postponed until 10:00 a.m. tomorrow. She then hurried off without taking any questions.

There'd been a development, I realized, maybe something big, but they weren't telling us. I glanced inside Dot's. Hank was on the phone, his face expressionless, and Kelly was stuffing flyers back into a box. At least for the time being, they were as out of the loop as the rest of us.

Since I'd signed up to receive automatic news alerts from the sheriff's department, I'd hear eventually if anything major had gone down. But this meant that I'd have zip from law enforcement for the post tonight. I breathed a sigh of relief that I at least had my interview with Cody coming up.

As the media vehicles departed with a roar, I parked

myself against my Jeep again, nursing a bottle of lukewarm water and watching the daylight fade. There were still a few volunteers milling around, but eventually they took off as well. And so did Hank and Kelly, locking the door of Dot's behind them.

I was alone in the lot now, accompanied by nothing except the sound of cars whizzing behind me on Route 9N. Finally the truth smacked me in the head. Cody was a no-show.

Damn.

The only thing I could think of at this point was to head to his house and see if he'd talk to me there, which would also provide my first chance to see part of Shannon's usual jogging route. I'd already programmed my GPS with the family address on Wheeler Road, which ran between Route 9 and Route 9N.

The area turned out to be heavily wooded, with homes set far apart. I'd seen the word *successful* used to describe Cody Blaine in the news coverage, and the house at 192 Wheeler backed that up. It was a large modern design of glass, stone, and what appeared to be cedar, set fairly far back on the quiet road, with woods rising behind it in the rear. The only light was the one burning just above the front door. Maybe Cody was picking up the kids at Kelly's in-laws. Or perhaps he wasn't staying here at all, avoiding the press who'd show up if they knew he was in residence.

Odd, though, that no one would be stationed at the house in case Shannon staggered home in that fugue state her family had envisioned.

I pulled into the Blaine driveway, backed out, and headed toward Route 9N. Wheeler Road had a fairly wide shoulder, and it was easy to envision Shannon running here, breathing in the crisp air, thinking about how to decorate the next batch of cupcakes she'd make for her kids.

And then, rounding a bend, I *saw* her. A woman in dark shorts and a white T-shirt, streaking up the road in the same direction I was going. Even in the waning light I couldn't miss her long blond hair, tied in a ponytail and bouncing hard behind her with each step.

It was Shannon Blaine. And it looked as if she was running for her life.

CHAPTER 2

I BRAKED, SHIFTED FAST INTO PARK, AND FLUNG OPEN THE door.

"Shannon," I yelled, scrambling out of the Jeep and tearing up the road toward her. "Shannon, wait."

She finally swung around, so fast her ponytail slapped her lightly in the face. Maybe she *had* been in a fugue, wandering through the area for two full days, always just far enough ahead of searchers to elude being seen.

"Shannon, are you okay?" I called, short of breath. "Let me help you."

As I closed the distance between us, she backed away from me, and I spotted the alarm in her eyes.

"My name's not Shannon," she said, catching a breath.

And now, only a few feet apart, I realized that I'd been mistaken. Even in the dim light, I could tell that her eyes were brown and not that dazzling green I'd noted in Shannon's photo. How stupid to let my imagination play a trick on me.

"I'm so sorry," I said. "From the back you looked just like Shannon Blaine."

She narrowed her eyes, still considering me warily. "I don't even know who that is. I—I'm not from here."

"Um, okay," I said. I realized she must be a tourist. "Shannon's a local woman who went missing on Monday, possibly from this exact road. Actually, I'm not sure it's safe for you to be out alone like this. There's a chance that she was abducted."

Her eyes widened briefly, but then she shrugged dismissively.

"I'll be fine. I don't have far to go—just up the road."

"Are you staying at the Lake Shore Motel?" I'd spotted it on the corner of Wheeler and Route 9N. The owner was the guy who reported seeing Shannon jogging—every day except Monday.

She hesitated before answering. "Yeah."

"I was actually planning to stop there to speak to the owner. Why don't you let me give you a lift?"

She shook her head quickly, the ponytail bouncing. "Like I said, I'm fine. . . . But thanks anyway."

She spun back around and broke into a run again, pumping her arms in rhythm with her legs. I noticed that she wasn't wearing reflective gear, so she seemed to be at risk in more ways than one. But she'd made it clear she didn't want me butting into her business.

I retreated to the Jeep and took off again, giving the jogger a wide berth as I passed. I caught a brief, final glimpse of her in the rearview mirror before she was swallowed into the gloaming.

I reached the Lake Shore a few minutes later. It wasn't hard to see why the owner was able to keep tabs on Shannon's runs. The front office, I noticed, was at the end of the one-story white clapboard building, facing Route 9N, and its front wall was taken up almost entirely by a window. Though there were a few cars in the parking lot, a blue fluorescent sign announced vacancy, and my guess was that the motel, like the one where I was staying, wasn't even half full. I'd read that business slowed drastically in the Lake George area after Labor Day, but that there was always another burst of tourism in October, people taking in the peak of the jaw-dropping fall foliage.

The counter in the small reception area was being manned by a skinny guy in his early twenties, dressed in a white short-sleeved button-down. I guessed that he wasn't the owner, who was probably off duty now if he usually had the morning shift, but the desk clerk could at least direct me to him.

"What can I do for you?" he asked with a tired smile. A TV droned behind the half-closed door to his right, and I wondered if he'd been watching the tube in there before I arrived.

"Is the owner around? I'm a reporter, and I'd love to interview him about Shannon Blaine."

Since the guy had already given at least one interview, I was pretty sure he would be game for another. What I'd discovered when I first started on the crime beat was that people on the fringes of a story—and sometimes even those in the thick of it—were almost always eager to get their faces on camera or their names in print. Unless, that is, they had good reason to stay on the down low. And even then, people who should have kept their mouths shut sometimes made the mistake of talking their asses off.

"Uh, you'll have to come back in the morning," the clerk said quickly. "He works the desk seven to two."

"Oh, gosh, I have to file the story tonight—and it would be great to have a few quotes from him. Could you call him and ask if I could possibly swing by his home?"

His mouth dropped open, as if I'd just asked him to strip to his tighty-whities.

"He doesn't like me to bother him after hours."

"It's really important. We're trying to help the police find this woman."

"Um, okay. Give me a minute, will you?"

He slipped quietly into the room behind him and shut the door. The wait at least gave me a chance to glance out the plate-glass window, keeping my eyes peeled for any sign of the jogger I'd encountered.

The desk clerk finally reemerged along with a pale, beefy man, probably in his late forties.

"Terry Dobbs," he announced, letting his eyes sneak briefly up and down the length of my body. He was wearing khaki pants paired with a light flannel shirt, and his gray hair stood up in small tufts on his head, as if he'd been roused from a nap in front of the TV when the clerk popped in. "What can I do for you?"

I thanked him for his time and explained the purpose of my visit, giving my spiel about *Crime Beat* and our desire to assist in the search for Shannon.

"Happy to help," he said. "We're all hoping for the best." The way he puffed his chest up suggested he was as eager for the attention as he was to assist, but hey, after being ditched by Cody Blaine, I didn't really care about his motives as long as he didn't go making shit up.

He cocked his head toward the clerk. "Gary, why don't you grab your smoke break now so I can chat with this nice young lady. I'll keep an eye on the desk."

Gary beat it, and after producing my notebook and pen, I sat in one of the straight-backed chairs in the reception area, gesturing for Dobbs to take a seat in the other one.

"I read in the *Post Star* that you often see Shannon running by the motel," I said. "But not Monday morning. Is that correct?"

"Yup, that's right. No sign of her on Monday."

He'd crossed one leg over the other, casual-like, but I sensed he was on alert, as if he was being careful with his words.

"Is it possible that you were dealing with a customer at the same time Shannon ran by and you didn't catch a glimpse of her for that reason? Or maybe you were on a call? Or a bathroom break?"

"Mondays are quiet as a tomb this time of year. I pretty much had my eye on this window the whole morning."

"Of course, she could have taken another route that day."

"Coulda. But it would have been the first time. Never seen her miss a day. Except Sundays. Church day."

So it was possible Shannon Blaine had been abducted before reaching the Lake Shore Motel. Or that she'd never made it out of her house alive.

"Got it," I said. "Any thoughts about what might have happened to Shannon?"

He shrugged. "I hear they're entertaining all kinds of theories. That she's got amnesia and is wandering around the woods. Some pervert grabbed her. She ran off with another guy. Or even that the husband's behind it all."

"Is there one theory you favor more than the others?"

"Nope. I just hope they find her. She looks like a real nice lady."

I wondered if he ran his gaze up and down her body as he'd done to me.

"Just one last question, if you don't mind, Mr. Dobbs. Did you ever see her running with anyone else? A female friend? A guy?"

"Nope, always alone."

I thanked him again for his time and pulled out a business card, asking him to please contact me if anything else occurred to him. While I'd been talking, I'd kept one eye on the lit parking lot, and there was still no sign of the blond jogger. She should have been here by now.

"Oh, Mr. Dobbs," I said, turning back to him. "I met a woman on the road who looked a bit like Shannon and she said she was staying here. Do you know who I'm talking about? Blond. In her early thirties."

He pursed his thick pink lips and shook his head slowly back and forth.

"No, nobody like that here."

Okay, that was weird. Perhaps the blond jogger simply had remembered her motel being at the end of Wheeler when it really wasn't, or else she had lied to me because her place of lodging wasn't any of my damn business. And, of course, it wasn't.

From the Lake Shore I headed south on route 9N, passing seemingly endless motels, fast-food restaurants, and retail outlets, as I approached the village of Lake George, the center of town. It was time to crank out my post for the day, but I found myself in a quandary. Thanks to Cody ghosting me and the sheriff postponing the press conference, I had almost nada to show for my half day on the scene. I felt like a reporter covering a royal wedding who'd managed to snag only a quote from the guy who'd groomed the horses.

And that wasn't a good thing. *Crime Beat* was hardly in the same league as *Vanity Fair* or the *New York Times*, but the writing was good for a true-crime site and the reporters seemed to be scrappy, ready to turn over every stone in their research. Dodson Crowe would be expecting a certain quality from my first piece of reporting for him, and I needed to deliver.

Finally, just as I pulled into the village, I had a brainstorm: I'd write my post from the first-person point of view. Though I'd used that approach in my book, it wasn't a style *Crime Beat* writers typically employed. In this case, though, I thought I could make up for my lack of good quotes by offering plenty of impressions, even the chilling moment when I'd spotted the blond jogger on the road.

I found a spot for the Jeep right off Canada, the main drag in town, and after grabbing my laptop, I searched on foot for someplace to park my butt. The village was pretty charming, with one- and two-story commercial buildings, many with rustic-style peaked roofs. A few shops were still open, with racks set outside and souvenir T-shirts flapping in the evening breeze.

After finding a café, I settled in a booth, ordered a sandwich, and banged out the post. I described the fraught scene at Dot's, the palpable fear of the local residents I'd interviewed, Kelly's hopes that her sister was simply in a disassociated state, and my frustrations over being stood up by Cody even though I assumed it was for a good reason. I'd swiped one of the flyers with Shannon's photo earlier that day, and from time to time as I typed, I stared at those riveting green eyes.

Where are you, Shannon? I wondered. Where in the world did you go?

Though I wasn't going to allow my imagination off the leash yet, it was time to review, and perhaps reconsider, the probabilities in the case. According to Kelly, her sister hadn't appeared to be under emotional duress or suffering from severe mommy burnout, so that weakened the idea of Shannon simply splitting on her own. As for the injury angle, it seemed unlikely to me that Shannon had done a face-plant on the road and was now wandering the woods with a head wound.

That left stranger abduction, a decent possibility, despite Kelly poo-pooing it.

And it also left Cody. Now that I'd seen the guy's good looks in the flesh, it wasn't hard to imagine him as a magnet for women, someone who could have cheated on Shannon and wanted out of the marriage without a lot of ugly strings attached. Though two sheriff deputies had conducted a brief search of the Blaine house after Cody reported his wife missing, I was sure law enforcement was now itching to make a more thorough inspection, not only of the house but also of the family garage and vehicles. They would want to conduct tests with luminol, which highlights traces of blood even if there's been a thorough attempt to bleach them away.

But they couldn't do it simply because of that itch. They needed either Cody's permission or a search warrant indicating there was probable cause that a crime had been committed there.

I didn't add any of this speculation to the post. It was too soon for that. But tomorrow I was going to see what I could learn about any girlfriend in the wings, either from the moms at the school or employees of Baker Beverage.

Over a cappuccino I reviewed what I'd written, cleaning up grammatical errors and polishing the prose as best as possible in the little time I had. Finally, I attached it to an email to Dodson and hit send. I had to admit that I felt a little giddy delivering the first daily reporting I'd done in ages. I just hoped that he wouldn't have an issue with my first-person tactic.

By the time I left the café, in danger of someone sweeping under my feet, the combo of caffeine and deadline jitters had left me wired, as if tiny firecrackers were exploding in my bloodstream. I decided to walk for a while and attempt to unwind. Though most of the shops had finally closed for the night, a handful of restaurants remained open, and there were still a few folks ambling along Canada Street.

A couple of blocks later I found myself in front of a small tavern. Through the front window, I could see it was half full with what looked like a local crowd, dressed for early fall in plaid shirts and turtleneck sweaters. I decided to spring for a glass of wine.

There were a few empty stools at the bar, and I slid onto one and ordered a California cabernet from a friendly, bearded bartender. A string of colored lights had been strung above the row of bottles behind the bar, and it gave the place an enchanting, almost magical look.

As I glanced around I realized that the row of picture windows on the rear wall faced the lake. Since it was dark now, all I could see was a slim necklace of lights, which were probably affixed to the ends of piers and boat docks. Maybe there'd be a chance for me to come back here for lunch one day and really take in the lake. I'd read that the first Europeans to come upon it were Jesuit priests, one of whom dubbed it Lac du Saint-Sacrement, though after winning the French and Indian War, the British renamed it after King George II. But long before either the French or the British were around, the Mohawk Indians called it Andiatarocte, meaning the place where the mountains close in.

I'd taken only a sip of wine when I heard my phone ping,

and I grabbed it from my purse. A text from Dodson. Bracing myself, I opened it.

Like the first person. Stay with it. Posting now.

Okay, good. I could relax at least and focus on the eighties hits playing on the sound system.

The pat on the back from Dodson, however, hardly put me in a celebratory mood. A young mother was missing, and even if she was still alive, it was unlikely that she'd be found unharmed.

After dropping the phone back in my purse, I caught the eye of a woman at the end of the bar, perched on a stool six or seven spots away from me. She was middle-aged, probably late fifties, slightly heavyset, with short, coarse brown hair, and still wearing her hip-length unbuttoned coat, the kind my mother used to call a "car coat."

I'd seen this woman before, I realized—at the volunteer center, where she'd arrived midafternoon and spent a few minutes talking intently with Kelly. Thinking she might be a family friend worth debriefing, I'd said a hasty goodbye to the Baker Beverage deliveryman I had been interviewing and made a beeline in her direction. But she'd been faster than me, taking off in her car before I could reach her.

I had another chance now, however. Though she clearly knew other patrons—she'd lifted her hand in a wave a couple of times—she was on her own, a half glass of white wine set in front of her. I grabbed my own glass and moseyed down to the end of the bar.

"Excuse the intrusion," I said, "but I'd been hoping to talk to you at the volunteer center today and never had the opportunity. Do you have a minute now?"

The woman raised a dark, bushy eyebrow.

"What about?" Not rude, but hardly friendly, either.

"About Shannon Blaine's disappearance. I'm a reporter. My name's—"

"I know who you are," she said bluntly.

"Did Kelly mention me?"

"No, but I recognize you. Your reputation precedes you."

"I hope in a good way," I said. Maybe she'd read *A Model Murder*, or had seen me discussing it on TV. I smiled, hoping to diffuse the odd tension permeating our encounter.

"I guess that depends."

"On what?"

"Whether you think crime reporters should be behind the scenes, gathering the facts, or out in front, showing up on places like CNN and the *Today* show."

It hit me then that she was another reporter, though I didn't recognize her. I was briefly tempted to say something snippy, like "Oh, come on, let's not be a player hater," but that would have only worsened the situation.

"Who do you work for?" I asked.

"The *Glens Falls Post Star*. Probably too small potatoes for you to know."

"Of course I've heard of it," I said, hoping that by switching the tone I could appeal to her sense of collegiality. "Are you by any chance Alice Hatfield?"

"Yup," she said, looking surprised but still guarded. "That would be me."

"Well, nice to meet you. I guess you know I'm Bailey Weggins."

She nodded.

Fine, I thought, I'll take my toys and go home. But I intended to leave on a high note.

"Your reporting has been terrific. See you around."

She leveled her hazel eyes at me.

"Thanks," was all she said.

I returned to my perch and tried to enjoy the last of my wine. The crowd shifted again, and Alice Hatfield vanished from my line of sight. I was used to reporters being competitive but generally not pissy, except of course Matt Wong. Hatfield was making him look like one of the Care Bears.

Ten minutes later, I was back in my Jeep, headed to the Breezy Point. There was still some light traffic in the village, but before long I practically had 9N to myself. The wind had kicked up and it sent herds of dead leaves scurrying across the road ahead of me. Most of the motels and businesses were dark, clearly closed for the season.

The Breezy Point might as well have been. There were only three other vehicles in the parking lot—and lights peeking out from the doors of just two of the units.

When I stepped out of the car, the air seemed even crisper and smelled like fall—piney and mossy with a hint of wood smoke. I couldn't wait to crawl under the covers.

Key in hand, I hurried toward the door to my unit. From behind me I heard the scrape of a shoe. My heart jumped.

"You've got a lot of nerve," a male voice said.

I spun around, my heart in my throat. Cody Blaine was standing five feet behind me, and even in the dimness of the parking lot, it was hard to miss the fury in his face.

CHAPTER 3

INSTINCTIVELY I TOOK A STEP BACKWARD. HE HAD ONLY about four inches on me, but right now I felt every one of them.

"Cody," I said, trying to keep my voice even. "What's the problem?" Had I somehow misunderstood our meeting time or place?

"I want to know why you wrote those things about me."

"What things?" Wait, he must have already seen my post.

"That bullshit on the website. Trying to ramp everything up so it's really juicy. You said I blew you off today. You made it sound like I've got something to hide."

"I didn't say you blew me off. I said you never returned to meet with me, but you probably had plenty to take care of."

"You also said that the cops always wonder about the husband."

"They do; that's just a fact of life."

My hands were lightly fisted, I realized, and I forced

my fingers to relax. If I was going to defuse the situation, I needed to appear calm myself.

"Look, I'm sorry," I added. "And though I'm here as a reporter, I'm moved by your situation. I want our coverage to play a role in helping find your wife."

He took a step closer, muscling into my space, and glared at me.

"You have no freaking clue what my kids and I are going through," he said.

I didn't like the hostility I felt radiating off him. The guy, after all, might be a killer. I let my eyes dart quickly to the right, to the office. It was brightly lit, but from this angle I couldn't tell if anyone was at the front desk.

"You're right. But I imagine it must be beyond horrible."

"Then why aren't you digging up stuff? Looking for leads? Isn't that what reporters are *supposed* to do? At least the ones who are any good?"

He shifted back slightly on his heels, easing out of my space bubble a little.

"I *am* looking for leads, that's why I wanted to meet with you. But you can talk to me now, and I promise to help in any way I can. Had you noticed anything different or secretive about Shannon's behavior lately?"

"So now you're suggesting she was having an affair."

"No, I'm wondering if she was under any kind of stress."

"If she was depressed or especially stressed out, she never showed it. And she'd never willingly leave our kids."

"Didn't it seem odd not to hear from her while you were at work on Monday?"

"I tried her around midday but it wasn't a big deal when she didn't call back. I knew she had a lot of errands to run that day."

"What about the possibility of someone keeping tabs on her? Did she ever mention noticing anyone weird when she was running? Or anyone in her life saying or doing something that seemed hostile?"

"If she had, don't you think I would have shared that with the cops? What I'd love to see is reporters making themselves useful, turning up fresh information."

"Do—"

"I can't stand here all night. My kids need me."

He turned his back to me and strode toward a silver Lexus. I waited until he'd chirped the door open and then quickly let myself into my room. After placing the chain lock on, I nudged the curtain aside with my pointer finger and watched the car buck backward from its space and then practically tear out of the parking lot.

I wrenched off the cap from a bottle of water I'd stashed in the cooler and took two big gulps. Cody Blaine's visit—the way he'd popped out of the shadows, the anger in his voice—had unsettled me, and my heart was still thrumming.

What had the encounter really been about? I wondered. A desperately concerned husband who didn't like the way he was being portrayed, *or* a guy who was totally on edge because he'd bludgeoned his wife to death in the kitchen, dumped her body deep in the woods, and couldn't handle having his buttons pushed?

I let out a deep breath. Right now I had no clue. But I didn't like the guy.

After changing into a T-shirt, I grabbed my composition book and laptop, peeled back the duvet, and slid into bed. First, I scribbled my impressions of Cody while they were still fresh. Though I rely on those slim reporter pads for doing interviews, I find that when I'm on a story, jotting down observations in a marble black-and-white composition book with a number two pencil somehow manages to clarify my thinking and enables me to see emerging patterns.

Next, I clicked on the link for yesterday's press conference. I'd already viewed it twice before I'd left the city, but I wanted to check out Cody's behavior more closely now that I'd had a couple of interactions with him.

Though his confrontational attitude tonight hadn't served him well, I still had to hand him an A for his performance in front of the crowd. He had positioned himself just to the right of the sheriff, and listened intently to the remarks, his face pinched in serious distress. After the sheriff concluded, Cody took a turn at the mic. He was composed, but you could hear the anguish in his voice, which broke more than once.

"Shannon," he said. "If you are hurt or in any kind of trouble, we are here for you. And if someone has taken you, I want to say to that person, 'Please, Shannon's kids need her, and I need her. I plead with you to let her go.'"

There wasn't a single red flag, at least from what I could see. In fact, his behavior was in stark contrast to the way Scott Peterson had acted in the days following the disappearance of his wife, Laci, back in 2002. I was still in college at the time, but the case had fascinated me and I'd devoured every detail.

Peterson, I remembered, had betrayed no anguish, refused to be interviewed about Laci, and hadn't participated in either the search efforts or the press conferences. It wasn't a surprise to most of us who'd been following the case when it turned out he'd murdered her.

I leaned back against the wooden headboard, reflecting. Was Cody just a far better actor than Peterson? He certainly seemed *smarter*. Even tonight, as he stood there with his boxer briefs in a twist, I couldn't miss the air of sophistication about him. I would have to see how I felt as the days progressed—and more facts emerged.

Next, I reread Alice Hatfield's stories about the case in the *Post Star*. They *were* good, well researched and compellingly written, which wasn't always a guarantee with a small-town paper. It would be smart for me to find a way to win her over and encourage an exchange of information going forward.

I checked the clock on my phone. It was after ten and Beau should have arrived in Bogotá by now. As if I'd somehow managed to communicate with him telepathically, my phone pinged with a text. Just landed. Clearing customs. Love you. Wc tomorrow when settled.

Love you, too. Miss you already, I wrote back, relieved to have heard from him. Though violence in Colombia had declined significantly since the Pablo Escobar days, street crime and muggings were still a problem, and I felt more than a twinge of worry.

My eyelids were drooping by this point, and after double-checking that I'd bolted the door, I turned off the light and wiggled down under the duvet. Though my thoughts were churning, I fell asleep quickly from sheer exhaustion.

By half past seven the next morning, I was at the local elementary school, a one-story redbrick building. Since I'd managed to arrive on the early side, I stood for a while in the parking lot, pretending to read content on my phone so I wouldn't look too conspicuous. About ten minutes later, the drop-offs began, not only via family minivans and SUVs, but several school buses as well. Near the entrance of the building, people clustered briefly to chat—moms in jeans or tracksuits and little kids hoisting backpacks featuring images like the Little Mermaid and the *Jurassic World* T. rex. I was looking for any woman dropping off a child who appeared to be between six and nine years old—the ages of Noah and Lilly Blaine—and who also had a friendly face. Buddy, an old crime-beat reporter I'd worked alongside when I was first in newspapers, always said that zeroing in on the right person to talk to in a crowd made him feel like a lioness eyeing the weakest gazelle in the herd.

Soon enough, I spotted her: a sweet, guileless-looking woman, probably in her mid-thirties, who had just emerged from a red minivan with a boy of nine or ten. The pair meandered up one of the cement walkways, and I followed behind, pausing when she bear-hugged him under the portico at the front of the school.

When another mom yelled, "Hi, Missy," and she paused

to chat with her, I hung back. Two minutes later she began to retrace her steps toward the van, and I made my move.

"Missy, excuse me," I called out as she crossed the grass. "Have you got a minute?"

She spun around, her face already set in a receptive smile, though her expression clouded once she realized that the words had come from a stranger.

"Someone told me you might be able to help me," I said, reaching her. "I'm a reporter covering Shannon Blaine's disappearance, and I'm eager to talk to a few of her friends."

"Oh, gosh," she said. "I feel awful about the whole thing, but I don't really have much to offer. I barely know her."

"Sorry, maybe I have you confused with someone else. Do you happen to know the names of any of her friends?"

"Um, she's kind of private from what I've heard, and I don't think she pals around with many other mothers. I mean, there's her friend J.J., who the paper mentioned. You could ask her."

"But apparently she's still somewhere in the Adirondacks and can't be reached."

"Oh no, she's back now. I just saw her up on the grass." Missy swiveled her head toward the school and pointed her chin up. "She's over there. The woman in the pink jacket."

My heart already skipping, I followed her gaze until I spotted a woman with honey-colored hair standing under the portico, deep in conversation with another mother. So J.J. was back. And the word didn't seem to be out yet in the press corps. I had no freaking clue why the gods were blessing me this way, but I wasn't going to question it.

"Great, thank you, Missy. Have a good day."

I turned but didn't make a beeline toward J.J. quite yet, deciding that my best strategy would be to corral her in the parking lot so our exchange would be more private. I was close enough to see that J.J. was attractive, though not in the refined way Shannon was. She was fairly big-boned, the kind of woman you could picture not only riding a horse but also mucking the stall cheerily. She didn't look very happy this morning, though I couldn't blame her. Her friend was missing.

She finally nodded solemnly to the other parent and then started to move, but instead of heading to the parking lot, she began to move in the opposite direction, following one of the cement paths running across the school lawn.

I broke into a sprint until I almost caught up and then followed her as the sidewalk looped around to the far side of the school. When it eventually intersected with a village sidewalk, J.J. hung a left. She was walking home, I realized.

She eventually made another left, down Elm Street, and I decided to strike while I had a clear field. I called out her name, and she turned around, her expression guarded. After closing the gap, I quickly introduced myself and added, "I'm sure it's been awful to come back and hear the news. Would you have a few minutes to talk?"

"Did you *follow* me?" she demanded. I could see why the idea would upset her, but I had a funny feeling it wouldn't take a lot to work J.J.'s last nerve. Now that I was up close, I had a sense from the set of her jaw and the look in her wide-set eyes that there was an edge to her.

"I actually dropped by the school for another reason and happened to see you leave," I said. "We're trying to paint a really vivid picture of Shannon for our readers, and it would be so helpful to include your impressions."

She threw her head back disdainfully. "My best friend is missing. How are my *impressions* supposed to get her back?"

"The more information about Shannon that's out there, the greater the chance that someone will call in a legitimate tip about her whereabouts."

I was waiting for another blunt retort, but instead her shoulders sagged and her expression softened.

"I'll talk to you," she said, "but it has to be tit for tat. I need to know what's going on. All the sheriff's office wanted to do was pump me for information."

"Absolutely. I've got info to share."

"We can do it at my place. I need a hit of coffee."

I walked alongside her for a half block to a cute, yellow-painted clapboard house with white shutters and a front porch lined with pots of orange and yellow mums.

After unlocking the door, J.J. ushered me through the living room into a sparkling white, nicely appointed kitchen, and as she poured us each a mug of coffee, I slid onto a barstool at the counter. There were echoes of kids in the kitchen—a wicker basket of sneakers by the back door, school photos and award ribbons tacked on the fridge by magnets. But no masculine vibe. I remembered Kelly mentioning that J.J. was divorced.

"I really appreciate your time, because I can only imagine how tough this is for you," I said, pulling out my notepad and pen. "How did law enforcement finally get ahold of you?"

"I actually got ahold of *them*," she said, after taking a slug of coffee. "I'd been staying in the Adirondacks without any cell service, and when I stopped in a town for lunch yesterday, I saw that my phone was blowing up with calls and texts. I drove straight to the sheriff's office yesterday afternoon."

That probably explained the canceled press conference.

"I heard you and Shannon spoke by phone on Monday. Did she say anything that might hold a clue to where she is?"

"No, but it was all very quick. Hi, bye, see you in a couple of days."

I studied her face as she spoke, alert for any sign that she was lying. There was still the possibility that if Shannon had run off, she'd been assisted by J.J.

"Did she say she was going for a jog?"

"No, but I assumed she was. She does every day."

"Did—?"

"OK," J.J. interrupted, raising a hand. "It's time for the tat part. I need to know what the hell is going on. I've tried to reach Cody, but he hasn't returned my calls, and neither has Kelly."

I took her through the highlights that I'd garnered from the news coverage and my afternoon at the volunteer center. I sensed from her expression that some of it was new to her—and that it was scaring her even more.

"Those poor kids," she said. "Do you think the cops are really doing everything they can?"

"It seems that way, and there are a ton of volunteers, coordinated by a guy named Hank Coulter. Do you know him?"

"Yeah, I know him. Used to head the Lake George police before they disbanded it and put the village under the county sheriff's office. He can be gruff, but people always felt he knew what he was doing."

"And what about Cody?" I asked. "Is he a good husband?"

J.J. pulled back in her stool, narrowing her pale-blue eyes. "Are you thinking there's a chance he's responsible?"

"That's always a possibility in these situations." There was another possibility occurring to me now, too, but I didn't raise it with her. Sometimes a husband has an affair with his wife's best friend and then plots to remove the wife from the picture.

J.J. pinched her thumb and forefinger together and tapped the counter a couple of times. "Off the record—isn't that how you guys put it?—I don't like him and never have. He's got this too-cool-for-school swagger, like he owns the world. *But*, that said, Shan's crazy about him, and she's been a perfect wife for him. As far as I know, he's never given her any reason to think he was catting around."

Which didn't mean, of course, that there wasn't a girlfriend tucked in the wings.

"Ever any sign of domestic abuse?"

"No way. And Shannon and I went to the local beach a lot— not so much this past summer but every other summer—so I would have noticed something like that."

"Why not so much this summer?"

"Since March she's been helping Cody out a little at

work—at Baker Beverage. They're expanding, and she said he needed her to lend a hand in the office. It's only part-time, but it takes up a chunk of her week."

"I saw the house. Cody's business must be doing well."

She paused for a drink of coffee, but I wondered if she was also choosing her words. "Seems to be. They've got a big boat. Condo in Florida. Take pricey vacations with their kids."

Was J.J. envious? I wondered. It couldn't be easy for her as a single mom.

"How did they meet, do you know?"

"In the Caribbean, actually. Shan was in her twenties and looking for a fun change of scenery, so she took a job doing marketing for a resort down there. Cody had just finished a tour in Afghanistan and ended up working at the same place."

"And he's from Texas?"

"Yup. Near Fort Worth."

"How'd they end up coming back here?"

"Shannon was a little homesick, I think. Plus, not all that long after she met Cody, she ended up pregnant."

"Was he happy about it?"

"I guess so. Apparently they'd already decided to make it official. They had the wedding down there—one of those destination deals—and moved here in time for Noah to be born."

"Do you mind if I switch gears for a sec? I'm wondering if Shannon does any kind of volunteer work, like an activity that could have inadvertently put her in proximity with someone unsavory?"

J.J. lowered her gaze, tapping her fingers again. "She volunteers in the school library but not as much as she used to—because of her work at Baker."

"Was Shannon feeling stressed or upset about anything lately?" Cody had told me he didn't think she was, but women didn't always share inner turmoil with their husbands.

"Not stressed. Maybe a little preoccupied, but who isn't when they have kids at home? Besides, why would that even matter?"

"I'm just wondering if maybe life got too crazy for her and she needed a break . . . and now doesn't know how to come back."

J.J. was already shaking her head before the words were out of my mouth.

"No way. Even if she *was* a stress mess, Shan would never abandon Noah and Lilly that way."

But her eyes suddenly flickered.

"What?"

"There's something I told the sheriff, but I don't want this showing up in any article of yours."

"You have my word."

"That day on the phone? She seemed kind of off, like she wasn't really focusing on the conversation. She didn't take any interest in my trip, which was unusual for her."

"Did you ask her if something was the matter?"

"Yeah, but she told me she was fine, just had a lot to do that day."

A chilling thought jumped out at me. "Could someone have been in the house with her when you called?"

"No, nothing like that. But something seemed to be on her mind."

"About her personal life maybe?"

"Look, as I told you, she didn't say. And now, no offense, but we need to shut this down. I want to head up to Dot's to help out."

"Understood," I said, sliding off the stool. "Does Shannon have any other close friends?"

"Shan's not one of those people who needs a gaggle of friends. We have each other, and that seems to be enough for her."

"What about her sister—are they tight?" I was thinking of the little stink bomb Matt Wong had dropped about Kelly.

"They've had their issues, but again, I don't see what that has to do with anything."

"Just curious. They don't get along?"

"When Shannon moved back here from Anguilla with Cody, her father immediately brought him into the family business, and then a few years ago, when Mr. Baker became ill, he turned it over to Cody to run. Kelly resented that."

"Would she have wanted her own husband to work there?"

"Doug? He already runs a chiropractor business. The rumor was that Kelly would have liked it for herself. I hear she doesn't love some of Cody's choices, but the proof's in the pudding, as they say—the business seems to be booming. Now if you don't mind, I really need to split."

She began moving toward the front of the house.

"So you were camping in the Adirondacks?" I said as I

trailed behind her. The back of my brain had been noodling over what she'd said about having no cell reception, which seemed odd to me—why would a mother with young kids go someplace where she couldn't be reached?

"Not camping. Off the record again, that was a little white lie. The place where I was staying is a cabin my dad built. After he died this spring, my mother decided to sell it, and I've been promising to spruce the place up for her. I'm a real-estate stager, just so you know. It was my kids' days at my ex's house, so I figured I'd just go up there and start the process. I didn't love not having cell service, but I figured the kids would be fine for a day and a half."

"Why the camping story?"

"Because the less my ex knows about my damn business, the better. A guy I'm seeing was planning to meet me the night I arrived."

"And you didn't see any reports on TV while you were up there?"

"We never bothered with a TV there." She swung open the front door. "Bye."

"Thanks again for your time," I said, handing over a card and extracting my fingers just in time to prevent them from being pinched by the closing door.

I needed to be on the move myself. I'd stolen a peek at the kitchen clock and seen that it was going on nine. There was a stop I hoped to make before the press conference at ten.

From J.J.'s house, I jogged back to the school and headed to the address I'd found for Baker Beverage Distributors, about four miles south of the village of Lake George. Cody probably wouldn't be around today, but I was hoping to chat with a few more of the employees.

The building was set back a bit from the road, on a couple of nicely landscaped acres. It was huge and industrial-looking, covered with metal siding, though there was a natty striped awning over the door to the front office, placed there, I assumed, to make that section look inviting for clients. I pulled into a small lot by the office, though I could see a larger parking area along the rear half of the building, filled with big beverage trucks emblazoned with soda and beer logos.

I was halfway to the office door when I noticed the sign in the window. "The office is closed this week, but deliveries are being made. If you have any questions, please call and leave a message and someone will respond shortly."

I sighed in frustration over making the trip for nothing. I knew some of the staff were helping in the search, but I hadn't realized that Baker would actually be closed.

Dot's was so packed when I returned that I was lucky to grab a parking spot. A podium had already been set up a few feet beyond the overhang, and the place was abuzz with press and volunteers obviously eager for an update. I spotted both Wong and Alice Hatfield, plus J.J., who was talking solemnly to another woman. And Terry Dobbs, the owner of the Lake Shore Motel, was in the mix today. Volunteering, I wondered, or simply rubbernecking?

I managed to snag a spot for myself toward the front of the crowd, not far from the podium. From this vantage point I could see that Sheriff Ed Killian was already present, positioned beneath the overhang, along with two deputies. With him were Kelly; her husband, Doug; a girl of about twelve or thirteen, who appeared to be their daughter; and Shannon's mother, her glazed eyes suggesting she had attempted to quell her angst with heavy meds. Right next to her was a man in a white clerical collar—a priest or minister. I recalled what Dobbs had told me about Shannon not running on Sundays because it was a church day. This was probably her pastor, here to lend support to the family.

Cody was up in front, too, though removed slightly from the others. Perhaps as the hours had passed, the family had grown suspicious, and they were now keeping a slight distance, both literally and figuratively. A woman I didn't recognize was standing directly behind Cody—an attractive redhead, probably in her mid-thirties. As I observed, Cody turned and spoke to her in a neutral manner, one that suggested she might be his assistant, the one who had supplied a partial alibi for him on Monday morning. Nothing about their body language suggested anything more intimate, but I would have to keep my eye on their interactions.

At exactly one minute after ten, Sheriff Killian strode assuredly toward the podium. He was about fifty, handsome in a sheriffy way, and lacking the potbelly so common in men in his age group. He had an imposing presence, due in part to his high, felt-covered campaign hat, which made him appear to be around six feet nine.

He cleared his throat. "Good morning, ladies and gentlemen," he said, his voice husky and his tone sober. "I want you to know that we are still aggressively searching for Shannon Blaine. At this point, unfortunately, we do not have any active leads. I do, however, have one significant development to report, thanks to our search efforts."

He paused, as if giving us time to catch our breaths.

"Late yesterday afternoon, one of the searchers found Shannon Blaine's earbuds about a mile from her home."

CHAPTER 4

A COUPLE DOZEN HANDS SHOT UP, LIKE A MOB OF CURI-ous meerkats, but the sheriff raised his own hand in a "Let me finish" gesture.

"The earbuds were located in a section of brush several yards off Wheeler Road. Though we'd searched Shannon's jogging route previously, we decided to cover the area once more now that we have additional volunteers.

"We are fairly certain that the earbuds belonged to Shannon because, according to her husband, she'd put a dab of pink nail polish on them to differentiate them from his or those of the kids."

Even from several yards away, I noticed Cody flinch at this small reminder of everyday life—or at least everyday life before Monday.

My mind whirred. The earbuds seemed to confirm that Shannon *had* left for a jog that day, and that something bad had happened to her along the way. In other words, she hadn't simply gone on the lam, bored or frustrated with life.

"Unfortunately, at this time, we still have no concrete leads regarding Shannon's whereabouts," Killian added. "We're continuing to look at all possibilities, including foul play. I want to add that the fund for the safe return of Shannon Blaine, established by family and friends, is now at fifty thousand dollars. . . . I have time to take a few questions."

The hands shot up again, with various reporters barking for Killian's attention.

"Sheriff!" Matt Wong shouted. "Are you thinking Shannon was abducted and the earbuds fell off in a struggle?"

A murmur rippled through the crowd.

"That is certainly one possibility, but, without any evidence, I'm not going to speculate about that."

"Gina Tesco, Channel Six News," a woman's voice called out. "Do you believe Shannon could still be alive?"

"Shannon Blaine is still considered missing." As Killian uttered those words, I saw Shannon's mother desperately clutch Kelly's hand. "And it's our goal to find her. We are using all resources available to us. We continue to coordinate search teams and employ the use of the sheriff's department's helicopter. And we will follow up on any information that seems credible. As of today, we have received roughly one hundred and fifty tips to the hotline."

Killian pointed a finger toward a male reporter midway back. "Bill?"

"Have the tips included possible sightings worth investigating?" he inquired.

"There have been reported sightings, but none have checked out so far."

"Sheriff, back to the earbuds." It was my good buddy Alice Hatfield. She'd topped her car coat today with a black crocheted beret, befitting the morning's cooler weather. "Why do you think searchers failed to notice them the first time they went over that area?"

"We didn't have as many searchers on Tuesday morning as we did yesterday. And it's also possible the earbuds ended up under leaf cover, which later shifted with the wind."

I shot my own hand up.

"Sheriff Killian, Bailey Weggins, *Crime Beat*. Isn't there still one other possibility? That someone tossed the earbuds along the road, perhaps even *after* Monday, to make it look like Shannon had been jogging there?"

Heads swiveled in my direction. I think most people immediately caught my drift. Sure, the earbuds could have been knocked off her if she'd been snatched while jogging, but if Cody had murdered Shannon in their home, he may have planted the earbuds immediately afterward, or even later, when the police's interest in him began to intensify.

There was even a far-fetched possibility, I realized, that Shannon had placed them there herself, as part of a plan to fake an abduction.

"Ms. *Wiggins*, did you say?" the sheriff said, sounding more curious than snide. He joined a force of about a hundred people who had mispronounced my last name in my lifetime.

"Weggins."

"Yes, Ms. Weggins, that is also a possibility. But as I said, I'm not going to speculate. Next."

I shifted to the left a little, hoping to catch a glimpse of

Cody's reaction to my question, but my view of him was now blocked.

The sheriff fielded a few more questions. Was the lake being searched with sonar? (Answer: "No, we are holding off on that effort for the time being.") Were registered sex offenders still being interviewed? (Answer: "Yes, that is ongoing.") And, last, had the Blaine home been searched again, and if so, was luminol used? (Answer: "We are not going to speak on areas that might impact the investigation. . . . That's all for today.") He promised that there would be another press briefing tomorrow, the time to be announced.

As the crowd dispersed, with reporters hurrying back to their vans to prep for their stand-ups in front of the cameras, I studied the players around the podium. I could see Cody now, speaking in what looked like hushed tones to Hank Coulter and still appearing very much like a husband who was worried sick.

The priest seemed to be murmuring something to Shannon's mother, words of comfort that surely wouldn't be able to soothe her at all. From what I'd seen over the years, people whose loved ones are found murdered are never the same, though many of them manage to regain a degree of normalcy down the road. But if a loved one vanishes, never to be seen again, life is never, ever normal or good again. The family and friends left behind are unable to stop wondering and agonizing.

The mother nodded dully a few times. The priest gave her arm a squeeze and moved off in the direction of a burgundy SUV. I hurried toward him.

"Father, may I have a word?" I asked. "I'm a reporter with

an online publication called *Crime Beat,* and I'd love to ask you about Shannon. Does she belong to your parish?"

"I'm not actually a priest," he said pleasantly enough. "I'm a deacon. Tom Nolan. And yes, Shannon's a parishioner."

"Oh, sorry for the misunderstanding. Can I ask the name of the church?"

"St. Timothy's. The Catholic church here in Lake George."

Up close, I realized that he was a near doppelgänger for one of my brother Cam's college friends, a charming Irish-Catholic guy who'd had Kennedy-thick hair and big white teeth that seemed to be jockeying for room in his mouth.

"I'd love to give our readers a fuller sense of Shannon as a person. Do you have a moment now?"

"Unfortunately, I have to be back for a meeting at the parish center." He hesitated. "But if you want to stop by in an hour or so, I could probably spare a few minutes. As long as you're aware I'm not interested in gossip or anything of that nature."

That seemed to be code for "FYI, I won't be throwing any shade at Cody Blaine."

"Totally understood. Shall I meet you there?"

"Yes, it's right next to the church."

As he drove off, I glanced back at the action. Though the sheriff had announced he wasn't going to respond to additional questions, a cluster of TV reporters were trailing him to his vehicle, launching useless queries his way—I guess mainly so that their camera crews could catch them strutting their stuff.

Cody, I noticed, had slipped inside Dot's, but the red-haired woman I'd seen him speak to earlier was still hanging outside, waiting, it seemed.

Okay, I thought. Let's figure out who she is.

"I'm so sorry for everything you're going through," I said as I approached her. "Are you family?"

"No, I'm Mr. Blaine's assistant," she said. "Can I help you with something?"

I gave her my spiel and said I'd love her impressions of Shannon.

She smiled sadly as the breeze whipped a few strands of her hair around her face. "Shannon's wonderful—in every way. We have to find her and bring her home."

"Have you spent much time with her?"

"Not a lot, but she does come to the office a few days a week now." She swiveled her head in order to see into the interior of Dot's, and Cody, catching the movement, motioned for her to come inside. She nodded agreeably.

"Excuse me," she said. "I'm needed inside."

"Of course. And would you mind telling me your name?"

"Riley," she said. "Riley Hickok."

I had to find a way to have a longer conversation with her, though my hunch was that she was fiercely loyal to her boss. Was that loyalty based on more than a regular boss/assistant relationship? I watched as she hurried into the building and strode quickly toward Blaine. Though Riley was attractive, she wasn't in the same league as Shannon, and yet that hardly ruled out the notion of an affair. What's that old line? *Show me a beautiful woman and I'll show you a man who's tired of fucking her.* So crude but so often true.

Once Riley was inside, Blaine seemed to rattle off a set of instructions to her. Nothing about their body language suggested anything more than a working relationship. But they both had to know that curious eyes were watching.

"Good question about the earbuds." I heard a woman's voice coming from behind me, and spun around to find Alice Hatfield standing there.

"Thanks," I said without cracking a smile.

There had to be a reason she was massaging my ego after offering me a cold shoulder in the bar.

"I mean, you went where most people from here are afraid to go," she added, her voice deeper than I'd noticed previously. "It seems no one in town wants to so much as hint that Cody might have something to hide."

"Why is that, do you think?"

"People like him apparently—at the office and in town . . . and speaking of which, I want to apologize for being so rude last night."

I was glad she was going there. At the least it meant she could be a possible resource, willing to share info on the area.

"Apology accepted."

"Feel like grabbing a cup of coffee? There's a spot about ten minutes up the road, right on the lake."

A chat with her could provide valuable background about the residents of Lake George, if, that is, she had an inclination to spill. But for all I knew, something big was about to go down right here at the volunteer center and Alice Hatfield was attempting to lure me off the premises so a colleague of hers could grab the scoop for the paper. She must have read the wariness in my eyes.

"No ulterior motive," she said with a smile. "I promise."

"Okay then. You want to lead and I'll follow you?"

"Sounds like a plan."

Shortly later I was headed north on 9N, trailing behind her red MINI Cooper. After about two miles, we exited to the right and navigated our vehicles down a narrow paved road. Our destination appeared to be the boathouse-style restaurant that was at the very end, right on the lake, alongside a marina with at least thirty gleaming white powerboats of various sizes. Alice led me to a set of wooden steps and we climbed to the deck.

It was my first full view of the lake, which was absolutely stunning. When I'd been researching the area back in Manhattan, I'd stumbled upon a description of it that Thomas Jefferson had offered in a letter to his daughter. It was "without comparison," he'd written, "the most beautiful water I ever saw . . . limpid as crystal."

Yet another thing the guy had been right about.

The surroundings were equally riveting. On the eastern side of the lake, directly across from us, the low green mountains dropped right to the shoreline. As the range continued farther north, the color shifted to a faded blue, like a piece of duck cloth left too long in the sun.

"Do you have loons here?" I asked Alice as we walked

across the deck. Though there were at least ten tables set outside, there wasn't a single customer.

"Yes, more and more thanks to conservation efforts. And bald eagles now, too. . . . Why don't we grab a seat?"

A waiter emerged from inside and said that though they weren't officially open, he'd be happy to bring us coffee. His manner toward Alice suggested he was familiar with her.

"Do you generally cover this area for the paper?" I asked.

"No, I'm assigned stories pretty much as they arise, though seniority guarantees I land the good ones when they turn up. But I actually live a couple of miles down the lake in a winterized cabin, so I have the advantage of knowing people in this neck of the woods."

"I can see why you'd want to live up here," I said, nodding toward the lake. "It's pretty special."

"Well, at least during *parts* of the year. Winter's a bitch. They can organize all the polar bear plunges they want, but it still doesn't make it any fun to be here in January."

She pulled off her beret and made a futile attempt to unflatten a severe case of hat hair.

"Do you have family here?"

"Not anymore. Husband died five years ago. Son's in Chicago. . . . Look, let me say it again. Sorry about being rude last night. I've actually read your book and really liked it. I guess I was just in a pissy mood."

"Because of something to do with the story?"

"In a sense. As bad as I feel for the Blaine kids, this is a super-compelling case. As you can imagine, we can go for a while with nothing much to cover up here, when all we have for news is the health department's annual 'Be tick smart' campaign. Finally, there's something I can sink my teeth into, but I've got a crowd to contend with."

"You mean the other reporters?"

"Yeah. They're just doing their jobs, but some of them are working my last nerve. Did you see the one from Channel Six today? Gina Tesco? At the presser on Tuesday, she nearly mowed down a couple of people on her way to the front. She looked like an inebriated bridesmaid trying to make sure she caught the bouquet."

I laughed out loud. "And then to add insult to injury, a reporter from some *website* shows up in a flippy skirt and mules."

It was her turn to laugh, a full-throated one that showed she really meant it. "If you want to freeze your butt off, that's your business. But after you and a few others arrived, I realized the story was definitely going national. *Dateline* is probably packing up their vans at this very moment, and you can bet they'll try to muscle anyone local out of the way."

The manager slipped back out onto the deck, toting two mugs of coffee along with sweeteners and a little pitcher of milk. It wasn't even seventy degrees, but I found it invigorating to be outside with a warm mug in my hand, watching a few motorboats crisscross that lovely, limpid lake water.

We both took a moment to sip our coffee, and I studied Alice without being too obvious. I was sticking to my guess of her age as late fifties. She wasn't an unattractive woman, but she'd done little to enhance her appearance. Her hair was frizzed on the ends, her bushy dark brows were in serious need of grooming, and she didn't appear committed to the final step in the directions for foundation and blush—the one that said, "Now blend."

"You mentioned something back at the volunteer center that intrigued me," I said. "About local people not wanting to suggest that Cody Blaine could be behind his wife's disappearance. Could they be thinking it but not saying it out loud?"

"Not sure. I've crossed paths with the guy a couple of times socially, though I only know him to nod to, but I hear he's a good boss, generous with bonuses, that sort of thing. And reportedly a good family man, too. So people may actually be reluctant to even entertain the idea."

"Should they be less reluctant?"

"We're talking off the record, aren't we?"

"Uh-huh."

"The stats are in favor of the husband being guilty as sin, right? And Cody's got only a partial alibi. So yeah, suspicion is warranted."

"Have the cops been able to get their hands on any security-camera footage from homes along her jogging route?"

"Motels and restaurants have cameras but not so many private homes do, and from what I hear, the police came up empty. So there's no proof she left the house alive after returning from the school drop-off. And as you suggested, the earbuds could have been planted, to confuse the authorities."

"By the way, how'd Cody end up with the Baker family

business?" I'd heard one version from J.J. but was curious if there was another.

"He went to work in sales for Baker when he moved here with Shannon. The father apparently thought he walked on water and asked him to take over the whole company when he became ill. Congestive heart failure, if I remember correctly. Shannon, Kelly, and the mother share in the profits, too. I haven't found out yet if there's a stipulation that he'd be out of a job if he and Shannon divorced."

"So what do *you* think? Has he killed her?"

Alice tugged one side of her mouth up in a half smile, and I caught a twinkle in her eye.

"You know, just because you're from the big city doesn't mean you're the only one who gets to ask the questions."

"Okay, I'll go first with that one. Yes, there's a good chance Cody offed his wife. But it's also not uncommon for women to be abducted by predators. So we can't rule that out."

Alice nodded.

"Plus," I added, "I'm struck by Cody's demeanor. In cases where the husband's guilty, he often gives himself away. Cody Blaine looks distraught, and he also seems fully engaged in the search for his wife."

I didn't mention the incident last night, which I was keeping to myself for now, waiting to measure it against what emerged over the next few days.

"Maybe," Alice said, "he watched those other dudes on YouTube, saw what they did wrong, and decided he didn't want to end up on *America's Dumbest Criminals*."

"Is that what you think?"

She smiled slyly. "You said you'd go first, I didn't say I'd go second. . . . Kidding, kidding. The jury's still out for me. There's something about the guy I don't like. He seems a little slick to me, someone who's more sizzle than steak—like one of those Texas guys who people describe as all hat and no cattle. It's not hard for me to imagine that he more or less charmed his way into the family business."

"I know what you mean about him. I guess we'll have to see if a motive emerges over the next day or so. A girlfriend. A big insurance policy for Shannon. If the police have any leads on either, they're not giving them away."

I watched Alice's face closely to see if she had knowledge on either of these points, but it betrayed nothing. She glanced at her watch. "Unfortunately, I need to skedaddle," she said. "There's another story I'm covering this week."

Skedaddle. I hadn't heard that word in ages. While Alice was clearly a pro, a sharp, dogged reporter who didn't want to be muscled out of a scoop, she also had a folksy, homespun quality. Like maybe she'd crocheted that black beret herself. The brisk manner, I suspected, was partly for show, part of her professional persona, and not reflective of the kind of woman she was after five—or whenever it was she called it a day.

She signaled for the check through the window, and as I started to insist on paying for my own coffee, the manager gave us a wave that indicated there'd be no charge.

We walked down to our cars, exchanged cell numbers, and said goodbye.

"See you around campus," she said as I unlocked my Jeep. "And, look, in the interest of playing fair, there's something I should tell you. A post of mine is going on the paper's website in about ten minutes reporting on the family's life insurance situation, compliments of a source of mine. Cody had a policy on himself for $500,000 and a supplementary policy for Shannon for $50,000. That wouldn't give him much of a payday for killing her."

Alice didn't wait for a reply, simply offered a fast wave, jumped into her MINI Cooper, and took off. I smiled to myself. A little voice told me to be vigilant with her. She might be folksy and salt of the earth, but I suspected she could also be as wily as a Lake George trout.

Sitting in my Jeep, I mulled over what she'd told me about the insurance policy. That removed only one of Cody's potential motives. There was still, however, the possibility of an affair. If Cody had a girlfriend, killing Shannon would prevent a messy divorce that might impact his life with his kids and his stake in Baker Beverage.

It was time for a chat with Tom Nolan. Before setting off, I did a quick search on my phone about what the role of a deacon entailed. While growing up in the Boston area, I had a bunch of Catholic friends, but I hadn't been super familiar with all the customs of the religion. Deacons, it turned out, were ordained by the church, worked on a volunteer basis, and could officiate at services such as baptisms, wakes, and funerals, though they weren't allowed to say mass. Unlike priests, they were free to marry.

I returned to the main road, swung left, and headed

south to the village. The sky was a perfect blue and the sun bright. From inside the car, it would have been easy to think it was a balmy summer day.

I found St. Timothy's Roman Catholic Church easily, but as I darted up the steps of the parish center, I nearly collided with Tom Nolan rushing out of the building. He held the door and smiled distractedly in my direction. It was clear he didn't recognize me.

"Hi, it's Bailey Weggins," I said. "You told me to drop by."

"Oh, yes," he said, focusing now. "I'm so sorry, but I forgot about a meeting I had for my regular job."

"Can I walk you to your car at least?" I said. He might be having second thoughts about agreeing to speak to me, and I needed to snag whatever comments I could.

"Um, sure," he said as I fell into step with him in the parking lot.

"What can you tell me about Shannon? Do you know her well?"

"Not very well, no. I'm more acquainted with her mother and sister, though Shannon and I have chatted a few times after the ten o'clock mass. She's a terrific person. Very thoughtful."

"What about her husband? People have told me they have a good relationship. Is that your sense—?"

"Now, now." He shot me a warning look. "I said I wasn't going to engage in any gossip."

"*Has* there been gossip?"

"No, that's not what I meant. And besides, I don't really know them as a couple. Cody isn't a member of the congregation."

"Oh, only Shannon then? Does she come alone to services?"

"For the most part, yes, though she was here with her mother a few weeks ago."

He had plucked the car key from a pocket of his crisp black slacks and was obviously eager to bolt.

"Has she been doing volunteer work with the parish? I'm wondering about an activity that could have put her in proximity with someone who developed a fixation on her."

"No volunteer work yet. That would probably come in time."

"In time?" I wasn't following.

"Shannon only joined the parish a couple of months ago. Or I should say rejoined."

"She was a lapsed Catholic?" I asked, my curiosity aroused.

"That's right. But very committed now."

"So it was around the middle of summer when she rejoined?"

Nolan sighed. "I don't see how her religious convictions are relevant. It's really a very personal matter."

"Off the record then." We were at his car now, and he chirped the key. "Please, this could be important to the case."

"That Shannon's a Catholic? I certainly don't see—"

"If Shannon was searching for meaning recently, it could point to the fact that something was troubling her. And that she may have eventually felt a need to escape."

"Yes, it was in the middle of the summer," he said. "I'd say mid-July."

"Have you shared that with the sheriff's department? It might prove valuable."

"I haven't, no." He swept a hand through that thick brown hair of his. "But I'll address it."

Back in my car, I jotted down a couple of notes in my composition book and took a minute to sketch out a time-line of Shannon's recent months. Around March, according to J.J., she started working at Baker Beverage; in mid-July, she became a churchgoer again. And in late September, she vanished. Why the sudden return to Catholicism? I wondered. J.J. had sworn Shannon wasn't stressed, but perhaps something *had* been eating at her, a concern that eventually led to leaving her life behind.

It was after noon by this point. After picking up take-out tacos and returning to the Breezy Point, I tore off my jacket and composed my next post, naturally including the earbud news but not revealing what I'd learned about Shannon and the church. It seemed smart to keep that to myself for now.

The moment I hit send, I felt overtaken by a wave of fatigue. I'd hardly been working my ass off, but the day had been mentally draining. I flopped on the bed and closed my eyes, promising myself no more than a ten-minute catnap.

It must have been far longer than that because when I woke with a start, the room was dim and utterly silent. I pushed myself up on an elbow, taking a few seconds to recall where the hell I was. Right, the Breezy Point Motel in Lake George.

I fumbled for the bedside lamp and switched it on, casting

a small pool of light around the room. My head hurt, a result
of napping too long.

From the desk, my phone suddenly rang. Beau? I wondered. He'd promised to call when he was settled, but I
hadn't heard from him today. I stumbled toward the desk
and grabbed my phone. Not Beau. Number blocked. I answered, wondering if the caller might be one of the locals
I'd given my card to.

"Bailey Weggins?" The voice was deep and weirdly quiv-
ering, and I couldn't tell if it belonged to a man or a woman.
The speaker, I suddenly realized, was using a voice-altering
device. My pulse quickened.

"Who is this?" I demanded. Super-dumb question—as
if a person using a vocal disguise was going to tell me who
they were.

"Do you want to know what kind of Catholic girl Shannon is?"

"What *kind*?" Could it be Tom Nolan on the other end?

"You'd be surprised if you knew."

My heart was racing by this point. "Do you know where
Shannon is?"

"Go to Sunset Bay."

"Wait, *what*?"

"Sunset Bay."

"But where in Sunset Bay? Please—please tell me."

"You'll find it. And you'll see the kind of Catholic girl
she really is."

And then the call disconnected.

CHAPTER 5

I FROZE IN PLACE, STARING AT THE PHONE. FINALLY, I jerked my head toward the door, relieved to see the chain link was in place.

Had I just been pranked? Was Matt Wong or another reporter trying to divert my attention and have a cheap laugh at my expense?

It didn't feel that way, though. The call had seemed too sinister.

I grabbed my composition book and a pen and quickly jotted down what I'd heard. Where was Sunset Bay and why was it important for me to know what kind of Catholic Shannon was? Was it possible that something weird was going on with St. Tim's, which had led to her disappearance, and the caller wanted the word out? The tone of voice had been taunting, though, hardly reflecting a desire to help.

And no one besides Tom Nolan had known I'd been probing on that subject.

But hold on. People had seen me talking to Nolan in the

parking lot after the press conference, and anyone observing us could have easily guessed I was asking about Shannon's role in the parish. And I'd given out business cards to a horde of people in the past two days, even to some of the canvassers I'd interviewed.

I scribbled down a few names: Cody, Kelly, Hank, J.J. They'd all been at the press conference this morning. Perhaps it actually had been Nolan himself calling, wanting to pass along additional info about Shannon without me knowing it was from him. And yet wouldn't he have realized it would be suspicious coming so soon after our conversation?

And what, he just happened to have a voice adapter in the glove box of his car?

I tossed the notebook aside. There was no way at the moment to determine who the caller was, or if it was even someone I knew. What I needed to do was figure out what he or she was talking about.

I grabbed my laptop next and typed in "Sunset Bay." It turned out to be a hamlet by a small bay of Lake George and near the town of Bolton, only a fifteen-minute drive north from my motel. Back in the 1920s the location had featured a tony hotel known as the Sunset Bay Inn, but it had burned to the ground in the 1950s and had never been rebuilt.

I searched next for "Sunset Bay, Catholics" but nothing popped up, other than a mention of a Catholic church in Bolton—St. Mary's, which, from its website, looked to be more of a chapel. It was possible that Shannon had attended mass in Hague when its schedule lined up with hers on a given Sunday, though from the little I knew from old friends, people generally didn't jump from one parish to another. They stayed put, unless they moved or were traveling.

Another thought: Since Shannon's home was roughly equidistant from the Bolton church and St. Tim's, there was a chance that St. Mary's had been her original parish but that she decided to switch churches once she'd recommitted. Except Kelly and Shannon's mother belonged to St. Tim's, so it was likely her childhood parish.

And if St. Mary's was relevant, anyway, why hadn't the caller mentioned Bolton rather than Sunset Bay?

Next, I searched the Internet for everything I could find about lapsed Catholics, even reading a few blogs by people who'd reclaimed their faith. Age sometimes was a factor. There was nothing like a fear of dying to make someone rethink the way he or she was approaching life. Shannon was only thirty-four, though, so it was hard to believe that was the reason.

One of the blogs had been written by a man who had lost his sister and had rekindled his faith in order to help him make sense of her death and ease the despair it had caused. Shannon's father had passed away a few years ago, but if grief were her primary motivation, she probably would have turned to the church sooner than this past July.

So what had motivated Shannon to go back? I wondered. Was it because of turmoil in her life, and had that same turmoil compelled her to seek an escape? And could the answer shed any light on her disappearance?

I stood for a minute in the center of the room, swigging a bottle of iced tea and thinking. Then I grabbed my car key. Night was falling and my stomach was rumbling, but I didn't want to wait until tomorrow to check out this lead. Five minutes later I was on the road, with my Jeep pointed north.

The word *hamlet* turned out to be generous. Sunset Bay, or at least the main part of it, consisted simply of a dozen white clapboard buildings, including a general store, diner, and ice cream "parlour." Just beyond were a few sleepy looking motels and unpaved roads shooting off in several spots toward the lake. There was no point in traveling down any of them tonight because it was too dark to see much.

Before heading back, I drove north for two more minutes to the town of Bolton and quickly found St. Mary's. It was locked up tight for the night.

Clearly, if I was going to discover what the caller had been talking about—and if it *wasn't* a prank—I was going to have to learn more about the area first.

Maybe someone at Dot's would be able to help with relevant info. Like Hank Coulter, Captain Command Center and former chief of police. Granted, he'd chosen to be tight-lipped on the subject of Shannon, but perhaps he'd feel differently about Sunset Bay. Though it was now close to seven and I knew he was probably gone for the day, I set out for Dot's on the off chance he was still manning the phones. Drawing close, I saw to my dismay that the lights were off and the only vehicle in the parking lot, a black pickup truck, was preparing to exit.

I slowed, curious. As the truck passed me on the left, I caught a quick glance of the driver, who was Coulter himself.

He was alone but moving his mouth, probably using Bluetooth to talk on the phone, and he appeared agitated.

Something was up.

I pulled into the lot and shifted into park so I could check my phone. No alerts from the sheriff's department, no news on the *Post Star* site about Shannon, either. Should I follow Coulter's car? I wondered.

My phone pinged before I could decide, and I was surprised to see a text from Alice Hatfield. And even more surprised when I opened it:

> They're searching the Blaine house. You might want
> to get over here.

Okay, this was big. The only way the cops could have obtained a search warrant was by convincing a judge they had probable cause, that they believed evidence of a crime would be found on the premises.

This was probably what Coulter was jawing about, tipped off by one of his buddies still in law enforcement. I quickly turned the Jeep around and hightailed it to the house on Wheeler Road. Sure enough, as I neared the Blaine place, I saw that the front yard was aglow with lights. Several police vehicles were parked in front, along with a solitary TV van and, just behind it, Alice's red MINI Cooper. She was leaning against the hood, her attention focused on the house. As I pulled my car in behind hers, she swiveled her head and flicked her chin up in greeting.

"Thanks for the tip," I said, approaching her on foot. "Did I do something to deserve it?"

"I figured I owed you one after last night."

"Much appreciated. Do you know what grounds the cops used to obtain the warrant?"

"No warrant necessary. According to my police source, Blaine gave them the okay to have a second look." Now it was her turn to grin. "I think your suggestion that the earbuds could have been planted got under his skin."

"Are you serious?"

"The guy seems hell-bent now on proving that he didn't harm his wife. Regardless of your question, with each day she's missing, the spotlight on him intensifies, and now it's in his interest to seem as cooperative as possible."

I cocked my head toward the house. "Have you tried going up there and asking questions?"

"Yeah, and they gave me the deep freeze. Said I can wait until the press briefing tomorrow."

"I think I'll mosey on up there for a closer look."

"If your toes get cold, I happen to have a big thermos of coffee."

"Thanks, I'll definitely consider the offer."

As I walked away, I noticed the wind for the first time, racing up the sleeves of my jacket. Fall definitely was closing in.

The police had strung yellow caution tape around the perimeter of the large yard, obviously to keep reporters from trampling onto the grounds, though the only media on-site besides Alice and me was the navy-jacketed reporter from the

Albany TV station and his camera guy. A couple of sheriff's deputies were standing ramrod straight on the other side of the tape, their thumbs tucked into their thick black belts.

Most of the action, however, was in the house. The drapes were drawn in every room, but even from this far back I could see shadows dancing behind the curtains of several rooms. Was Cody inside? I wondered. According to the law, he would have been allowed to stay and observe but not interfere. If he was in there, it was more than likely that he had an attorney with him.

A few minutes later, as I stood with my arms crossed, trying to keep heat from escaping, two New York State policemen emerged. They were obviously working in conjunction with the sheriff's department, and one was carrying two large paper bags, probably filled with items from the house, the other a large, official-looking leather case.

"Is it true Mr. Blaine gave you permission to search the property?" I called out, knowing the chances of an answer were slim.

"No comment at this time," one of the officers shot back. "The sheriff will take questions at the press conference."

"Do those bags mean you found something?" the TV reporter queried. He also knew he wasn't going to score an answer, but he needed video for eleven.

As expected, no response.

I watched the two cops drive off in an SUV and turned my attention back to the house. There were still shadows moving, both upstairs and down, but standing outside wasn't going to tell me who was in there.

I hoofed back to the red MINI and opened the passenger door.

"Does the coffee invitation still stand?" I asked.

"Yup. Jump in. Unfortunately, I can't guarantee there's not a bass hook poking out of the passenger seat."

"I have a lot of respect for a woman who fishes," I said as I settled into the front seat, keeping one eye on the Blaine front yard.

"Do you fish yourself?"

"No, never liked the worm part. I guess you could say my big outdoor hobbies are hiking and bird-watching, probably because they were things my father did. He died when I was twelve."

"That had to be tough. Is your mother still alive?"

"Yes, though she's currently off teaching in Nigeria."

"Wow, how'd she end up there?"

"She developed a big case of wanderlust when she turned sixty, and she's been traveling a ton and also accepting stints in far-flung places as a visiting professor. At least we get to stay in touch through the miracle of Skype."

By now Alice had handed over a paper cup of coffee and refilled the plastic cup from the thermos that she was drinking from. Part of me was still on alert, suspicious there was an agenda behind her gift of a lead and the coffee klatch invite. But maybe what I was seeing was simply the salt-of-the-earth side of Alice.

"So back to the action here," I said. "Did I miss anything before I arrived?"

"Not much. They brought out grocery bags, like the ones

they carried out a minute ago. It doesn't look like they're wrenching up floorboards."

"Do you think the fact that Blaine gave them permission means he has nothing to hide?"

Alice tore at a ragged cuticle, considering.

"Not necessarily. The guy's shrewd, and he's not going to expose himself unnecessarily. If he killed her in the house, he probably did it without spilling any blood, so he knows there's nothing in there to incriminate him."

Noticing I'd guzzled most of my coffee, Alice kindly refilled my cup.

"Does it always turn this nippy in September?" I said.

"At night, you bet. Though we usually end up blessed with an Indian summer at some point."

A thought began to bubble up in my mind. Alice clearly knew the area inside out, and so she'd be the perfect person to ask for insight about Sunset Bay. I'd be tipping her off to a lead that could prove to be a freaking gold mine, but without any context, that lead was in danger of becoming a dead end.

"You were nice enough to alert me to the search here, and now I'm going to return the favor," I said. "But in exchange I need you to answer something for me."

She raised a bushy eyebrow. "I'm all ears."

I told her about the phone call then and how it had probably been prompted by the caller spotting me with Tom Nolan.

"Whoa, hold on. That's *very* creepy."

"I know."

"I don't get the church stuff. Are we supposed to think her disappearance is related to her being a Catholic?"

"I have no clue. And there was no way to tell if the person really knows anything about Shannon's whereabouts or if it was just a crank call."

"It could actually be the killer, you know."

"Yes. Or someone who knows the killer."

"You going to let the sheriff in on this?"

"Not yet. I want to wait until I gather more information and make sure it isn't a hoax."

"That makes sense, I guess."

"And that brings me to my question. Do you have any idea what the caller was referring to? I searched online for anything related to the Catholic church in Sunset Bay but there's not even a chapel there."

Alice leaned forward and took a sip of her coffee. Even in the dark of the car, I could see her brow furrow.

"There's a chapel a couple of miles away, in Hague. Though if the person meant Hague, he would have said so."

"My conclusion exactly."

"The only other thing I can think of is that there *used* to be a place around there that was affiliated with the diocese. It was called Sunset Bay Retreat Center, so that might be why it didn't turn up when you searched under the word *Catholic*. They stopped operating at least ten years ago, maybe a little more, but the building's still standing."

"And it's abandoned?" Even through my jean jacket, I could feel the goose bumps sprouting on my arms.

"To my knowledge, yes, though I suppose it might have been sold and is now under development."

"How do I find this place?"

Alice sighed. "That's gonna be tricky to explain. It's at the end of an unpaved road that heads down to the lake, but there's a bunch of those, and I'd have to be there to remember which—" She paused. "You want me to show you, don't you?"

"Yes. First thing tomorrow . . . And if we turn up anything related to Shannon, we could both use it in our posts, okay?"

"Okay. And yes, we have to go really early. I have a lot of ground I want to cover tomorrow."

"Early it is," I said, and savored a last sip of coffee.

Maybe the call *had* been from Matt Wong trying to mislead me. But something in my gut told me it had been significant and I'd had good reason to feel shaken by the sound of that eerily altered voice. The caller knew something.

The question was what.

CHAPTER 6

I HAD A RESTLESS EVENING AFTER LEAVING ALICE, WIRED from a combo of caffeine, the fact that Beau was temporarily incommunicado, and, needless to say, the mystery caller's message replaying in my head. What if the retreat center actually *was* the place the person was referring to? And what if there was something, or someone, waiting there for me?

I managed to find an open take-out food place close to the Breezy Point, and while eating a soggy chicken Caesar salad at the desk in my room, I toyed with the idea of alerting Killian about the call but decided to wait until I'd secured more info. Hoping it would calm me, I closed out the night with a hot bath, using the so-called "massage" soap bar that had been placed on the rim of the tub. It featured raised dots that I assumed were supposed to soothe my weary arms and legs, but rubbing them along my skin felt about as close to a massage as having my body licked by a puppy.

Right before crawling between the sheets, I shot my mom

an email, checking in. Mentioning her to Alice had made me realize it had been a few days since I'd reached out.

The next morning, I was headed toward Sunset Bay by seven thirty, stopping briefly for coffee and a muffin along the way. As soon as I pulled into the hamlet, I spotted the red MINI parked in front of the diner where Alice and I had agreed to meet. She lowered her window as I approached the car.

"I showed up on the early side and did some reconnaissance," Alice said. She was wearing the same black beret from yesterday. "I had a hard time figuring out the right road after all this time, but the guy who runs the diner told me which one it is. You want to jump in with me or follow in your car?"

"Why don't I drive us both? If something weird is going on there, it's probably best not to show up in a convoy, and my car is less conspicuous."

"By the way," she said after she'd parked herself in the passenger seat with her tote bag at her feet. "I made a call last night to someone I know in the area and he says they definitely haven't done retreats here in years. I'm not sure we're going to discover anything, especially if it's all locked up."

"Yeah, it's a long shot. If we come up empty, can we take time to look around Sunset Bay? Maybe this place holds a different clue about Shannon."

"Sure."

As I fired up the Jeep, Alice glanced at me.

"Last chance to turn this over to the cops."

"Let's wait to see if we find anything. That way they can't accuse us of sending them on a wild-goose chase."

I drove past the hamlet's cluster of blink-and-you'll-miss-them clapboard buildings. Narrow roads shot off through the trees on the right, and before long, Alice directed me onto one named McAllister Road.

As we descended toward its banks, the lake disappeared briefly from sight, blocked by masses of firs, poplars, and maple trees, and then burst into bold, blue view again farther down the road. We reached a dead end a minute later, the water sparkling directly in front of us. To our left was a huge and impressive gray stone house, with five gables, four chimneys, and a wraparound porch.

"Yup, this is it," Alice said.

"You've been here?" I said, killing the engine.

"I drove down here with a friend years ago, when it was still up and running. She'd gone on a retreat here when she was in high school and she wanted me to see the house, though I'd noticed it when I was fishing up this way. She said the kids thought it was haunted."

It *did* look haunted, with all those spooky gables and darkened windows. The house must have been a single-family home at one point, a summer retreat for one of the millionaires who had vacationed here in the early part of the twentieth century.

"How did the Catholic church afford to have a place like this?"

"It was gifted to them, apparently. . . . You wanna look around, right?"

"Yup."

We climbed from the Jeep and took a moment to survey

the scene. There was absolutely no one in sight, and the only sound was from the water lapping against the rotting boat dock behind us. The air was as brisk today as it had been last night, and I was glad I'd layered a sweater under my jacket.

"I asked the diner owner if he'd heard reports of any activity around here lately," Alice said. "He said no, for what it's worth."

In unison, we started toward the house, trudging through the thick, overgrown, and yellowed grass, and climbed onto the porch. The weather had done a number on it, splintering many of the planks and causing others to pop up at the ends. The double wooden doors were battered, too, and a metal chain had been wrapped around the two knobs and secured with a now-rusted padlock. It didn't look like it had been touched in years.

"Let's check the windows," I said. They were shuttered on the inside, but there was about an inch or so gap in most pairs of shutters, enough to peek through. We split up the job, with Alice taking one section of the porch and me the other. Peering inside, I saw that the floors were coated with dust, and that the few furnishings that remained had been tarped with old white sheets.

"From what I can see, no one's been here anytime lately," Alice announced as she rejoined me a few minutes later.

"Same here."

"So maybe your caller was talking about another place in Sunset Bay. Or simply pulling your leg altogether."

"Wait, what's that?" I'd strolled toward the very end of the porch, past the last window, and I could make out the edge of another building behind us. I leaned out over the railing. It was a simple one-story clapboard structure, not much fancier than a large shed, except that there was a stone fireplace chimney at the left end. The woods rose up behind it, like a long, dark curtain.

"I don't even remember that from the time I was here," Alice said, reaching my side. "Maybe it hadn't been built yet."

"Let's check it out."

We descended and made our way around to the other building. The light suddenly dimmed, and I looked up to see that a mass of dark clouds had gathered without warning and was now driving over the sun, transforming the lake from blue to pewter gray.

I glanced over my shoulder with a chill. There was a chance, I realized, that last night's caller was watching us. He might have followed me from the Breezy Point, eager to see how I did deciphering his clue. I needed to keep my guard up.

We reached the building and pressed our faces against its grimy windows. It appeared to consist of one big room, a rectangular space now totally empty except for a few folding chairs leaning forlornly against the far wall.

"Must have been used for meetings or lectures," Alice concluded.

I moved toward the front door, and as soon as I reached it my heart skipped. It was open, but no more than a sliver. I pressed my hand to the weathered wood and pushed. The door eased open several inches with a long, low creak. Hearing the sound, Alice spun in my direction.

"Jesus," she said, catching sight of the opening.

I brought a finger to my lips in a shushing gesture.

"Is somebody in there?" she whispered.

"I don't know, but we need to find out."

"I've got a flashlight in my tote bag. Let me grab it."

While she hurried back to the car, I studied the building, holding my breath. Could this really be where Shannon was? I certainly didn't relish the idea of going inside. If she was hiding here of her own free will, it meant she'd become unhinged and we could end up in a difficult confrontation. If she'd been abducted, well, then, the situation might prove a whole lot scarier. There was also, I knew, the chance that we'd find Shannon's body inside.

And, of course, there was still the chance that this wasn't the place the caller had meant at all.

As soon as Alice returned with a flashlight big enough to explore a mine shaft, I eased the door all the way open and we stepped inside.

Alice slowly trained the beam around the room. With that and the little bit of daylight seeping through the windows, we could see well enough, and yet there was really nothing more than what we'd glimpsed from the outside. As the beam of the flashlight briefly settled on the floor, we caught sight of a field mouse zipping along the baseboard.

Then something else caught my eye. There were marks on the floorboards where the layer of dust had been disturbed, as if someone had walked through here—and not all that long ago. I supposed it could have been a rep from the diocese collecting chairs or other furniture that had been left behind.

Or it could have been someone else.

My stomach knotted as a warning flare launched in my head.

"Look," Alice whispered behind me. I turned and saw that she was now facing the short wall on the right and directing the beam at two doors several feet apart from each other. Together, we tiptoed toward the closest one.

With Alice still holding the light, I tugged open the first door. Behind it we found a small half bathroom, both the sink basin and toilet bowl brown with mineral stains and reeking of sulfur. There was no indication that either had been used recently.

Maybe a storage room, I thought, as I reached for the next door, but as soon as I eased it open, the beam of the flashlight fell onto a staircase plunging into darkness. To a basement. Oh, beautiful. Just what I was hoping for.

"Should we check it out?" Alice asked, with an expression that said, "I'll give you a thousand bucks if you say no."

I could relate to her fear. The idea of going downstairs practically made my knees weak. But there was a chance that Shannon was below, and if she was still alive, she would need our help immediately.

I nodded. As Alice stepped ahead with the flashlight, ready to descend, I motioned with a finger for her to wait. I tiptoed to one of the old folding chairs and carried it back, then leaned it against the open basement door. The last thing we needed was for it to slam shut with us on the wrong side.

Since Alice had the light, I ended up following her down

the stairs, both of us cautiously hugging the wall as we went. After about a dozen steps, the basement opened up beneath us.

It turned out to be finished, with fake wood paneling and a row of small, high windows at the rear, which allowed a tiny bit of sunshine to creep in. Even before Alice directed the beam around, I could see the space was empty except for a couple more folding chairs and a decrepit whiteboard easel. It smelled as if mold was growing in every crevice.

"Nothing here," Alice said.

Except, I realized, as my pulse began to race, the dust on the paved cement floor had been disturbed, too. There appeared to be fairly fresh footprints, and they led toward the wall at the far end.

"Run the light over there, will you?" I told Alice, pointing with my chin.

It was more fake wood paneling, with a small furnace at one end and the base of the fireplace at the other. The scuff marks, oddly, stopped at the middle of the wall. As Alice bounced the beam over the surface, I finally saw the three cut lines. We were actually looking at a door in the middle of the wall, one that was flush with the paneling. A tiny metal latch poked out from the seam on the right.

"It's got to be some kind of storage space," Alice said, seeing it, too.

"Right. We'd better check inside."

I didn't have a good feeling. Someone had been down in the basement lately and either had removed objects from the storage space or put something there.

I crossed the floor, reached out, grabbed the little latch between my fingers, and pulled.

It didn't budge at first, and I wondered if the door had been sealed. I jiggled the latch back and forth. Finally it stopped fighting me, and I heard a shifting sound behind the door and pressure against my arm. Whatever was inside was trying to get out.

I lurched back, and the cupboard door flew open. Something dark, and long, and slippery spilled out, slamming against my thighs. A huge trash bag.

I jumped back another step as the bag fell partially on my feet. It landed with a thud but also a squishy sound, and then I heard the end burst open with a pop. A smell hit me like a punch in the face, making me retch.

I knew that smell. I knew it from stories I'd covered and a few awful moments I'd faced in life. It was the putrid smell of a decaying human body.

CHAPTER 7

B EHIND ME ALICE GAGGED.
"What— Is it *Shannon?*"

"Probably." I had to fight like a bitch not to chuck my breakfast. "But we gotta leave."

Alice gagged again, and the beam of the flashlight caromed around the basement. As I turned to flee, the beam bounced briefly over the open closet.

"Wait," I said. Holding my breath, I reached back to steady Alice's arm and trained the light on the rear of the closet. I couldn't believe what I was seeing. There were two more black trash bags lying on top of each other, though not as stuffed-looking as the one at my feet.

"Jesus," Alice said, following my gaze.

"I know." I grabbed her elbow. "Let's go."

We scrambled back across the basement and tore up the stairs. By the time we were out of the building, my lungs felt ready to explode.

"You okay?" I asked after a few gulps of oxygen.

Alice nodded, gasping for air herself.

"Man, this is awful," she said finally. "What the hell was in those other bags?"

"I don't know. But I bet not anything good."

I pivoted, searching the area with my eyes. Was someone out there, watching our every move?

"We need to call 911 pronto," Alice said.

"Let's do it from my car, though. Whoever wanted me to find this place may have eyes on us now."

"Jeez, good point."

We took off at a jog to the Jeep, and after locking us in, I reached 911, explaining that another reporter and I had stumbled upon what seemed to be human remains, possibly belonging to Shannon Blaine. Keeping an eye out the window, I gave the dispatcher the name of the road and explained we would be waiting at the base of it, right by the lake.

As I dropped the phone in my lap, I noticed how clammy my hands were. Though I'd always realized an outcome like this was in the cards, the reality was crushing. That lovely young woman, with two little kids pining for her return, was most likely inside the bag that had burst out of the closet and opened at my feet. And it had clearly been foul play that had put her there.

"Love how you used the word *stumble*," Alice said. "Killian's gonna take issue with *that*."

"I know he'll be pissed, but it's not like we were given any reason to think the worst. We weren't even sure if this was the place the caller was referring to." I turned toward Alice so I could look her in the eye. "I'll take full responsibility, but you might be blamed for tagging along. Is that going to create problems for you in town?"

"Nothing I can't live with. And thank God we *did* investigate." She directed her gaze toward the two structures we'd come from. "I wonder why the killer picked this spot. Maybe he went on retreat here years ago."

"Or he's just familiar enough with this area to know about it."

Alice lifted one bushy eyebrow. "Cody's from Texas, of course, but he's lived here long enough to have heard about the place. Shannon might have even gone on retreat here and told him about it. And he might be the one who called you."

"But if he murdered his wife, why would he want her body found?"

"Remorse? Guilt?"

"Then why not just turn himself in to the police?"

"Well, then the caller could have been a friend of his he confessed to, and the person decided to lead you here."

"Yeah. But if it was someone trying to do the right thing, why make those taunting comments about Shannon being a good Catholic girl?" Despite how distorted the voice had been, I kept coming back to the tone, which had made me picture a sneer on the caller's face. "No, it must have been the killer. . . . And shit, what if there are other bodies?"

"I counted two more bags. You?"

"Same. Though did you notice how much thinner they looked than the first one—not the bags themselves but the contents? Maybe there's only evidence stuffed in those. From the crime scene."

"Or there *are* two more bodies, but he had time to dismember those. . . . You know what this means, of course. We could be talking *serial killer*."

I nodded. That horrifying possibility had occurred to me, too.

Off in the distance, I caught sight of a motorboat slicing across the lake. It was hard to believe that as we sat near this horrible grisly scene, life was proceeding normally for other people.

"That would fit with the phone call," Alice said. "Don't serial killers like to broadcast clues, practically begging to be caught?"

"Some do, yes, but not all. . . . Have any other women been reported missing in the past few months?"

When I'd done my research on the area before driving north, I certainly hadn't turned up anything like that.

Alice slowly shook her head. "No, not that I've heard of—and I certainly would have caught wind of news like that at work."

I thought suddenly of the blond woman I'd seen jogging on the road, and my stomach clenched. But if she had gone missing, wouldn't her family or friends have tipped off the authorities to that fact?

"What if the guy's a trucker?" Alice said. "Or someone else who covers long distances for work and ends up here periodically?"

"Meaning?"

"He murdered two other women in different locations, and because this seemed like a safe dumping place, he hauled their bodies here. On his last trip he killed Shannon and added her body to the pile."

"Yeah, it's possible. But I've always heard that serial killers like to stick to what's called a killing field. And how would this one have known about the retreat center?"

"Could be a guy who's originally from the area and moved away. He might have even come here on retreat as a teenager and known it was closed now."

I bit my lip, considering her theory. "But it has to be someone who's around here *now*. Because he—or at the very least someone who knows him—had to have been aware of my talking to Tom Nolan about Shannon, about her being a Catholic. And then he got his hands on my cell number somehow."

"And what's all this Catholic stuff about? What the guy said to you. And this place. What if—?"

She didn't have a chance to expand because the quiet outside the car was pierced by the roar of engines. We swiveled our heads to see two sheriff's department vehicles shooting down the road in our direction. I felt relief but at the same time I had to remind myself: *Prepare to have your butt kicked—and hard.*

We climbed out of the Jeep and walked briskly toward the spot where the two vehicles had jerked to a stop. Before we even reached them, another car came barreling down the road, spraying dirt everywhere. This one, according to the logo on the door, belonged to the state police.

Sheriff Killian exited one of the first cars.

"What the hell is going on?" he demanded, stepping so

close I caught a whiff of menthol from his aftershave, which I should have been thankful for after the rancid smell from minutes ago.

"We found what I assume is a corpse in the basement of the smaller building," I said, as calmly as I could manage. "It fell out of a closet, in a large black plastic bag. We saw two other bags as well."

He locked eyes with me, his expression incredulous, as if I'd just told him the Loch Ness Monster had reared its head above the waterline of the lake shortly before he arrived.

"You told 911 it was Shannon."

"I said it might be Shannon. We didn't look in the bag, of course. But it was clear from the shape and the smell that there were remains inside."

"And do you want to tell me what in God's name made you come down here?"

I quickly explained about the call, and that it had inspired me to research Sunset Bay, trying to determine if something around here was connected to the church. This place popped up on the radar.

"Sheriff, I need to take partial responsibility," Alice interjected. "When Bailey asked me if I had any clue what the caller was referring to, I told her about the center and offered to drive her here."

Nice, I thought. She wasn't afraid to take the heat.

"You know, Alice, I would have expected more from you," Killian said. "Not from Ms. Fancy Pants. Those big-city folks play by their own rules, but I thought you were in a different league."

Killian glanced back at two deputies and cocked his head toward the building in a gesture that said, "Let's go." After commanding a third deputy to remain with the cars, he swiveled back to Alice and me and bored in with slate-colored eyes. "Stay put," he commanded. Then he and the two deputies strode up the bank, their polyblend pants making swishing sounds in the tall, dry grass.

I leaned against the hood of the car and considered how I could defuse the situation with Killian. He knew I was from New York, which meant he must have checked me out online after I lobbed the question at the press yesterday. I *hated* the label he'd just tagged me with in his huff. I should have told him that though I owned a few cute dresses and some killer shoes, I was hardly a fancy pants.

Almost fifteen minutes passed, and though there was no sign of Killian, one of the deputies eventually emerged from the smaller building, flashlight in hand, and began an inspection of the exterior of the big stone house, fruitlessly jiggling the front door lock a few times. Finally, Killian and the other deputy stepped out of the small structure, and Killian joined the guy inspecting the larger building while the other deputy trotted down to Alice and me. He explained that we would both have to drop by the Warren County municipal building in order to make statements to the sheriff once he returned. Alice could drive herself there. I was to go with him.

"But what about my car," I protested. "And Alice's is at the diner."

"You can leave yours at the top of the road and find a

way to retrieve it later," he said, unmoved by my plight. "The sheriff ordered me to accompany you. We'll get Ms. Hatfield back to her vehicle."

Alice turned to me. "Call me when you're done. I'll give you a lift."

"Thanks." I was clearly in the hot seat, and I appreciated her support.

The ride to the municipal center took about twenty minutes. I rode in the passenger seat, not the rear of the vehicle, but, still, at stoplights people craned their necks for a better glimpse of me. I'm sure they wondered if I'd pulled some bitch chick move, like tried to crush a cheating bastard of a boyfriend with the front end of my car.

I assumed I'd be in for a long wait once I was deposited at the location, since Killian would be up to his ass in body bags for a while. Or technically speaking, contractor bags. They were thicker and sturdier than regular trash bags, and I knew from some research I'd done for another story that they were available in a variety of sizes, even six feet long.

Was it really Shannon inside the one that had tumbled out? If she'd been snatched by a serial killer while jogging, she also might have been raped and tortured. I cringed as I wondered how long she'd been alive and terrified before being killed.

And if there were bodies in the other bags as well, this story was going to blow up big-time. I felt a wave of guilt over the next thought that popped into my head: traffic for my *Crime Beat* posts would explode, too. This story had more layers than Dodson could have imagined, and I was smack in the middle of it.

I ended up waiting close to two hours for Killian. I'd been without food or caffeine since my meager breakfast, and I could feel my energy flagging. I used part of the time to jot notes in my composition book. I also replayed my brief conversations with Nolan, trying again to recall who was in the vicinity at the press conference, but except for the main players, it was a blur of nameless faces.

When Killian finally arrived, his expression was beyond grim. I bet he was wishing he'd hit retirement age before ever coming across a scene as grisly as the one he'd encountered this morning.

Two people trailed him into the sterile interview room, a deputy whom I didn't recall from the scene, and a female state trooper.

"Start from the beginning," Killian said bluntly. "With the phone call. And don't leave anything out."

"Of course," I said. I wanted him to see me as an asset, not a thorn in his side. "I've been reviewing everything in my mind so I can be as thorough as possible."

I shared every detail I recalled and showed him my phone so he could see when the blocked-number call had originated. The state trooper made a note of my number and service provider. I also explained that the caller had probably been at the press conference yesterday and seen me speaking to Tom Nolan, or that Nolan had mentioned our conversation to someone.

"By the way," I said, "I suggested to Mr. Nolan that he tell you about Shannon rejoining the church in case it was relevant."

Killian's expression gave nothing away, so I had no idea whether the deacon had followed through.

"And how do you think the caller managed to get his hands on your number?" Killian asked.

"I've handed out my business cards to a lot of people this week, including many of the volunteers. One of them could even have left one lying around Dot's. Other than that, there's no easy way for a stranger to have access to it."

"Here," he said, passing a pad to me. His skin, I noticed up close, was slightly weathered from sun and wind and maybe from trying to keep the peace as well. "Write down the names of everyone you remember handing a card to."

When I'd finished, he ran his gaze over the names and then dropped the pad back on the table with a thud.

"I've just gotta ask," he said, returning his gaze to me. "Is this the way you big-city reporters do business? Following up on leads that should go to the police? Because that's not how we do business here, and it's going to have to stop."

"I'm really sorry about that," I said, doing my best to appear remorseful. "But I figured the call might not be anything more than a prank. Or maybe a local person wanting me to turn up some gossip about Shannon. The idea of finding her remains seemed very remote."

I scrutinized his face, watching for any hint that I'd guessed wrong about Shannon's body being in that bag, but Killian continued to be all Robocop with his expression, revealing nada.

"If the person contacts me again, I'll share it with you immediately," I added.

Would there be another call? I wondered. The prospect was scary in one sense, but I couldn't deny part of me was hoping for another lead. As long as I was the conduit, I was at the center of the action. And the more contact I had with the killer, the greater my chance of learning his identity myself. Wouldn't Dodson go bananas for *that*?

Killian didn't appear mollified, but I sensed the lecture was over. I would have loved to have asked what was contained in the other bags, but it was pointless, since there was no way he'd disclose that information. I also briefly considered whether I should mention the encounter at my motel with Cody but decided not to. That conversation didn't seem relevant to what was now in play.

"Am I free to go now?" I asked.

"Yes. But I don't want to see a post from you before the press briefing later today. And I want a guarantee you'll leave out specific details. No mention of the Catholic reference in the call. No mention of the bag—or I should say *bags*. And needless to say, no more interference in any police operations while covering the story."

I didn't love the fact that I had to hold back in my post, but of course Killian needed to control the situation as much as he could. And at least he wasn't holding me on suspicion of being a fancy pants.

"You have my word."

As I rose to leave, the state policewoman lifted a palm off the table.

"There's something I'm not grasping," she said. "What made you so interested in Shannon Blaine's religion?"

"I was simply trying to learn more about her, and after I heard she'd started going to church again recently, I wondered if something had been eating at her enough to make her take off—or whether someone in the congregation had targeted her."

"And did you learn anything?"

I shook my head. "Nothing—except that she seems to have made the decision in July."

As soon as I was out of the building, I phoned Alice, and she promised to pick me up in twenty minutes. I was famished by this point and was close to eating my purse. But the extra wait turned out to be worth it. While I paced in front of the municipal center, a state trooper I didn't recognize emerged from the front door, his cell phone to his ear.

"There were three in total," I heard him say gruffly. He clearly had no clue who I was. "All 187. We've got a major situation on our hands."

The number 187 was code for the crime of murder. So there were definitely three bodies.

A horn beeped lightly, and I glanced over to see the red MINI pulling up to the curb. Alice, hatless now, waved.

"You survive?" she asked as I slid into the passenger seat.

"My ass is a little chewed up, but I'm alive. Needless to say, he never offered me a thank-you for my efforts."

"If it's any consolation, I didn't get one, either."

"Was he tough on you?"

"Not especially, though he warned me to stop doing his job for him. He seemed mostly interested in whether I thought you knew more than you were letting on earlier."

"Are you *serious*? He thought I knew what we'd find there?"

"Not sure what he was getting at, though I assured him you seemed completely taken aback by the discovery. I think he was mainly wondering why the guy picked *you* to blab to, and whether there was more to that story than you indicated."

"There isn't. And hopefully Killian understands that now that we've talked more. . . . Did you learn anything during the interview? Like whether it was definitely Shannon in the first bag?"

"They didn't give anything away. Though I put in a call to a law enforcement source of mine, and I may hear something later."

"It has to be her. And it looks like the other bags had bodies in them, too." I relayed what I'd overheard the trooper say. I felt I owed Alice one, not only for leading me to the retreat center but also for my having put her in the hot seat.

"Three, wow. So we're definitely talking serial killer, aren't we? And one who obviously wanted the bodies found."

"It looks that way. . . . I can't believe I'm suddenly feeling sorry for Cody Blaine." And I was. Earlier in the week I'd considered how much the kids were suffering, but this would be wrenching for him, too.

I also experienced a twinge of guilt. I'd never come out and suggested in my posts that he was behind his wife's disappearance, but I'd hinted at the possibility with comments like, "A woman is statistically more likely to be killed by a male partner than anyone else."

"Okay, I'm merely spitballing here," Alice said, "but couldn't *he* be a serial killer, one who decided to make his wife his latest victim?"

"Of course, anything's possible, but serial killers generally don't target women they're close to. They may even have wives or girlfriends who have no clue what they're actually capable of."

"I love a girl who's got her serial killer facts down pat," she said. "So I guess the next question is who's in the other two bags?"

"Exactly. Any more thoughts on that subject?"

Alice touched a finger to her lips, deliberating.

"Well, as we already discussed, they can't be local," she said. "Or we would have heard about them being missing. So they're from at least fifty miles away. And if we're really talking serial killer, I would guess the other victims are women, too."

"I wonder if they were also Catholics, like Shannon. I keep coming back to where they were found. And what the caller said. . . . By the way, Killian mentioned there would be a briefing today but didn't say when."

"It's at five o'clock. At Dot's."

"Thanks. And thanks for everything else, Alice. I ended up roping you into a gruesome discovery and creating a big headache for you."

"Yeah, but I got to share in the scoop, so I owe you a thank-you, too."

We finally reached McAllister Road in Sunset Bay, and Alice pulled up behind my Jeep. There was a cluster of TV vans and a small throng of rubberneckers bunched nearby, but two state police vehicles and several officers were preventing anyone from moving closer.

"See you at the press conference," I said.

"I'll be there with bells on. And, Bailey, as you said earlier, this guy who called you may be watching."

"I know, but I'm not super worried. He had a specific use for me, and I fulfilled it."

Helicopters were buzzing overhead as I slid out of the car, probably attached to TV news teams. Word had gotten out that something big was happening in Sunset Bay. Before departing the hamlet, I parked again and hurried into the nearly empty diner, where I ordered a tuna sandwich and two coffees to go.

"Any idea what's going on down the road?" the sixty-something counter guy asked me. "Awful lot of commotion."

"It seems to have something to do with the old retreat center," I said, leaving it at that.

"The Catholic place? But that's all shut down."

"I'm not sure what's up. . . . Any idea why they stopped running retreats there?"

"What I heard was that the diocese ran low on funds—it's gotta be over ten years ago. They maintained the property for a while, though, hoping to start up again, but since then they've let things go."

"Why not sell the place?"

He shrugged a bony shoulder. "Apparently the woman who willed it to the church had a stipulation about it not changing hands."

I thanked him for his time and paid for my food. I also

made one additional stop on my way back south—the Lake Shore Motel, where the desk clerk from the other night was holding down the fort. I asked if a woman with long blond hair had ever shown up and registered, but he insisted no guest fit the description. Please, I thought, don't let her be in one of those bags.

Back at the Breezy Point, I wolfed down my food while racing to write up my next post. I'd have to wait until after the press conference to send it to Dodson, though at least that would allow me to incorporate any disclosures from Killian. I thought back to my initial post in the first person, which had turned out to be a fortuitous choice. I'd become part of the story today, and I wouldn't have to suddenly and awkwardly insert myself into the copy now.

Next, I placed a call to Bonnie Peets, a forensic expert in New York I often turned to for insight, and left her a voice mail asking for her assistance as soon as possible.

I popped open the second cardboard cup of coffee and hopped online, hoping to confirm what I'd learned about the retreat center. According to property records, it was definitely still owned by the diocese.

As I nursed my lukewarm coffee, my phone lit up with Bonnie's number on the screen. After describing Shannon's disappearance and my discovery this morning, I asked her what the smell might reveal about time of death, among other things.

"First, I need to hear about the whole setup," Bonnie said. "Where exactly is the building located? What's the temperature inside and out, and also inside the closet? And could the temperature in the basement have been altered for any reason? By someone leaving the windows open, for instance?"

Right, good questions.

"The building's on the shore of a lake and hasn't been used in years. It's ranged between the low sixties and low seventies here this week, and so I'd guess the temperature in the basement—and the closet, too—has been in the fifties or sixties. There's an old furnace in the basement, to the right of the closet."

"What's on the other side of the closet?"

"The base of a fireplace that's on the main floor."

"And you say this woman disappeared four days ago?"

"Yes."

"And how did the body seem when it fell on you? Was there any stiffness?"

"I only had a second to feel it against my legs but no, it wasn't stiff."

"Based on those details, it seems likely she's been dead those four days. She's passed through rigor mortis, the period of about twenty-four hours when the muscles stiffen, and now they've relaxed again. The bacteria start breaking down the tissues almost immediately—that's what's causing the lovely putrefaction you noticed."

So most likely Shannon had been killed on Monday, the day she went missing. At least she hadn't been held hostage for days, terrified out of her mind.

"I assume you get used to the smell in your line of work, right?"

"Well, *I* never have." Bonnie chuckled. "Cops sometimes

burn coffee grounds to mask it but trying that once made me never want to drink coffee again."

Bonnie was a tall, elegant brunette in her mid-sixties, who looked like she could be a partner in a white-shoe law firm. It was sometimes hard for me to picture her during her preconsultant days, investigating gruesome homicides for the ME's office.

"Okay, here's where it gets even more interesting," I said. "There were two other trash bags in the back of the closet. From what I've managed to overhear, the police found bodies in those as well, though the bags looked thinner, not as full. Could the killer have chosen to dismember two previous victims but not the most recent one?"

"I'm not a profiler, so I can't speak to his MO, but sure, they could have been cut up . . . or maybe the bodies mummified. When that happens, the corpse gradually shrivels into a leathery, parchment-like mass. Then you're dealing with something thinner and lighter. You've seen pictures, I'm sure."

"Yeah," I said with a shudder. "What would make a body mummify rather than simply rot away?"

"Dry heat, for one. If the bodies were placed in the closet when the furnace and fireplace were still operational, you would have probably had the right conditions. It wouldn't have taken long to mummify, maybe just a couple of months."

Was that what was really in those bags? Mummies? But there was one detail that didn't fit.

"But the furnace probably hasn't been used in ages. The building was closed down a decade or so ago."

"It's possible the other two bodies were stashed in the

closet when the furnace was working. Have you considered that?"

My mouth dropped open in surprise. No, I hadn't.

"How stupid of me."

"If you *are* talking about mummies, the ME will at least be able to spot certain injuries, which wouldn't be obvious if the bodies were decomposed. . . . Look, sorry, but I have to split. I can call you back later if you want."

"No, that's all I need for now. Much appreciated."

As I ended the call, I finally exhaled. Alice and I had pondered the fact that no other women in the area were currently missing, but it now seemed we needed to consider ones who had gone missing a decade or so ago, when the center first shut down.

A thought skirted around the edges of my brain, elusive at first, but within a few seconds I'd managed to grab hold. It was an article I'd read the night I'd been handed the assignment.

Ten years ago this past summer, two twenty-year-old women had disappeared from a Lake George campground and were never seen again. Maybe they *hadn't* taken off, as the police had concluded then, but had been abducted, slain, and stuffed in the basement of the retreat center.

A breath caught in my throat. If the bags held the remains of the two campers, it meant there really *was* a serial killer at large.

But if that was the case, where had he been all these years?

CHAPTER 8

ISHOVED THE CHAIR AWAY FROM THE WOODEN DESK, LEAPED up, and paced the room, struggling to pull my thoughts together. From what I knew, there were several reasons a serial killer could go dormant.

He might have been convicted of another crime and been cooling his heels in prison. Or he could have vacated an area after murdering several victims, engaged in a homicidal spree elsewhere, and returned to the original site years later.

And sometimes, despite all those horror movies suggesting that serial killer behavior always *escalated*, some of them lost the urge to kill, or at least took a break, because of circumstances in their personal lives. The notorious Green River Killer murdered prostitutes during his difficult first two marriages, but his killings dwindled during his third marriage, a happy one.

Grabbing my laptop, I brought up the stories that had been written about the two campers years ago in the *Post Star*. Their names were Page Cramer and Amy Hunt. Both twenty at the time of their disappearance, they were pretty, feisty-looking young women. And though Amy had chestnut-colored hair, Page's was long and blond, similar to Shannon's.

They'd reportedly befriended each other in hairstyling school in Manhattan. Amy was originally from Glens Falls and returned there after completing the program, snagging a job as a stylist at Lillian's Beauty Salon. When another stylist job opened up, she had recommended her friend, and Page had moved to the town.

On the last Sunday of July, ten years ago this past summer, the two had picked up a rented tent and sleeping bags and driven Amy's car to a campground in Pilot Knob, on the eastern shore of Lake George. A few campers later reported spotting them when they arrived and again near lunchtime. At around seven that evening, they were observed by a witness going into a bar called Muller's in Fort Ann, a small town about twenty miles east of the campground. The bartender confirmed they were there but claimed they'd only drunk one beer each and hadn't spoken to anyone else.

That had been the last sighting of the young women. When they didn't show up for work on Tuesday, Amy's mother, who was already concerned because she hadn't heard from her daughter, contacted 911. The police found the tent still at the campground, but there was no sign the girls had ever slept in it. Amy's car was gone.

From the articles in the *Post Star*, all of them by a reporter named Luke Orsini, it sounded as if initially there'd been a serious effort to determine Page and Amy's whereabouts, but that ebbed after suggestions surfaced that the girls had talked about taking off, maybe for Canada. It was even insinuated that they'd gotten involved with drugs. The articles seemed to stop fairly abruptly, though there was a follow-up story in the paper five years later, also by Orsini, entitled "Still No Clues as to Whereabouts of Missing Girls."

I jotted notes as I read, including the name of one of Amy's friends, Kayla Underwood, who was quoted as saying that Amy would never have simply taken off. She was someone I needed to talk to. And when I had time tomorrow, I was going to hoof it over to the campsite and take a look. And check out Muller's while I was at it.

If the remains in the two extra bags were indeed those of the campers, the police would be looking for someone who had been in the region ten years ago. And at first glance, at least, that seemed to rule out Cody Blaine.

I returned to the desk, picked up my composition book, and thumbed through the timeline I'd jotted down for Shannon. She and Cody had moved to the area from the Caribbean just over eight years ago, shortly after they married and a few months before their son was born.

Next, I brought up Cody's bio on the Baker Beverage website in order to confirm that info. He'd apparently joined the company as a salesperson soon after his arrival here, was promoted to sales director and VP, and finally assumed his current position as president. His LinkedIn profile didn't tell me much more, other than the fact that his job at the Anguilla resort—as a food and beverage manager—had kicked off nine years ago. Prior to that he'd been in Afghanistan for two tours of duty.

Okay, that would have to be checked out. Though it was unlikely that Cody was a serial killer who'd also knocked off his wife—he hadn't even met Shannon ten years ago and therefore probably wasn't even familiar with the area back then—I needed to be absolutely certain he was out of the country that fateful July.

As I considered where to find the info—probably by calling army headquarters first thing Monday—my phone buzzed and I saw that Beau was trying to FaceTime me.

"Hey, you," I said as I beheld his face on-screen. It felt really good to finally be connecting with him.

"Hey, you, too," he said. His hair looked a little matted, like it might have been raining in Bogotá. "Great to be staring into those blue eyes of yours, even from this far away."

"How *is* it?"

"Totally fascinating. And the art scene is thriving."

"I was a little worried when I didn't hear from you yesterday."

"Sorry about that. Besides the fact that we're trying to cram in so much, my cell service has been less than ideal. I finally had a chance to read your posts today. Sounds pretty intriguing up there."

"Well, it's a lot more intriguing *now*."

I took him quickly through the high points of what had happened since my last post—from the mystery call yesterday evening to my minutes-old theory that the other remains might belong to Amy and Page.

"That's shocking," he said. "This could be huge."

"For sure."

"Well, that's good for you then. This is the kind of story you've been hoping for, right?"

His reaction relieved me, meaning he seemed to be taking my current situation—phone buddy to a killer and finder of dead bodies—in stride. We'd had several long, hard conversations this past summer regarding his growing anxiety about my work and the danger he believed it entailed.

In all fairness to Beau, I *had* landed in more than a couple precarious situations over the years, not only while covering crime stories but also while helping out a few friends in serious dilemmas. But I loved what I did, and I'd bristled at the notion that maybe I should be stepping back or choosing milder crime stories to cover. I was hardly going to start focusing on people who lied on their résumés or refused to recycle.

I did my best to help Beau see my point of view. And I'd seen things from his perspective, too. The tension had finally dissipated.

"Yeah, it's a good story," I admitted. "Though of course I feel horrible about these women."

"Why do you think the killer called you?" he asked.

"I assume he'd seen me around, asking questions, and managed to get his hand on my phone number."

"No, I mean, why would he want the bodies found?"

"I was pondering that with Alice—the reporter I was with. Some of these killers like to show off, even crave being caught. Maybe he realized he'd hidden Shannon's body too well and wanted to be sure it was discovered."

But even as I sent that last idea up the flagpole, I could see there was a sizable hole in it. If the killer hadn't cared that the first two bodies had remained undetected for years, why the need to showboat about Shannon's?

"I can see your wheels spinning even from two thousand miles away," Beau said.

"One thing suddenly isn't making sense, but I'll mull it over some more. . . . Beau, just so you know, I'm going to be super cautious. As long as the motel has other guests around, I feel safe here, but if that changes I'm going to switch."

"Good to know, Bailey."

Before we hung up, he offered his initial impressions of Bogotá and told me that his Spanish was proving better than he thought. We said goodbye, and he promised to call me the next chance he had.

In the hour before I needed to leave for the press conference, I perused additional local coverage of Page and Amy's disappearance on the Albany-area TV station websites— nothing there that I didn't know already—and tracked down a number for Amy's friend Kayla, which turned out to be easy enough. On LinkedIn, there was a Kayla Underwood working as an assistant manager at a car dealership in the town of Queensbury, just north of Glens Falls. It had to be the same woman. When I called and asked for her, I was told she was off that day but would be working tomorrow, starting at ten.

"Can I get a cell number for her?" I asked. That's one of the things I loved about tracking down people in sales. They never minded having their cell numbers disclosed because they didn't want to miss out on any opportunities. Two seconds later the guy read it off.

When I tried the number, it went straight to voice mail. "Hey, Kayla, my name's Bailey Weggins," I said in my best chick-eager-to-purchase-a-new-vehicle tone. "The dealership gave me your number. Can you call me? I'd love to connect today."

At four thirty I slipped on a jacket, locked the room, and headed south to Dot's. I was on the early side, but I wanted to meander through the crowd before Killian took the podium and eyeball who had congregated at the scene. If the killer had indeed observed me talking to Tom Nolan at the volunteer center, he might show up again here today.

It turned out things were already buzzing when I pulled into the lot, and I managed to snag a decent parking spot. The TV vans from the Albany area had been joined by ones from Syracuse, Rochester, and Binghamton.

I made my way toward the front of the ice cream shop. There had to be at least forty people outside, a mix of local residents and members of the press. I could feel the change in vibe from the previous two days. Though the earlier mood had been sober, it had been tinged nonetheless with a can-do spirit, as if the volunteers truly believed that if they looked hard enough and tacked up a zillion flyers, they could bring Shannon home safely. Today, a pall hung over the scene.

Once I was closer, I was able to see into Dot's. Hank Coulter was there, huddled with a small group that included Kelly and Doug, as well as Tom Nolan. No sign of Cody. Of course, if Shannon was indeed one of the victims, Cody had probably chosen to stay home with his kids.

"My, my, haven't *we* been busy," a voice said behind me.

I turned to find Matt Wong, with a natty red scarf knotted around his neck.

"What do you mean?" I said, deciding to play it neutral.

"Well, if you're going to be coy, I guess I'll have to be, too."

"Suit yourself, Matt." I started to move off.

"Off to meet your buddy Cagney?"

"Huh?"

"The Cagney to your Lacey."

"Ha-ha." I gave him my back and walked away. Clearly one of his local sources had alerted him to the fact that Alice and I had played a role in the morning's discovery.

For the next few minutes I wove through the quickly expanding crowd, keeping an eye out for anyone who seemed weirdly entranced with the goings-on, or, on the other hand, too detached. No one fit the bill, but a couple of times I had the fiercest sense that someone's eyes were on my back. Each time I'd turn, though, I didn't catch a soul looking my way.

Finally I neared the front and caught sight of Alice, again in her car coat and crocheted hat. She shot me a wry smile that seemed to say, "You doing okay?" "Can you believe this zoo?" and "Let's talk later," all in unison. I flashed her back a look that I hope translated as, "Yes, yes, and yes."

After locating a decent spot to stand in, I pulled a pen and notebook from my bag. The sky was overcast, and a gusty breeze whipped people's hair into their faces and sent papers scurrying across the parking lot.

At four minutes to five, the sheriff's SUV arrived. Killian

stepped out with a deputy, headed into Dot's, and emerged a few minutes later with Kelly, her husband, and Tom Nolan. All of them were bleak faced, and Doug was gripping Kelly's elbow. I had little doubt what that signified.

Killian strode toward the podium, where a dozen microphones were bunched together today. Before he could speak, the wind sent one of the Missing flyers skittering across the pavement of the parking lot until it plastered itself ominously against the podium's wood base. My phone buzzed in my purse, and I saw to my dismay that it was Kayla Underwood. I had no choice but to send the call to voice mail.

"Good afternoon, ladies and gentlemen, and thank you for your attention," Killian said, his voice as somber as a graveyard. "I have some significant developments to share with you today.

"Earlier this morning, the sheriff's office was called to a building on the banks of Lake George, near the hamlet of Sunset Bay. The building was once part of a complex called the Sunset Bay Retreat Center but was abandoned for use eleven years ago. Shannon Blaine's remains were found in the basement of that building."

The crowd let out a collective gasp, and I felt my stomach clutch. As sure as I'd felt that it was Shannon we'd found, it didn't make the truth any easier to digest.

"The remains were located, by the way, thanks to the efforts of two reporters, one of whom received an anonymous tip. We are, of course, investigating."

More gasping, this time accompanied by lots of head swiveling. I stared straight ahead toward the podium, avoiding eye contact with other reporters. I didn't want anyone to guess it was me until I could send off my post this evening.

"At this point, neither the cause nor time of death have been determined," Killian continued, ignoring the hands shooting up everywhere. "This is early stages still, and the investigation is unfolding. We wish to offer our heartfelt condolences to Shannon Blaine's family . . . and before I continue, I want to give Kelly Claiborne the chance to say a few words."

Kelly unhitched herself from her husband's grip and exchanged spots with Killian.

"On behalf of Shannon's entire family," she said, clearly doing her best to keep her voice steady. "I want to thank everyone for their efforts this week. The reward we were offering will now go to anyone with information that leads to the arrest of the monster who killed my sister."

That was it. She returned to her husband's side, and Killian took over the podium again. As a reporter shouted a question, Killian held up a hand to say, "Not now."

"I have another significant development to report today," he said. "In the same location where we discovered the body of Shannon Blaine, we found the remains of two other individuals, which appear to have been there for a considerable period of time."

All around me, people exclaimed in shock and disbelief.

"As of yet, we have not identified those bodies," Killian added, tapping the air with his hands to shush the crowd, "and I don't intend to waste my time or yours speculating. We will keep you informed as the investigation progresses. Since the volunteer center will be closing, all future press conferences on this case will be held at the municipal center."

What followed was a blizzard of questions, reporters wanting to know who owned the building, whether the killer could have worked there at some point, if there was any possible connection between Shannon and the other bodies, and so on. It wouldn't take long for people to link the news to the disappearance of the two campers years ago.

Though Killian disclosed that the property was owned by the Catholic church, he blunted most of the other questions with an "I'm not at liberty to discuss at this time."

So far, no one was picking up fully on the religious angle, but why would they? They hadn't heard what the caller had said to me, and as far as they knew, the retreat center had been selected as a dump site simply because the killer had known it was abandoned.

As Killian prepared to finish, I scanned the parking lot for the Claibornes. They'd slipped away from the front and were making a beeline for an SUV. I snaked my way out of the crowd and hurried in their direction.

"Kelly, I'm so sorry for your loss," I said softly, as our paths intersected.

"Thank you," she muttered. She seemed to be holding it together, but her face was as white as candle wax.

"I'm not sure the police have told you this yet, but I was one of the two journalists who found Shannon's body."

"You? Are you the one who got the tip?"

"Yes, that was me. Kelly, do you recall giving my business

card to anyone, or seeing someone pick it up from the table where you were sitting?"

She squinted, clearly trying to focus.

"I did leave it on the table but—I don't recall anyone picking it up."

So one of the volunteers or someone posing as a volunteer could have easily grabbed it.

"I know you need to get home to your family, but is there anything you can tell me about the retreat center? Did—did Shannon ever go on retreat there when it was in operation?"

"Look, my wife's in no shape to be answering questions at the moment," Doug said. With his tanned skin, sandy hair, and light brown eyes, he vaguely resembled a pair of chinos. He ushered Kelly into the car and then slid into the driver's seat.

I spun around, hoping I still had time to catch Nolan, but he was already in his own vehicle, nosing out of the lot. I'd have to pay him a follow-up visit at the parish house. I wanted to learn what he knew about the Sunset Bay Retreat Center, and also pump him for more details about Shannon's return to the church.

I glanced over to where I'd been standing earlier. The sheriff had backed away from the podium and the crowd was breaking apart, some people appearing shell-shocked, others looking fearful as they whispered frantically to each other. Alice spotted me and held up her hand, fingers splayed, suggesting we should talk in five minutes. I used the time to listen to the message from Kayla. She clearly thought I was a prospective buyer because she couldn't have sounded friendlier, and when I returned the phone call two seconds later, she answered with the same pep in her voice. I introduced myself and said I wanted to talk to her about Amy Hunt.

"I don't get it," she said, her tone suddenly cool. "Why now, after all this time?"

"I'd like to learn more about the case for another story I'm doing," I said. "I don't know a lot about Amy's situation, but it sounds as if the authorities didn't pay enough attention to her disappearance."

"Enough? Try zilch."

"I'd love to meet you and discuss it."

"Uh, sure, okay. I'll be at work by ten tomorrow, so I could meet you at the dealership then. It's not super busy in the morning."

She provided the address and signed off. I spotted Alice heading toward me, zigzagging through departing cars.

"You wanna grab a bite at Jake's after we both file?" she asked, reaching me. It was the restaurant where we'd had our first, very stilted conversation.

"Absolutely, but could you give me an hour and a half?"

"You bet."

I drove back to the Breezy Point and quickly updated the draft of my post with details from the press conference. I forwarded it to Dodson and asked if there was anything else he needed from me, since the story up here had exploded.

When I arrived at the restaurant, Alice was already seated at a table by the window, still in her coat and studying her phone. It was too dark at this point to see the lake through the glass behind us, but at least we'd be away from the bar noise.

"This is the kind of day when I really miss my husband,"

she said, once I'd flopped into a chair. "He'd be giving me a foot rub right now."

"Want me to make an attempt?"

She snorted and shrugged off her coat. "You'd probably cut your hands on my calluses. Besides, you've had an equally tough day, my friend."

We ordered wine and food at the same time, and as soon as the waitress moved off, I divulged my theory about the other two victims being Amy and Page.

"I've been wondering the same thing," she said. "Of course, that would mean their bodies have been there for a decade."

"If you do the math, it works out. Though they stopped doing retreats eleven years ago, the guy in the diner told me they kept the site functional for a while longer, hoping to start back up again. Amy and Page went missing ten years ago. The killer could have left the bodies in the basement at that time, figuring there was little chance of anyone besides him going into the storage space. The furnace must have been turned on that next winter, and the bodies mummified."

"Those poor things. I didn't cover that story myself—I think I had a bad case of Lyme disease then—but from what I recall, the cops really bought into the idea that the girls had simply taken off."

"I bet you they're not so dismissive now. How fast do autopsies happen in this neck of the woods?"

"The bodies will be sent to Albany Med and that place is pretty efficient. But as you know, these things take a lot more time in real life than they do on TV, so it's not like we'll be hearing tomorrow. My police source has promised to call me with anything he hears, though."

I shot her my best smile. "If I pick up the tab tonight, would you be up for sharing?"

"As long as it's solely for your own edification. I could never even post what he says and attribute it to an unnamed source, because people might suspect it's him."

"Got it."

Alice plucked a piece of bread from the basket and buttered it. "So how does all this make you feel about Cody Blaine?"

"I'd say that for the most part, the idea of him as his wife's murderer has left the building, but I'm trying to figure out the most expedient way to determine if he was out of the country ten years ago."

"Let me save you the trouble. I have a pal in the veterans' office here and he confirmed that Cody was in Afghanistan when the girls disappeared."

"Ah, so that definitely lets him off the hook."

"Yup. Like I told you, I don't love the guy, but I'm feeling pretty bad for him now."

Our wine arrived, and we each indulged in a long sip.

"Any more ideas about who the killer *could* be?"

"I know you didn't love my trucker theory, but to me that's still a possibility, and it explains the ten-year gap. Maybe he's been killing in different areas all these years."

I picked up the saltshaker and made circles on the table with it, pulling a thought together.

"But remember, the killer has to be someone—or closely connected to someone—who knew I was asking about Shannon going to church again. And that means a person who's been in the mix here lately."

"That's the kind of thought that makes me want to leave the lights on at night."

When our meals showed up, we switched gears—I could sense Alice needed a break from the topic as much as I did—and we talked instead about how we'd each broken into the field. Alice, it turned out, had worked in newspapers pretty consistently since college but had tabled her career for seven years when her son, Ben, was young. She showed me a couple of pictures of him. Nice-looking guy, now a college professor, and she clearly adored him.

"You've been a reporter for a long time," I said, taking a break from my crab cakes. "Have you found a way to keep days like today from getting the better of you?"

I wasn't simply making conversation. Despite how many gruesome stories I'd reported on, I was having a hard time preventing this morning's experience from weighing on me.

"Well, fortunately we don't get many as bad as this. But I've covered my share of horror shows. Kids abused and then put into foster care, et cetera, et cetera, et cetera. I find that every so often I have to detach, disengage completely. Or I go nuts."

"How do you do that?"

"Actually, that's one of the reasons I fish. I head out onto the lake with a cooler and stay for hours. It's my form of meditating, I guess."

"So you keep your focus on the fish? On catching them?"

"This is going to sound ridiculous, but for me the real disengagement comes when the fish *aren't* biting. I find it really peaceful to sit in the boat and do nothing but listen to the water lapping and the gulls calling overhead."

I could feel my expression turning wistful.

"What?" she asked.

"Remember I told you my father was a bird-watcher? He always said he loved the spaces *between* birds. When he was simply waiting for a birdcall or a rustle in the trees."

"It's the exact same thing, really." Alice chuckled. "My husband was all about the day's catch and frying it up for dinner. I never admitted to him that when I went out on the boat alone, I sometimes didn't even drop my line in the water."

We had just ordered coffee when Alice's phone buzzed.

"Okay, here we go," she said as she caught the name on the screen. "Give me a second."

I nodded as she rose from the table and positioned herself ten feet away, in the corner of the room. Less than two minutes later, she was back, her mouth agape.

"Can you say?" I asked. It was clear whatever she'd heard was big and I had to at least try to find out what it was.

"Yeah, but you're giving me your word, right? This is merely for background. We can't even hint at it."

"You have my word." My pulse had started to race.

"The remains in those other two bags? They were actually fairly well preserved. Just as your pal hypothesized, the bodies *had* mummified."

"Are they the campers?"

"They think so. They need to obtain DNA from some of their family members and make a comparison, but there's a tattoo on one body that fits with one Page Cramer had."

"Anything else?"

"No autopsy yet on Shannon, but from the bruising, it looks as if she was strangled. They'll probably announce that."

I winced. It was all so freaking sad.

"But here's the really crazy part," Alice continued. "There are cut marks on Shannon's body, probably made *postmortem*. And they seem to be on the other bodies, too."

"He stabbed them after they were dead?"

"Yes, but only on the palms of the hands, and the tops of the feet."

"*What?*" Somewhere in the back of my brain, a thought was knitting together fast, based on bits and pieces I'd read over time. "You mean like—"

"Yeah," Alice said. "Like stigmata."

CHAPTER 9

FOR A MOMENT I SAT THERE STOCK-STILL, STUNNED. WHY would the killer feel a compulsion to mark his victims that way?

"Do you know anything about this type of phenomenon?" Alice asked.

"Nothing beyond a few references I've seen in books."

Alice fished her phone from her purse and asked Siri to fill us in.

"Okay, here's Wikipedia," she said, peering intently at her screen. "'Stigmata is a term used by members of the Christian faith to describe the manifestations of bodily wounds, scars, and pain in locations corresponding to the crucifixion wounds of Jesus Christ, such as the hands, wrists, and feet.' Um, let's see . . . 'Stigmata are primarily associated with the Roman Catholic faith. . . .'"

"From what I've read, the wounds on so-called *real* stigmatics are supposed to have appeared spontaneously."

"Right. Oh, this is interesting," she said, still reading.

"'A high percentage of all stigmatics—perhaps over eighty percent—are women.' So the killer must be a religious nut, right? He leaves the bodies at a former Catholic retreat center. And now this."

"And the phone call," I reminded her. "Mentioning what a good Catholic Shannon was."

"Jeez, this is adding up to be pretty freaky."

"Any word on cause of death for Amy and Page?"

"Nothing yet."

We asked for more coffee and batted theories back and forth for a while longer, but I could feel myself growing restless, eager to be in a setting where I could think without old songs by Foreigner and Bon Jovi pounding in the background. I also wanted to settle back in my motel room, with the dead bolt firmly in place, before it grew too late. I flagged the waitress for the check.

"Bailey, I know I'm in danger of becoming a nag, but please be extra careful," Alice said when we stepped out onto the sidewalk. I appreciated her concern. I kept telling myself I'd served a purpose for the killer, and he might want or need me to continue in that role, which meant my life wasn't in any danger. But the news Alice had revealed tonight had unnerved me.

Our cars, it turned out, were in different directions, and before parting, we embraced in a hug. As ugly as the day had been, it had bonded the two of us.

Two minutes later, I was headed north on Route 9N. The road was nearly deserted except for the occasional car coming south. My high beams picked out the motels and fast-food stands closest to the road, but everything else was swallowed by darkness.

As I drove, I let my gaze dart regularly to the rearview mirror. Just once, a vehicle appeared behind me, but it pulled off after a couple of minutes onto a side road.

When I swung into the parking lot of the Breezy Point, a light was burning inside the office, but I didn't see anyone moving around in there. Surely there had to be a clerk on duty someplace.

I maneuvered into the parking spot in front of my unit, killed the engine, and twisted in my seat, scanning the lot. There was only one other car, parked way at the other end, in front of a unit with a faint light seeping out from the edges of the window shade. Well, at least *somebody* was around. I jumped out of the Jeep and quickly let myself into the room.

After flicking on the lights and shaking off my jacket, I checked Twitter for alerts from a variety of news sources. With the discovery of the three bodies, the Shannon Blaine story had exploded and was now online everywhere— including CNN, *People* Crime Watch, and the network TV websites. By tomorrow the area would be flooded with fresh troops of reporters. Maybe the killer would reach out to one of *them*. As much as I'd been creeped out by the call, the idea of another reporter securing a fresh clue from him didn't please me.

Next, I scrolled through a few vaguely scholarly articles about stigmata, including one that claimed that most historical cases of stigmata were likely either self-inflicted or psychosomatic.

None of which explained why the killer would want to mark his victims in that manner.

I toyed with a few possible motives for his actions. He might have been mistreated by a parent with extreme religious beliefs. Or he'd been abused—sexually or otherwise—by a member of the clergy. Since there was a possibility he'd gone to a retreat once at the Sunset Bay center, he may have even been abused *there*.

Surely the police would be combing through whatever records still existed from the center and following up with attendees, as well as with people who had supervised, instructed, or counseled there.

They wouldn't be sharing that info, but there was one person who might at least help me understand the killer's mental state: Marc Horton, a former FBI profiler who was always kind enough to take my calls. Though it was too late for a conversation now, I shot him an email asking if we could talk tomorrow.

This new development also added urgency to my desire to follow up with Tom Nolan. In addition to wanting to learn if he'd informed anyone about our brief conversation, I was eager to hear what he knew about the retreat center. Had he ever heard a parishioner mention having been there when younger? Had *Shannon* ever been there? I'd have to swing by the parish center at some point tomorrow.

A few days ago, I'd wondered whether Shannon had been experiencing a spiritual or emotional crisis that had led her back to the church and then spurred her to go on the lam. It hadn't played out like that at all, but I still wanted to know why she'd gone back, because it might factor into the killer's motive.

There was still the chance, of course, that Shannon had been abducted randomly by a sexual predator who'd spotted her jogging, one who just happened to have a religious obsession. He might have learned of her faith only after reading about her disappearance in the news. The fact that she had recently rejoined the church could be nothing more than coincidence. But as Buddy, my old newspaper colleague, used to say, believing in coincidences was on par with thinking that stuffed animals came to life when you weren't looking at them or that pulling the blanket up around your neck in bed kept you safe from harm.

Perhaps J.J. might have insight worth sharing. I needed to grab more time with her, and with Kelly, too, if I could ever manage to dislodge her from Doug's side.

I stretched my weary arms and legs and then turned my attention back to my laptop, rereading the *Post Star* coverage about the two campers. I found nothing I hadn't noted the first time. I also searched for anything I could find about Page's family, who were reportedly from Florida, but I had no luck in that department, either. Hopefully Amy's friend Kayla would prove to be a valuable resource.

My eyes, I realized, were strained from being in front of a screen for so long, and every muscle in my body begged for rest. I was also desperate for a break from the thoughts churning endlessly in my brain about the contents of those black contractor bags.

I double-checked that the bolt on the door was in place,

and after slipping into a T-shirt, slid between the sheets. Warm air whirred from the heating unit. Normally that kind of sound would have annoyed me to death, but tonight it managed to act like white noise, and before long, I felt myself drifting off to sleep.

And then I was wide awake again. I sensed a sound had woken me and I strained to hear. Nothing at first. I scooted up in bed. Okay, there it was—footsteps on the walkway not far from my door. My heart bounced inside my chest.

I reached for the lamp but thought better of revealing I'd been awakened. Instead, I froze in position listening. It was silent outside again, and I wondered if my imagination had gotten the better of me. But then, soft as a whisper, more footsteps, coming closer.

I fumbled for my phone on the bedside table and grasped it, just in case. The footsteps ceased again. Whoever it was must have stopped directly in front of my door. My eyes had adjusted to the dark by now, and I stared at the doorknob, waiting to see if it jiggled.

The knob never moved. But I could have sworn that the door itself shifted ever so slightly, as if someone were leaning lightly against it.

CHAPTER 10

ISLID QUIETLY OUT OF BED, CELL PHONE IN HAND, AND TIP-
toed to the window. As I reached toward the curtain,
I heard footsteps again, this time receding. I pulled the
curtain to the right. There was no one in sight, but the
window allowed me only a partial view of the parking lot,
not the walkway on either side of my unit.

I used the room phone on the bedside table to call the
front desk. It rang five times, ten times, twenty, as if each
ring was being sucked into a black hole. Finally, a man
answered, his voice surprisingly chipper.

"Can I help you?" he asked.

"You're the desk clerk?"

"I'm Dale, the night manager. Sorry about the delay, I
was emptying trash in the dumpster out back."

"Were you walking in front right before that? I could
hear someone on the other side of my door."

"Hmm, that wasn't me. A guest checked in a few minutes
ago. That's probably what you heard."

"Are they in a room right near mine?"

"A couple of doors down. I wouldn't worry. We don't have any trouble in these parts."

Really? I guess he didn't follow the freaking news.

I thanked him for his help and returned to the window, teasing the curtain back again. There was nothing to see.

Maybe the footsteps I'd heard had belonged to the late-arriving guest, but why had he or she lingered by my door? What if the killer had discovered my whereabouts in addition to my number and was skulking around out there?

I didn't drift off to sleep until well after two, and when I stirred awake around seven, I felt ragged. Before showering, I cracked open the door and surveyed the scene. A white Camry was now parked directly in front of a unit four doors down from mine, confirming that another guest had indeed shown up last night. But that didn't explain the lingering.

I was desperate for coffee and food, and before I headed to my meeting with Kayla, I stopped at the small café in the village I'd eaten at my first night here. The place was almost full by the time I arrived and smelled comfortingly of morning joe, maple syrup, and buttered toast. I made a beeline for the only table available by the window and ordered an omelet and coffee.

I was savoring my first slug of brew when I noticed that Hank Coulter, his jet-black hair gleaming in the sunlight, was sitting five or six tables away with four other guys around the same age. His back was mostly to me, but he must have sensed my eyes on him, because he unexpectedly turned and surveyed the room, slowly stroking his chin.

It didn't take long for his gaze to settle on me. I caught a flicker of recognition in his eye, but he offered nothing to acknowledge my presence, not even a quick nod.

It would be smart to have a conversation with Coulter—after all, he would have been on the police force at the time Amy and Page disappeared, perhaps even chief at that time—but it didn't seem wise to muscle in on the breakfast with his bros. I decided to watch for him to leave and corral him then. Though I would have to brace myself for a possible tongue-lashing. He would have heard from his contacts that I'd played junior detective and had gone to Sunset Bay yesterday without alerting the cops about the phone call.

But corralling proved to be unnecessary. As I was about to dig into my omelet, Coulter rose from his chair and headed in my direction. His plaid shirt looked to be the size of one of those tartan blankets you see at tailgate picnics or tossed over a leather chair in a man cave. I was sure he was going to take down a couple of juice glasses or mugs as he snaked his large frame between the tables, but his thighs seemed to read the space like sonar, and he cleared the area without a mishap. Two diners saluted him with "Morning, Chief."

"Mind if I sit?" he asked when he reached me.

"By all means," I said.

He lowered himself into the chair across from me, making the wood groan in protest. "Pardon my ignorance, but do you say your name *Wiggins*?"

"Weggins, actually."

"My apologies then, Ms. Weggins." His tone was oddly

friendly. Maybe he was simply toying with me before whipping out the lash.

"Not a problem."

He smiled, running a hand up and down the front of his shirt.

"Well, I want to make sure I've got it right, because everyone in this town owes you and Alice Hatfield a debt of gratitude. That retreat center was far enough away from the main search area that I'm not sure anyone would have thought to check there."

Okay, this was not what I'd been expecting.

"I appreciate you saying that, but it wasn't anything heroic. I was just following up on a tip."

"I spoke to Alice Hatfield and she told me you took the call seriously, that you went the extra mile to figure out what it might mean. And though they're not in a position to thank you at the moment, the family is grateful, too. As horrible as it is to lose Shannon, not knowing her fate would have been hell on earth."

I heard the fatigue and resignation in his voice. He may have once been the police chief, but he'd known Shannon's family, and this was clearly personal for him. A part of me was still waiting for the other shoe to drop but there was no hint of that.

"You're right. I've covered families that had to endure that. Do you know much about the center, by the way?"

"Not a whole lot. I got called up there a couple of times when I ran the force. A young priest drowned in the lake one morning, oh, probably fifteen years ago. Sad story. He apparently had a seizure while swimming."

"Seems like the killer must have been pretty familiar with the place. Any theories?"

"You mean do I think it's someone local? Off the record, could be. But we have a lot of repeat tourists, so it just as easily could be an out-of-towner who knows the lay of the land."

"And what about the other victims—any thoughts there?"

"I've never seen the advantage of idle speculation. We need to let law enforcement do their job, and thanks to the resources at their disposal these days, we'll know the identities soon enough."

"Some people are saying it's the two female campers who disappeared ten years ago."

He smiled, but tightly this time, his full lips whitening.

"That would certainly provide well-deserved answers for their families. But like I said, I'm not one for theorizing before the facts are in. Besides, I need to let you get back to your omelet."

"I appreciate you taking the time to come by. Do you happen to have a card with you?"

"I was just about to offer you one."

He drew a wallet from his back pants pocket and produced a card before weaving back through the tables to his pals.

I finished my omelet, which was lukewarm by now and tasted like a rubber band. There was still an hour before I was due to meet Kayla, so I ordered a second coffee to go. I drove through the village to the southern tip of the lake, parked, and popped the lid off the cup.

It was sunny today and fairly warm, one of those Indian

summer days Alice had alluded to. The lake was especially gorgeous, a deeper, more stunning blue than even the sky or the mountains that rimmed its borders. Above me to the right were the restored remains of Fort William Henry, which the British surrendered during the French and Indian War, an event captured so vividly in *The Last of the Mohicans*.

A horn blew, loud and long and guttural. I swiveled enough in my seat to see one of the big tourist steamboats, the *Minne Ha Ha*, push off from its dock, water gushing from the paddle wheel at the back.

Despite the scenic distractions, my conversation with Coulter stayed top of mind. Earlier in the week he'd seemed dismissive, and yet this morning he'd sounded like he wanted to pin me with the Rebel Alliance Medal of Bravery. The needle on my bullshit meter had bounced a couple of times while he was speaking—during those comments about the pointlessness of speculating—but maybe I was being unfair.

At exactly nine forty-five I set off for Queensbury, an area that, according to Google Maps, encircled the northern and eastern part of Glens Falls. I discovered ten minutes later that it wasn't a classic town with a central business section but a sprawling area that at first glance seemed to consist of mostly theme parks, fast-food stands, and factory outlets. I found the dealership wedged between a CVS and a family-style Italian restaurant, on one of those four-lane roads that's a feature of suburban sprawl.

I pulled into the lot a few minutes past ten. Though there didn't appear to be any customers yet, I spotted a cluster of sales guys through the plate-glass window, all decked out in spiffy cobalt-blue shirts.

One of them approached me as soon as I entered, but I told him I was looking for Kayla. The second I said her name, a young woman crossed the floor toward me, dressed in a black leather skirt, black jacket, and a white button-down shirt opened at the collar to offer a fetching sliver of cleavage.

"You're Bailey?" she asked bluntly, and I'd barely nodded when she announced, "Let's take this outside."

I followed her through the doorway to the far side of the lot, where she finally turned and faced me. She was pretty, about thirty, with olive skin and dark, shoulder-length hair worn in waves. Even with her jacket on, I could tell she was in great shape, that she probably worked out regularly.

"Thanks for seeing me, Kay—"

"Did you know when we talked?" she demanded. "That they might have found Amy?"

"The press conference hadn't even started when I first called you," I replied, dodging the question. "And they don't know for sure yet whether it's Amy and Page."

"It's them, I know it. Please tell me heads will roll."

"Whose heads?"

"The heads of the cops who didn't take it seriously."

"Was it the sheriff's office?"

"Yes, and the state police. But the guy who always seemed to be in charge was from the Lake George police. Something Cutter."

"You mean Coulter? Hank Coulter?"

"Yes, that's right. He let everybody think the girls just blew town."

No wonder Coulter hadn't been in the mood for speculating about the two missing women.

"You didn't buy the idea that Amy went off looking for an adventure?"

"Without letting her mother or her friends know? Not on your life."

"Why do you think Coulter was so quick to believe that?"

"Because this asshole Page used to date claimed she'd told him she was sick of the area and wanted to start fresh someplace else. I'm sure he said that to get even with Page for dumping him."

"What's the ex-boyfriend's name, do you remember?"

"Pete Hannigan. You won't find him around here, though. I heard he moved to the West Coast."

"What about the girls' family members? Do you know where any of them are?"

Kayla's eyes glistened, and for the first time I caught a glimpse of the grief wedged beneath the anger.

"Amy never knew her dad, and her mom died a couple of years ago from a heart attack. I'm sure the stress finally got to her. But at least she didn't have to go through *this*."

"What about Page's family? I read she was from Florida."

"From all I know, her family's still there. And for what it's worth, I never liked Page. She was a mooch if you ask me, a real user, and she was always boxing Amy off from all her old friends. But Amy dug her because she seemed so cool. Page walked around as if she were Miss South Beach or something."

She shot a glance toward the plate-glass window of the dealership, checking out what was going on inside.

"There were photos of Page and Amy in the *Post Star*. Is that how Page looked at the time, do you know? With long blond hair?"

Kayla squinted, "Yeah, the paper had an accurate photo. Why, because that other woman was a blonde, too?"

"Right. One more question. Were either Amy or Page Catholic?"

"What does *that* have to do with anything?"

"I'm just looking for anything that they could have in common with Shannon Blaine."

"Amy wasn't a Catholic. But she was spiritual, if you know what I mean. She believed in being good to people, and to animals. And even the planet. I have no clue about Page. From what I knew her main religion was worshipping herself."

"Okay, thanks," I said. "I should let you get back to work."

"You know what kills me," Kayla said, her voice rising again. "No one ever gave a flying fuck about Amy. But now that some soccer mom is dead, too, everyone's in a tizzy."

"It's not fair, I know. But at least the police may finally learn the truth about what happened to her and find the person who took her life."

"But if they'd cared enough back then to look for her, maybe she wouldn't be dead."

"If it's any consolation, *I* care. I'm headed to the campsite now, the one where Amy and Page were going to stay. And to the bar they were seen in that night."

"Good," she snapped. "And then maybe you'll see for yourself."

"See what, Kayla?" Goose bumps had popped up along my arms.

"Amy's idea of enjoying nature was keeping a cactus plant on her coffee table. It never made any fucking sense that she'd plan to spend a night in a campsite like that one."

CHAPTER II

KAYLA HADN'T BEEN KIDDING.

The small, wooded campground was on the eastern side of the lake, only ten miles from the village, and yet upon my arrival I felt like I was deep into the Adirondacks. The spot felt isolated, off the beaten path, though there were a couple of tents bivouacked amid the trees.

I wandered for a couple of minutes through the grounds, taking in the mossy, mushroomy scent of early autumn. As my feet swished through the dry leaves, it was hard to picture Page and Amy deciding to spend two days and nights here. Maybe Amy had developed a taste for the outdoors without Kayla knowing about it, becoming a girl who loved L.L.Bean gear and the smell of Sterno in the morning, but that didn't gel with the images I'd seen of her and Page in the *Post Star*. With their cute clothes and blown-out hair, they'd looked like city girls biding their time upstate.

Even more improbable as a destination for the two women was Muller's. The bar turned out to be a full twenty-five-minute drive southeast from the campground, situated in the tiny, not-very-picturesque town of Fort Ann. The bar itself, in a tired, three-story brick building, looked like a total dive.

I slid out of the Jeep, and in the distance to the east I could see a row of soft-hued mountains. Not the Adirondacks anymore. I was looking at the Green Mountains of Vermont.

I climbed the saggy steps outside the bar and swung open the door, letting the refrains of a mournful country-western song spill onto the porch. The lights were low inside, but I could see the place was mostly empty, except for a half-dozen guys on barstools, a couple with the tops of their butt cracks smiling rudely in my direction. The place smelled musty, with a top note of BO.

It took a minute for me to focus, and as soon as I did, I saw the bartender's eyes flickering in surprise.

"What can I get ya?" he asked, moseying over.

I was briefly tempted to say "a cooties shot" but asked for a Bud instead. I figured being a paying customer would afford me an ounce of leverage.

The bartender thrust his hand in the cooler, yanked out a Budweiser, and set the bottle and a glass on the greasy wooden bar.

"I've got a question, too, if you don't mind," I said.

"Try me, and we'll see how I do."

By this point a couple of the dudes at the bar had turned their heads to investigate.

"I'm wondering if by any chance you've worked here for at least ten years?"

He snorted. "You mean 'cause the 401(k) plan is so damn good? Nah, I've only been here a couple of years."

"What about the owner?"

"You doing an oral history on the town's hot spots?"

I smiled again. "No, I'm trying to track down information on a girl named Amy Hunt. She disappeared ten years ago, after stopping here."

The song about heartaches and regrets had ended with a long, woeful chord, and the place went deadly still. The only sound now was from the buzz of a neon beer sign above the bar. And I could have sworn I saw the shoulders on one of the customers tighten. There was, I realized, something vaguely ominous in the air, like the barometric pressure had suddenly nose-dived.

"The current owner's had the place for maybe five years," he said. "And the dude he bought it from is dead."

"Have you heard about the case, though? Amy apparently stopped by with a friend around seven o'clock on a Sunday night."

His lips parted for a split second and then pressed back together, like he was about to answer one way and then changed his mind.

"Nope," he said finally.

I didn't see any other options at this point. I thanked the bartender, setting my mostly full glass on the bar. Unlike Sheryl Crow, I didn't like a good beer buzz early in the mornin'.

Back in the Jeep, I brooded over the scene in the bar. What in God's name had Amy and Page been doing in such a dump—and so far from their campsite? If they'd wanted better action than watching chipmunks scamper around their campsite, why not head to a bar in the village of Lake George, which would have been about ten minutes from the campsite?

An explanation I couldn't ignore: they'd come here to meet up with someone. And perhaps that person was responsible for their disappearance. He could have forced them into his car when they left the bar, though there were two of them and they reportedly had consumed only one beer each. But then what became of *Amy's* car, anyway?

I was a few minutes out of town when my phone rang. It was Marc Horton, the former FBI profiler. I could tell from the Bluetooth sound effect that he was probably in his car as well.

I ran him through the case as quickly as possible, ending with the tip Alice had received about the stigmata-like cuts on the hands and feet of the victims.

"Freaky," Horton said when I'd finished.

"I thought freaky was the name of the game for you."

"Yeah, well, this one sounds especially so. Many serial killers desecrate their victims before or after, but in my own work I didn't come across much religious stuff."

"Would you guess the killer is someone with a religious obsession?"

"Might be. The marks must have a specific meaning to the person who did it, and he's sending a message to someone. It could be that a clergy member abused the killer. Something going on in his mind about that experience eventually triggered him to move into acts of violence."

"Could the killer still be a churchgoer today?"

"Yes, or he could have left because of the abuse. Or he might actually *be* a clergy member."

Okay, I hadn't gone to that place yet, but as soon as I did, Tom Nolan's face flashed in my mind. I needed to factor Horton's words in when I spoke to Nolan later and also find out what other clergy were affiliated with St. Tim's.

"What if," I said, the thought forming as I spoke, "the killer saw these women as martyrs of sorts? Or . . . even sinners who needed to be punished?"

"Anything's possible, but remember, you might be talking simply about someone who's mentally ill and has his own narratives going on, ones with no basis in reality. He could simply be hearing voices and think God is telling him to do what he did."

To my dismay I heard Marc's GPS announce that he'd arrived at his final destination.

"Do you need to go?" I asked him.

"Yes, but call me later if necessary. And keep me posted, will you? You've got my curiosity piqued."

"Will do."

"And, Bailey, watch your back, okay? You're out there, he knows who you are, and you never know what can trigger one of these guys. Have you thought about asking law enforcement for protection?"

"Uh, okay, let me consider that."

I probably wouldn't, though. I didn't feel like a target, and Killian needed every hand on deck to search for the killer.

I thanked him again before I hung up and took a different route back, picking up the Adirondack Northway until the exit for the village of Lake George. Five minutes later I was at St. Tim's.

As I parked I caught a glimpse of a dark-haired man emerging from a side door of the gray stone church, and I scrambled out of my Jeep, thinking it might be Nolan departing the premises. To my surprise it turned out to be Cody Blaine. I watched as he strode toward the parking lot with eyes fixed on his phone. He'd probably stopped by to make funeral arrangements, I realized.

At last he raised his head and spotted me. We locked eyes, and he held my gaze as he crossed the blacktop in my general direction, aiming for his silver Lexus.

"I'm really sorry for your loss," I said as he reached his car. Up close, his pale handsome face was an ashy shade of gray, as if grief and exhaustion had taken their toll. What was that phrase J.J. had used about him? *Too cool for school.* He certainly didn't appear that way at the moment.

"Thank you," he said. Fatigue bled into his voice, too, but there was nothing hostile in his tone. He hesitated, studying me. "Look, I should apologize for the other night. For confronting you that way. All I wanted was for people to help me locate my wife."

"No apology necessary," I answered, relieved that he wasn't holding a grudge.

"Is it true that you were the one who discovered Shannon?"

He seemed to be working with bare basics the sheriff had shared with him, clearly too busy and distraught to be reading my posts now.

"Yes, with another reporter."

"So you did what I asked that night. You tried to find her."

"I wish I could take more credit, but I was only following a lead. I'm glad I did, though."

"Do you have any idea at all who the caller was?"

"None, unfortunately. Whoever it was used a voice adapter."

"The fucking bastard. I wish I could kill him with my bare hands."

"Had Shannon ever mentioned the retreat center to you? Do you know if she'd stayed there when she was growing up around here?"

"I can't recall it ever coming up."

I nodded toward the church. "I know Shannon was a Catholic. Were you here to make arrangements for Shannon's funeral?"

"Yes, though we don't know when we'll have her body back. It's a never-ending nightmare."

He looked off, momentarily distracted by a pickup truck roaring up the road. It would be rude to detain him much longer, but this was my chance to ask about a subject that wouldn't stop gnawing at me.

"Tom Nolan told me she'd recently rejoined the church."

He eyed me warily. "That's right. So what?"

"Part of me wonders if her killer is someone she met at church."

"You mean another *parishioner*?"

"Maybe. It seems like a pretty big coincidence that

Shannon recently started going to mass again and then her body is discovered at a Catholic retreat center. Did she ever mention anything odd that happened at church?"

He shook his head in dismay. "No, nothing like that. She'd go to mass for an hour every Sunday and come straight home."

"Do you have any sense of why she started participating again?"

"She never spelled it out for me, probably because I'm not religious. Shannon's whole family is Catholic, and it was once a big part of her life, but by the time we met, she'd lost interest. I figured it was probably something she wanted to share again with her mom now that she was growing older."

"I see."

Cody raked a hand through his cropped hair. "I really need to get a move on. I'm sure you understand."

"Of course. Thanks for talking with me. And again, I'm so sorry for your loss."

He motioned to turn and caught himself. "I trust you mentioned this theory of yours to the sheriff."

"I threw it out there. I'm sure they have it under consideration."

"I'll make sure they do."

He nodded goodbye and slipped into the Lexus, shoulders slumped. He was probably going home to be with his kids, fix them boxed instant mac and cheese for lunch or heat up one of the casseroles that neighbors had dropped off. Maybe Kelly would be lending a hand. That was one of the things you discovered the more tragedy you saw. No matter how devastating the event, life went on, which meant funeral arrangements had to be made, meals had to be served, kids had to be put to bed for the night.

As Cody drove away, I crossed the parking lot to the parish center. One story high and T-shaped, it was a less attractive building than the church next to it, probably built on a budget. I pushed open the glass door and stepped into a large white lobby with a wooden crucifix hanging high on the wall. The only furniture was a single navy-blue wingback chair and a small side table featuring a pot of yellow mums, which gave off a vaguely unpleasant herbal scent.

Beneath the crucifix was a set of glass doors, through which I could see a small library and a series of meeting rooms, all with the lights off. A door to my right, however, had a crack of light beneath it, and a woman soon emerged from behind it. She was in her late forties, I guessed, dressed in brown slacks and a lightweight beige sweater, her champagne-blond hair framing an attractive tanned face.

She smiled warmly at me. "May I help you, dear?"

"Yes, thank you. I'm looking for Deacon Nolan?"

"Tom? I'm afraid he's not here. He's generally only here on Saturday mornings. . . . Is this about a wedding? Father Jim is over at the church and could answer any questions."

That was funny. Me giving off a bridal vibe.

"No, actually, Tom and I have been in contact about Shannon Blaine and I was hoping to speak to him further."

"Oh, what a heartbreaking story. I know Tom has been meeting with some of the family members. Is he doing bereavement counseling with you as well?"

"No, I'm a reporter actually, the one who found the body. Bailey Weggins."

"Goodness, I read about that. It must have been very traumatic."

"It was, yes. Are you familiar with the place—the retreat center?"

"I've heard about it, but I've never actually been there. I moved to the area around the time it was closing. I'm Emma Hess, by the way. The parish house administrator."

"Nice to meet you. I hear it became too expensive to run the center, but the diocese wasn't allowed to sell it?"

"Yes, that's what I've been told. Kind of an unfortunate catch-twenty-two."

"And what about records of retreat attendees from the parish? Or people who worked there? Would you have anything like that here?"

"The police already talked to Father Jim about the matter, but he said there's nothing like that in our files. It's too far back."

"Father Jim is the pastor?"

"That's right."

"Are there any other clergy members in the parish?"

"Not presently. He and Tom do a wonderful job of holding down the fort here."

"Do you happen to have a cell number for Tom?"

"Yes, but it's better if you give me your number and I can have him reach out to you."

I withdrew a business card from my purse. I'd already given one to Nolan, but I didn't know if he still had it.

"You know, I'm just remembering," she said as she accepted the card with a slim, manicured hand. "Tom mentioned that his son has a baseball game later this afternoon, so it may take me a while to reach him."

So Tom was a family man. It looked like it might be tough to catch up with him today, but perhaps Emma might provide a portion of the information I was searching for.

"I'm sure he's extremely busy. Being a deacon must be very rewarding, though."

"Yes, and rewarding for us as well. With Father Jim in his eighties, Tom has been a great backup and a real godsend to the parish." She chuckled as she caught her turn of phrase. "Ha, in a manner of speaking."

"Tom mentioned he has a regular day job, too, but I forget what he said it was."

"He's in banquet sales for one of the hotels. It gives him a nice degree of flexibility."

"How long has he been a deacon?"

"Probably close to ten years, which I know because it was around the same time I started my job. He gives so much, and everyone adores him. I don't know what we would have done if we'd lost him."

A warning ping went off in my brain.

"Lost him?"

"He was very ill for a while, a few years back. With esophageal cancer."

The pinging started to sound more like a piercing car alarm.

"Oh wow. I bet that meant a lot of chemo and radiation. When was this exactly?"

"Five or six years ago, I'd say, and yes, it was terribly arduous. But Tom faced it brilliantly, and he's fully recovered. I know it seems I'm speaking out of turn, but Tom is open about his experience. He's a big believer in people sharing what they're going through—as part of healing."

"How thoughtful of him." My mind raced, scrambling for other questions, but a phone in the office rang, tugging Emma's attention.

"Will you excuse me?" she asked, already on the move.

"Of course. Thanks for your help."

Strolling back across the parking lot, I weighed what I knew about Nolan against Marc Horton's theory that the killer might be a member of the clergy. Nolan had been seriously affected by cancer for at least several years. During his treatment, he wouldn't have had much strength or stamina, which could explain a hiatus. Tom knew Shannon. And Tom surely would have known about the retreat center. What if Tom had actually become a deacon ten years ago as a way of repenting for the murders of Amy and Page? The possibility of Father Jim being a suspect, I noted, seemed highly unlikely, considering he was in his eighties.

J. J. Rimes was still on my list of people I needed to see today, but I headed to town first, where I grabbed a sandwich and checked for any alerts from the sheriff's office. There was only one, stating the sheriff would be issuing a press release on the case later today, but there would be no briefing. Maybe Killian wasn't in the mood for facing tons of questions he wasn't at liberty to answer.

Next I scrolled through a bunch of news sites. None of

the outlets had breaking news on the case, though several were presently linking the development tentatively to the disappearance of the campers. A few were running other theories up the flagpole—like the one Alice had first suggested about the killer being an out-of-towner who had hauled the bodies from another location and dumped them here.

But I still didn't buy it. Even if the killer had once lived elsewhere, he was clearly in these parts *now*.

Finally, I checked my email in-box. Several reporters had reached out, using a second email address of mine that was listed on my author website, and asked if they could interview me about discovering the bodies. I took a few minutes to respond, promising to call them later in the afternoon if time permitted. By doing so I'd be establishing goodwill, in case I ever was looking for reciprocity.

My good pal Matt Wong had written me a note, too, congratulating me effusively. Of course. I had the inside track now, and he wanted to make nice and see what info he could download from me.

The one message I was actually happy to see was from my friend Jessie Pendergrass, whom I'd worked next to during my short stint at *Buzz* magazine. "See from your posts you're in LG. I'm in Lake Placid for the weekend. Want me to stop by for lunch on drive back Mon?"

"Absolutely," I wrote back, relishing the thought of her company. "W confirm Sun." I assumed I'd still be in Lake George on Monday, but it would all depend on how the story evolved from here.

I'd just finished my meal and ordered coffee when Dodson Crowe phoned.

"I'd always heard you like to put yourself in the thick of things," he said, "but I wasn't expecting you'd actually find the body."

"Well, don't count on that for *every* story," I said, laughing.

"The site traffic's been outrageous. People are eating this stuff up."

"Frankly, I never would have guessed it would unfold this way. You want me to see how this plays out, right?"

"Definitely. And we need to leverage it even better than we have been."

"What have you got in mind?"

"Video. I want to shoot one with you tomorrow."

That was the last thing I wanted to be doing. In fact, one of the factors that had attracted me to *Crime Beat* was that it didn't feature lame reenactments of crimes and hyperactive, hardly-ready-for-prime-time reporters pumping stricken family members for quotes.

"I didn't think you did video."

"We're beginning to roll it out with a few stories. I hadn't planned on it for this one, but considering how big the case is now, I think we should put you on camera."

"Dodson, I have zero experience interviewing people on camera," I said.

"You won't have to interview anyone. I only want you to recap the story to the camera and we'll splice in photos and footage."

That didn't make it any better. Though I'd done my fair share of TV appearances, both when I worked at *Buzz* and when I was promoting *A Model Murder*, I found the experience about as much fun as a bikini wax. Besides, I could hear Marc Horton's words echoing in my mind: *You never know what can trigger one of these guys.*

"Um—"

"There's a videographer in Albany whom I've used for one of my other sites. I'm going to have him arrange to meet up with you midday."

Didn't sound like I had a choice.

"Okay," I said. "I'll give it a try."

Signing off, I checked my watch. Time to swing by J.J.'s. This being Saturday, there was a chance, I realized, that she was currently standing on the sidelines of a soccer game or dance recital, but as I pulled up to the house ten minutes later, I detected movement through one of the front windows. Maybe I was in luck.

I had one foot on the pavement when I caught sight of J.J.'s door swinging open. If she was on the move, I needed to catch up with her before she jumped in her car. But lo and behold, it wasn't J.J. who stepped onto the porch.

It was none other than Doug Claiborne. Kelly's Ken-doll husband.

CHAPTER 12

OKAY, SLOW DOWN, I WARNED MYSELF AS I STARTED to leap to conclusions. It was possible that Doug Claiborne's visit was related to recent events. Perhaps he was conferring with J.J. about what role she would play in a memorial service.

And yet his furtive movements suggested that he was on the down low. After the door closed behind him, he glanced quickly up and down the street and then bolted to a vehicle parked five cars up from the house.

It was definitely possible that J.J. and Doug were having an affair. In our previous conversation, J.J. had mentioned that she was seeing someone whom she'd arranged to meet at her family's cabin in the Adirondacks, but she hadn't told me his name. I searched through my tote bag for my notes from my first conversation with Kelly. Yup, Kelly had said her husband was out of town the day Shannon disappeared. If they were having an affair, it shed an interesting light on the Baker/Claiborne family dynamics.

At the very least, Doug's circumspect manner hinted that he and J.J. were doing something that they didn't want anyone else to know about—perhaps sharing information about the case. If so, I needed to determine what it was.

I let five minutes pass before I knocked on J.J.'s door. I wanted to make sure that she wouldn't suspect that I'd spotted Doug's departure. I'd spring that information on her at the end, even though it was bound to piss her off.

It took three rings for J.J. to answer. She was fully dressed when she opened the door, in black leggings, ballet flats, and a long denim top, but her hair had a more tousled, bedheady look than I'd seen on her before. Of course, she could have taken to her bed in grief over the death of her friend.

"Yes?" she said warily, clearly remembering me.

"Hi, J.J. I'm so sorry for your loss. Do you have a minute?"

"I really don't want to talk to the press anymore. I've had my name in the papers *way* more than enough."

"What if we speak off the record? I'm not looking for quotes as much as for background that can help track down Shannon's killer. I'm the reporter who found her body."

"I thought it was the reporter from the *Post Star*."

"We were together, but I was the one who received the phone tip."

"Okay, come in."

"Are your kids off doing kid things today?" I asked, trailing her into the quiet house.

"They're with their father."

Which meant she'd had plenty of privacy this afternoon.

Rather than taking me to the kitchen this time, she led the way to a spiffily decorated family room with cream-colored walls. The sofa was beige, covered in a nubby, suede-like material, and punctuated with ikat pillows in red, mango, and beige. A built-in unit featuring a flat-screen TV took up most of one wall, its low shelves neatly stacked with board games and DIY craft kits. I saw that J.J.'s real estate staging career definitely carried over to her home.

After dropping onto the sofa, she motioned for me to take the armchair facing it. Now that I was in better light, I could see that she looked spent, and not necessarily in a postcoital way. Her skin was blotchy and her eyes puffy, from either lack of sleep or crying, or both. All in all, she seemed less flinty today, too, softened a little by events.

"Thank you, J.J.," I said, "I really appreciate this. It must be such a tough time for you."

She said nothing for a moment; instead, she stared hard at me, her eyes dancing a little as if there was a question in her mind itching to make an escape.

"How did Shan die?" she said finally, her voice catching.

"I don't know. There'll be an autopsy, of course, and the police will release certain details, but perhaps not all of them."

"Do you think she suffered?"

"I don't—"

"What if she was *tortured*? Or *raped*?"

"J.J., I've covered my share of homicide cases, and I know that friends and family often struggle with questions like that. But it's best not to agonize over those details. Concentrate instead on everything good that Shannon brought into the world."

"You mean all the good that's now been *trampled* on? Noah and Lilly are going to be forced to live in this permanent horror show. I left Cody a message saying I'd pick them up anytime he needed help, but I can't imagine how I can look them in the eye."

"Let me get right to the point. I've been wondering if there may be a connection between Shannon's body being left at a former Catholic retreat center and the fact that she became reinvolved in the church a few months ago."

She frowned, obviously not sure what I was insinuating. Finally the point landed.

"You think someone from the church killed her?"

"I think it's a possibility. Did Shannon ever mention anything strange that had happened to her at church? Something that unsettled her?"

J.J. shook her head hard. "Nothing."

Cody's response to that question had been negative, too, so if someone from the congregation had been watching Shannon, *targeting* her, she clearly hadn't sensed anything wrong or at least hadn't felt enough unease to mention it to her husband or friend.

"Do you have any idea why she started going back?"

"No, she never said a word, not until one Sunday in the middle of the summer when I called and asked if she wanted to take the kids for a bike ride and she said she had to drop by church first. I asked what she meant and she said she'd started going to mass again. It didn't seem like something she was eager to discuss."

Funny that Shannon wouldn't have suggested her reasoning to either her husband or best friend.

"Can you recall anything that could have factored into her decision?"

"Not really. At first I thought it had something to do with her cousin Destin passing. She'd been really close to him. But he'd been dead a whole year by then, and I didn't have the sense that she was still actively grieving."

But as J.J. herself had indicated, Shannon was a private person. She might not have wanted her friend to know that she was still consumed by the loss. And her father had died only a couple of years before, which might have cumulatively felt like too much to her.

"So if not her cousin's death, what else could it have been?"

"I don't know. Maybe she was simply searching for answers."

"To anything in particular?"

"Look, I'm sorry, but I really don't know. You asked me before if Shan had been depressed or under stress, and I told you she hadn't. But looking back, she'd probably seemed a little preoccupied, like she had a lot on her plate. So maybe all she wanted was a way to chill once a week, give herself a break."

God as me-time. That was a concept I hadn't heard before. But her comment triggered a memory.

"Can we circle back to something you said to me the first day we talked? You mentioned that when you called Shannon the morning she disappeared, she sounded a little off—"

"Isn't it the police's job to be asking this kind of stuff?" She reached up to an eyebrow and smoothed it with the tip of a finger.

"Yes, the cops are asking plenty of questions, I'm sure. But good reporting can be an asset to the cops, turning up additional information that's extremely beneficial."

"There's really nothing more I can contribute," she said. "And—and I probably made too much of that the other day when I talked to you."

"What do you mean?"

She smoothed her eyebrow again, more lightly this time. "That thing I said about her voice, about her seeming distant. It probably meant nothing. I'm sure she was only eager to start her run."

Okay, this was odd. Why suddenly revise her impression?

"Well, if your instincts that day told you—"

"I don't really recall what my instincts were telling me that day. This has all been a mess. . . . Look, are we done here? I feel like my head is going to explode."

"Sure, but if anything occurs to you about Shannon and the church, or anything else, will you give me a call?"

She threw out an arm, flipping over the hand, in a gesture that said, "Whatever."

I rose and made my way out of the room, with her right behind me. When we reached the front hall, I paused, ready to drop the *I Know What You Did Last Summer* bombshell.

"Thanks again for your help, J.J.," I said. I turned to face her. "One more question before I go. Do you think Shannon's sister might have any insight into the church question?"

"Like I told you the other day, Kelly and Shannon weren't super close. But be my guest and ask her if you want."

"Are you friendly with Kelly yourself?"

"Friendly enough. Look—"

"I just ask because I happened to see Kelly's husband coming out of your house a few minutes ago."

Her whole body froze, as if under a spell from a sorcerer. There was no mistaking the expression that flashed on her face. "Busted," it said. I could sense her scrambling, trying to hatch a credible cover story.

"And your point is?"

"Just curious. Are you friendlier with him than with Kelly?"

Her pale-blue eyes darkened, like the lake water when a cloud crossed the sun. Flinty Girl was back.

"Oh, that's rich," she snapped. "I don't know what you people in the big city do when someone in your world dies. Maybe you just think, 'Tough luck,' and order another dirty martini. But up here we look out for each other. We console each other. We offer to help and send food. Good*bye*."

As soon as I stepped onto the porch, the door slammed so hard behind me that the Indian corn hanging on the outside clacked loudly against it a few times.

Back in the driver's seat, I jotted down our exchange while it was still fresh in my mind. My gut told me that something funny was definitely going on between J.J. and Doug. She'd reacted way too defensively for me to believe it was all about people clinging together in grief, and as for her line about sending food, Claiborne hadn't exactly dashed off with a ham casserole in his hot little hands.

If they were sleeping together, both in town and further upstate, what did that mean in the grand scheme of things? For starters, it meant that J.J. most likely had been keeping secrets from Shannon, and Shannon may have sensed it or outright suspected that there was something brewing between her friend and her brother-in-law. It was even possible that Kelly had confided in Shannon that she was worried about what her husband was up to.

Of course, if Shannon was at odds with her sister, she might not have cared if Doug and J.J. were having a fling. Yet that didn't gel with what I knew about Shannon. Regardless of whether she and Kelly were close, she probably wouldn't have liked seeing her sister hoodwinked and betrayed.

There was another factor I had to consider. J.J.'s weird revision of her impressions of her final phone call with Shannon. Maybe she had learned something in the past couple of days that had given her a reason to reassess Shannon's state of mind that morning. Something Doug had told her, perhaps? There was also the chance she was flat-out lying now, covering her tracks, but I couldn't think of why that would be. I watched her in my mind smoothing an eyebrow that didn't need smoothing. Had that been a tell?

I slumped against the seat and exhaled loudly. My work

always necessitated talking to the friends and relatives of dead people, and while I'd learned over time to steel myself for those conversations, at moments they could be wearing, particularly when they went around in circles or the other side seemed to be offering nothing but a pack of lies.

I'd talked to a number of people today, yet I had little to show for it. I wondered if I was becoming too absorbed in the idea that Shannon's death was tied directly to her return to the church. Perhaps, as I surmised before, the killer had a religious fixation but hadn't even been aware of Shannon finding her faith again.

Before I temporarily ceased tugging at that thread, however, there was one more person I wanted to consult with: Cody's assistant, the red-haired woman I'd spoken to briefly the second day I was here. It was a stretch to think Riley, who'd only worked with Shannon for several months, would know more than J.J., but it was worth a try.

Please own a landline, I begged. And she did. According to the white pages, there was a listing for Al and Riley Hickok on Pheasant Road in Lake George.

The house, which was less than a mile from J.J.'s, turned out to be small but attractive, with a sleek white motorboat sitting in the driveway. Unfortunately, when I rang the bell, there wasn't any response. I leaned across the stoop railing and peered through the picture window into the empty living room. It wasn't decorated to the nines like J.J.'s, but the furniture seemed nice enough: a couch, coordinating armchairs, a colorful area rug, and a huge flat-screen TV on the far wall.

It was only when I went to give the bell one more try that I caught sight of the note taped on the inner wooden door and partially obscured by the outer storm door.

Viv, tried to reach you on your cell but no response. Sorry, had to run to office for a couple of hours. Can meet later if you want. R.

It wasn't surprising that she'd blown off a friend in order to work on a Saturday. Baker Beverage had been closed for several days, paperwork had surely been piling up, and Riley probably decided to jump on the situation before she fell too far behind. Since Cody was clearly busy consoling his kids and making funeral arrangements, I realized that this might be my best opportunity to talk to Riley without him around.

When I turned into the driveway for Baker Beverage a short time later, I was struck once again by how attractive the setting was. Though there was an industrial feel to the building itself, the area was beautifully landscaped. Business was supposedly booming under Cody, but the clusters of lush, mature trees and scrubs on the grounds reinforced what Kelly had intimated: that it had done very well under the late Mr. Baker.

I spotted the car as soon as I rounded the final curve of the driveway—a dark green Audi parked in front of the building. Chances were good the Audi belonged to Riley and I'd made it in time.

I parked ahead of the other car and crossed the lawn to the entrance. A glance through one of the windows to the side of the door revealed a small, empty reception area with only a single light burning. Not unexpectedly, the door was locked. I rang the buzzer, hearing it pierce the silence inside. When no one responded after a minute, I tried again and also rapped on one of the windows, to no avail. I realized that if Riley's desk was tucked toward the back of the building, she might not even hear me.

I retreated, traipsed around to the parking lot, and wandered along the long side of the building, looking for another entrance. There was a door halfway down the wall, and I gave pounding another try, without any luck this time either.

A thought flashed across my brain before I even saw it coming: What if she was in there with Cody, doing stuff they shouldn't be doing, like screwing each other's brains out instead of bottling beverages?

I was just about to round the back of the building to see if his Lexus was hiding out there when I heard a woman's voice call out "Hello" from the front of the building. I darted back along the perimeter to the main entrance, and there was Riley, her brow knitted in consternation, holding the door half open.

"Can I help you?" she said with a tone that suggested she wasn't really eager to do so. Her dark red hair was gathered in a sloppy braid and she was dressed in jeans, sneakers, and a green turtleneck sweater the shade of her car.

"Riley, hi, do you remember me?" I took a couple more steps in her direction but not so close as to raise her guard. "We met outside the volunteer center the other day. I'm Bailey Weggins, the reporter from *Crime Beat*."

"Oh, hi, I didn't recognize you," she said, her tone softening. "Is there something I can do for you?"

"First, sorry to barge in like this. I didn't realize you guys weren't open today." In light of her wariness, it seemed wise not to mention that I'd stopped by her house and read the note on the door.

"We're never open Saturdays at this time of the year. I came by to deal with a backlog."

"I was hoping to ask you a few questions. I talked to Cody today at the parish center, and I told him that we're trying to do everything we can to help find the killer." It was a cheap trick, but I knew my carefully chosen words would make it seem as if I had Cody's blessing to pump her.

"I feel horrible about what happened to Shannon, but I'm not sure how I can help."

"I know she'd been working here part-time and I thought you might have observations to share."

"Observations?"

"A detail you noticed or a remark Shannon made. It's possible she'd crossed paths with the killer in the weeks before her death and mentioned something that could be relevant."

"But they're saying it was a serial killer, right?"

"Right, but it could still be a person she'd had previous contact with."

"Uh . . . okay. Did you want to come in for a minute?"

"Thanks, that'd be great."

She motioned for me to enter the reception area and then led me down a hallway into a far bigger space, which featured several glass offices along one wall and a center area with about a dozen workstations, separated with gray dividers. The recessed fluorescent ceiling lights were on, giving the place a weird, too-bright look.

"I wish there wasn't so much to catch up on," she said over her shoulder. "I don't exactly love the idea of being alone here right now."

"I don't blame you. It's a scary time."

"Do the police have any leads yet, do you know?"

"Not that I'm aware of—so it's smart to be cautious. Where—where do they do all the bottling?"

She pointed a long, slim finger toward a closed door in the far wall. "Through there. This space is for the sales and office staff."

We were at her workstation now, directly outside a large glass-fronted office that I assumed belonged to Cody. Riley settled into the desk chair and indicated that I should take the cushioned filing cabinet on wheels. Her desk was neat and well organized, and one of those mind-numbing Excel files was on her computer screen. I had a sense that she was the kind of kick-ass assistant who made sure the trains always ran on schedule.

"Have you worked for Cody long?"

"Since he took over as president three years ago, though I'd been an assistant to a bunch of the sales guys for a few months before that. When Mr. Baker retired, Cody asked me to work directly for him."

"And Shannon had been working here, too, right? Starting in March?"

"March? Yeah, I guess that's when it was. She worked from home for a while, though more recently she was coming in here on Tuesday, Wednesday, and Thursday. With the kind of stuff she was doing, she didn't have to be on-site every day."

"And what kind of stuff was that?"

"Marketing. Promotional materials, creating buzz for the company."

"Marketing?" I said, stifling my surprise. J.J. had used a phrase like *lending a hand* to describe Shannon's efforts at Baker, as if her duties had included filing and manning the phones when the receptionist went to lunch.

"That's what her background was in. She'd done marketing for the hotel she worked at in the Caribbean—and she'd helped her dad out here years before. I had the impression that she was pretty eager to restart her career now that her kids were a little older. And we were happy for the help, of course."

"Did you have much chance to talk to her during the past months?"

"A little bit here and there. I would have liked to have spent more time with her, but Cody keeps me pretty busy."

"Did she ever mention anything to you about going to St. Timothy's?"

"No. But Cody told me about it the other day. That she became a Catholic again. He's been planning a funeral service for when Shannon's body is finally turned over to him."

"Were there ever any times when Shannon seemed

nervous or upset to you or made a comment about feeling that way?"

"Not at all. She always seemed really sunny."

"And Shannon got along with everyone here? There wasn't any friction with another employee when she came on board?"

"Oh no, everybody liked her, and she worked hard. My husband's in sales here, and the ideas she had for the new promotional pieces were really super."

I glanced across the sea of gray, racking my brain. Was there something I was missing?

"Crazy question," I said, turning back to Riley. "But is anyone else who works here a Catholic?"

Riley bit her freckled lower lip. "I'm sure some people are—I think St. Tim's has a decent-size parish—but that's not the kind of thing that comes up in conversation. Mostly the guys here talk about football, basketball, and how big their boats are, which drives me insane."

She patted the desk with her hands, eager, it appeared, to return to that tantalizing Excel file.

"Well, I should let you finish up. If you think of anything else about Shannon, will you let me know? Even the most minor thing."

"Of course. . . . I'll walk you out."

I followed her back to the reception room. She looked tense, and something told me she wouldn't be staying much longer today herself.

"I can't believe they don't have any leads," she said, opening the door. "Can't DNA tell them who did it?"

"DNA helps solve a lot of crimes but investigators don't always find traces of it at a crime scene. And if the killer's DNA isn't in the system, there's no one to match it to."

"That's not encouraging."

"I know, but let's stay positive. With any luck they'll find him."

In the parking lot, I took a couple of minutes to jot down notes from the conversation. Nothing much stood out to me as significant, but my mind was snagging on the weird discrepancy between how J.J. had characterized Shannon's role at Baker and Riley's description of what she'd actually done there. Had J.J. been jealous of her friend's ambition and thus downplayed her efforts?

Before departing, I checked my phone for email and messages. Keith Windgate, the videographer Dodson had in mind to shoot me, had written to say he'd like to pick me up at my motel at noon tomorrow. Yippee. There was still no press release from the sheriff. And no word from Tom Nolan. He might have to be prodded.

Speaking of prodding, it was close to four and I needed to pound out my post. I pointed my Jeep north and headed back to the lovely Breezy Point. There wasn't a single car in the parking lot when I arrived, but as I killed the engine, the white Camry I'd spotted this morning pulled in a few spots away.

I quickly hauled my butt out of the car, and, pretending to check my phone, loitered on the walkway in front of my unit. I was curious to finally set eyes on who had possibly paused outside my door last night. I heard the Camry door swing open and glanced up.

I nearly dropped my phone as the driver emerged. It was the tall blond woman I'd seen jogging down Wheeler Road the day I arrived, the one who had been a dead ringer for Shannon Blaine.

CHAPTER 13

FOR A SPLIT SECOND, I THOUGHT MY MIND WAS PLAYING a trick on me, conjuring up an apparition of the jogger simply because she'd been tangled up in my thoughts. What was she doing *here*, at the Breezy Point? She'd obviously checked out of wherever she'd been staying, which I'd already determined wasn't the Lake Shore Motel.

Maybe she'd found the previous place lacking. Or maybe she'd been vacationing with a partner or lover and they'd had a major blowout last night, the kind where you not only call the person the greatest fucking asshole who's ever lived, but you also storm out, slamming the door so hard that pictures bounce off the wall. There's always a moment following one of those kinds of fights, as you are wheels up and headed south—or north or east or west— when you wonder if you'll rue your decision because now the day or the night or your entire vacation is ruined, but you let it go because the smug satisfaction you're experiencing makes mincemeat of regret. As a connoisseur of the cutting-off-one's-nose-to-spite-one's-face gesture, I could totally relate.

Well, at least the jogger hadn't come to any harm, as I'd initially feared.

She had her phone out, too, I realized, and was now studying it, seemingly oblivious to my presence. I considered calling out to her, but then she darted into the unit so swiftly that I didn't have the chance. Her license plate, I noticed, was from New York State. I discreetly snapped a photo of it with my cell phone, in case it might come in handy.

As I unlocked the door to my unit, my curiosity still piqued, my phone rang. Alice.

"So what do you think?" she said in lieu of hello.

"Hey, there. About what?"

"The news. The bodies."

"Oh jeez, I checked my freaking phone ten minutes ago, and didn't see anything."

"Just came in."

I put Alice on speaker and found the alert in my email, but she began reading out loud before I could scan it.

"'We now have reason to believe that the remains discovered with Shannon Blaine's are those of two local women who disappeared while camping on the eastern shore of Lake George ten years ago. This will have to be confirmed by DNA testing in the weeks ahead.' You want me to keep going? There's not much, just their names and stuff."

"So we guessed right."

"People in town are going to freak. Because three dead young women confirms the serial killer angle."

"And one who's living right in their midst."

"You think so?"

"I do. Things keep pointing to him being a local."

"If they don't find this guy, it could take a big bite out of the tourist business up here."

"Do you think that's why Coulter and the others were so quick to conclude the campers had taken off? I spoke to a friend of Amy Hunt's today and she claims she never thought for a second that the girls had simply blown town."

"Coulter's not everybody's favorite, but it's hard to believe he'd put the tourist business above trying to find those girls, dead or alive. The friend say anything else interesting?"

Knowing Alice, she was probably kicking herself for not having thought to quiz Kayla.

"Claims the skipping-town rumor was started by an ex-boyfriend of Page's with a chip on his shoulder. By the way, what can you tell me about Fort Ann?"

"Fort Ann?"

"Yeah, the campers stopped there the day they disappeared."

"You know that line in 'Hello' when Adele asks if the guy ever made it out of the town where nothing ever happens? I think she was singing about Fort Ann."

"That was my impression. I drove over there today, and even went to Muller's, the bar where they had a drink, which frankly was like the ninth circle of hell. It's hard to fathom why they'd choose a place like that—and one so far from the campsite."

"Maybe they headed along Route 149 thinking they'd

find a spot close by and when they didn't, they kept driving, waiting to stumble onto something. The only time I ever go over that way myself is when I'm aiming for Vermont. It's right on the border."

Vermont. Could *that* be where they were headed? But why go to the trouble of setting up a campsite if your plan is to split? None of it made any sense.

"You think the cops are ever going to drop any hints to the public about the stigmata marks?" I asked, grabbing hold of the conversation again.

"Probably not until they find the killer. I think my pal regrets spilling the beans in the heat of the moment. I told him I had the information under lockdown."

"You can count on me."

"I know. So what are your plans from here? Are you going to stick around for a while?"

Good question. On the phone, Dodson had agreed that we should see how the story played out, but there might not be enough action to warrant *Crime Beat* having me up here full-time for much longer. If Cody had killed Shannon and the police found enough evidence to arrest him, my job would have entailed filing at least another week's worth of stories as more details emerged. Then I probably would have headed back to the city, possibly returning later if there were any new developments.

But since there was an unknown killer at large, it could take days, weeks, even forever, for the authorities to find him. There would be no point in running posts when I hadn't any news to share.

"For sure, I'll be here into the first part of next week," I told Alice, "but if the case runs cold, my editor will probably tell me to split. I can always drive back up if there's a break in the case."

"I've got more research to do tonight, but what if I made you dinner at my place tomorrow? I'm right on the lake, and if the weather cooperates, we could eat on the screened porch."

"I'd love that, Alice." And I meant it. Nothing like finding bodies in trash bags together to turn you into soul sisters—and I suspected she was feeling the same way.

"Just a warning, though. Most of us haven't learned how to make a meal up here without massive amounts of carbs. You don't look like you eat many of those."

"Oh, actually, that's exactly what I'm in the mood for. . . . You following a hot lead tonight?"

"Wouldn't you like to know? Nah, just sitting at my dining table going through stuff online, seeing if there are pretty young women missing farther afield. I figure the cops will be able to use their database to track down any relevant cases that involve actual murders, but there might be victims who disappeared under similar circumstances and whose bodies haven't turned up yet."

"You still think the guy might be from out of town?"

"I'm not wedded to the concept, but the ten-year gap keeps bugging me. I want to see what I find."

"How far away are you searching?"

"I started with surrounding counties and now I'm working my way outward."

"The old reverse-onion strategy."

"Yeah, but if I don't turn up anything in the next few hours, I may bag it. . . . Shall we say seven tomorrow? I'll text you my address."

"Great. I'll pick up a bottle of wine."

After signing off, I took a minute to toss Alice's latest strategy around in my mind. I'd told her on Friday that serial killers often felt most comfortable having their own killing field, but there were certainly exceptions. I recalled reading about one who had worked along miles and miles of an interstate highway on the Eastern Seaboard, leaving each body not far from the road. It took law enforcement a long time to realize the connections because the killer had struck in four or five different states. But that was years ago. If there were similar victims elsewhere in this case, the police surely would find them through database searches.

And yet I couldn't warm to the notion that such a crime spree had happened around Lake George. To me, at least, it still felt like the killer was from here, was here *now*, watching the action, taking in everything that was going on. And most likely reading my posts.

As I started to toss my phone on the desk, I realized Nolan had still not returned my call, so I phoned over to the parish center and reached Emma.

"I did give him your message," she said, "and he promised to be in touch. I know today has been very busy for him."

"Will he be at the parish center tomorrow?"

"I assume he'll drop in. He'll be participating in the ten o'clock mass with Father Jim."

"Thanks." I would have to catch up with him there.

I needed to scramble now and churn out my post. I texted Beau saying I hoped we could FaceTime later, and for the next hour I devoted my attention to writing the story, focusing mostly on the news about Amy and Page.

By the time I'd sent it off, my stomach was growling but I didn't have the psychic energy to go trolling for another take-out spot. I wolfed down a handful of cheese-filled Ritz Bits I'd brought from New York as emergency rations and used the next hour to sketch out notes for what I wanted to say in the video tomorrow, and then I managed to reach two of the reporters who'd asked me for quotes about finding the bodies, spending a couple of minutes on the phone with each of them.

Finally, I returned Matt Wong's call.

"Sorry I haven't stayed in touch since you got here," he said. "You know what it's like when you're in a new job and under an insane amount of pressure."

"No problem. What can I do for you?"

"Just wanted to say congrats. Pretty amazing, you getting a call like that."

"A totally lucky break."

"So what was the scene in that basement like? It must have been pretty grisly."

There was a small piece of information I wanted from Wong, and the only chance of securing it would be to cough up a morsel from my end first. But I had to be careful about what I divulged. Killian had demanded I keep pertinent details about the crime scene under wraps, and I had my journalistic turf to protect as well. Just because Wong was suddenly acting all nicey-nice didn't mean I wanted to swap info with him in the same way I had with Alice.

"Unfortunately, that's one area I can't discuss, Matt. The cops insisted. I take it you heard that they think the two other bodies are the missing campers?"

"Yeah, that's already old news."

"I could pass along an interesting nugget in that department if you like." I thought fast, ransacking my brain for a slim bone I could toss him without it costing me anything.

"Let's hear it then."

"Can I ask you a question in return?"

"You can ask. I can't guarantee I'll be able to answer."

"Okay, when the two campers disappeared ten years ago, one reason the cops believed they'd simply taken off was because an ex-boyfriend of Page's claimed she'd talked to him about doing that. But he apparently held a grudge against Page and may have made that stuff up. It seems the cops were too quick to buy into the theory."

"That's *it*?"

"To me, it's certainly worth checking out."

"All right, all right. What's your question?"

"On my first day here, you said that even the sweetest-looking sisters might secretly hate each other's guts. What did you mean by that, exactly?"

"You're still noodling over that?"

"Well, it's a pretty loaded comment. Were there problems between Kelly and Shannon?"

"Maybe. But what does it matter now anyway? It's not like Kelly's a serial killer."

"No, but I'm curious."

"Okay, I heard Kelly say something kind of nasty. About Shannon."

I waited silently, knowing he couldn't be prodded.

"It was an hour or so before you showed up," he said. "I was coming from behind the building—nature called and they wouldn't let anyone use the head in the ice cream place—and I overheard Kelly talking to her husband. She said, 'It's too bad Shannon can't be here to enjoy this. She would be loving all the attention.'"

That *was* nasty.

"Any chance it was only a bit of gallows humor, a way to try to cope with the nightmare?"

"Her tone was pretty snide. But like I said, it hardly matters now."

He was right, but I was still curious, particularly in light of a possible Doug–J.J. affair. I wanted, simply for my own sake, to get the right bead on the family dynamics.

"Well, thanks for sharing," I said. "I appreciate it."

"You up here for much longer?"

"Probably for a bit. Not sure at the moment."

"Why don't we grab a drink? I'm sure we can both be of service to each other."

"Uh, sure. Let's touch base later about that." I'd rather spend a night cleaning out my wallet, but Wong had provided an interesting nugget, and it would be smart for me to stay on his good side.

As I hung up, his comment about Kelly stayed with me, and I decided I needed more time with her. Even if she and Shannon had actively disliked each other, she might be aware of who her sister had come into contact with during her last weeks.

I texted Alice, asking if she had Kelly's cell number and would be willing to pass it along. She offered it up two minutes later, adding, It better be a really GREAT bottle of vino.

Before the phone was even out of my hand, I saw that Beau was trying to FaceTime me.

"Hey, you," I said, answering. His hair was mussed in a cute, sexy way, as if he hadn't had a chance to comb it all day. "So good to see your face again."

"Likewise. Sorry not to have called earlier. I've been a bit crazed."

"No problem, I've been racing around, too. Is it cool there?"

I could see that he was wearing his beige cowl-necked wool sweater.

"Yeah, and rainy, too, but that fortunately hasn't stopped us from covering a lot of ground."

"Have you managed to interview most of the painters you hoped to?"

"Yeah, and I have some good news. Remember that reclusive painter I mentioned? He finally agreed to let me shoot him. We're heading out to his finca tomorrow. That's what they call a country house here."

"Oh wow, that should be fascinating."

"How about you? Your posts have been great, but the case is sounding stranger than ever."

"Yeah, really disturbing. It's been nice for me to hang with that other reporter, Alice. Her company is keeping me sane."

"Is Dodson happy with your posts? He certainly should be."

"Yes, though speaking of him, I could use your help. He's making me do a video tomorrow, giving an update, and I'm dreading it a little."

"You'll be great, Bailey. You handle TV really well."

"But I've never had to do anything straight to the camera. Any advice?"

"Up your energy to about fifty percent more than feels natural, otherwise it can seem flat. And don't worry about memorizing anything. It's fine to glance at your note cards or iPad when you're talking. If you own the fact that you're using them, it'll end up looking more authentic."

"Great tips. Are you almost ready for bed? Though, wait, it's an hour earlier there, right?"

"Yeah, but I'm beat. By the way, I'd love to come back to Bogotá with you on vacation one day, and then head up to the beach in Cartagena for a few more days."

It wasn't unusual for the two of us to brainstorm travel plans for the future, but we were still sorting out how our relationship would be defined down the road. This past summer Beau had been pretty clear that he wanted us to make things official before too much more time passed. I loved him in a still-giddy way, and from the day we met, I'd sometimes imagined us married. But I was divorced, from a guy who had turned out to have a secret, disastrous gambling issue (read: bookies calling our apartment in the dead of night and threatening him with tire irons), and though I really trusted Beau and wanted to be with him, the idea of *marrying* again had begun to make me skittish.

"That would be awesome," I said. "I'd love to go back with you."

He smiled so broadly at the response, I felt a pang of guilt over the part of me that had grown mysteriously commitment-shy.

"Have a good night, Bails. And stay safe."

"You too, babe."

After signing off, I inhaled another handful of crackers and reviewed my notes for the video tomorrow. Though I probably would never feel totally at ease in front of a camera, I was at least less terrified than I used to be. I could still recall the excruciating morning of my first appearance on the *Today* show, when my body seemed weighted down with dread. Friends had advised me to just be myself, which seemed ridiculous. I mean, it wasn't as if I planned to go on the air impersonating someone *else*. The irony was that by the time the show's stylist finished with my short, flat, blond hair that morning, wielding a curling iron and a silo-size can of extra-firm-hold spray, I actually *did* resemble another person, someone with a do so high I could have been hiding a litter of kittens in there and no one would have guessed.

I'd simply have to suck it up tomorrow and do the best job I could. And it was only a web video, I reminded myself.

Though it was still fairly early, I stripped to a T-shirt, ready for bed. Before slipping between the covers, I poked open the curtain and peered across the parking lot. Besides the Camry, I could see two other cars, both of those parked in front of units in the butt end of the L-shaped building. No one skulking around tonight, at least as far as I could see.

I let the curtain drop, grabbed my laptop and notebook, and climbed into bed. I checked my email one last time for any alerts from the sheriff's department, but if there was news, they weren't sharing.

Law enforcement could very well be closing in on the killer without dropping hints, but the direct opposite could be true too. There was more than an outside possibility that the person who'd slain the three women would never be apprehended, that the crime scene wouldn't cough up the kind of forensic evidence that would point anywhere.

And though the killer might murder again down the road, there was a chance he'd lie low for a while again, living what appeared from the outside to be a normal, ordinary life.

If there were no developments, I would probably be back in the city by midweek. It would be tough, I realized, to leave without seeing any resolution or justice for the three dead women—and knowing there might *never* be.

Before I switched off the bedside lamp, I thumbed through my composition book, rereading the day's notes. Elements continued to unsettle me. How had a girl like Amy, who reportedly wasn't an outdoorsy type, ended up pitching a tent in a remote campsite? And why had she and Page later chosen a place as skanky as Muller's for a drink? Perhaps the camping had been an experiment, and the two had wandered into the bar after not finding anything else. But it all felt off to me.

I dragged my laptop across the comforter and typed the words *Fort Ann* into the search bar, in case I'd missed something on my last search, but nothing struck me as relevant.

Just for the hell of it, I also googled Route 149, the rural road I'd been traveling on today. And suddenly, things turned interesting.

According to reports in both the *Post Star* and a Vermont newspaper, there had been a slew of drug busts along the road over the past dozen years, most of which occurred after the police pulled over vehicles for routine traffic violations. It turned out that sleepy Route 149, as well as Route 4, where Muller's was located, were thoroughfares for transporting heroin, fentanyl, cocaine, and prescription painkillers from New York City and downstate regions to Vermont, a state that had been ravaged by an addiction crisis.

What if Amy and Page had been involved in drugs, even operating as mules? They might have gone to the campsite and/or to Muller's as part of doing business.

Did that mean the killer was a drug user or drug dealer? Or—as crazy as I knew it sounded—was he a religious obsessive who targeted the girls because drug users and dealers were sinners and needed to be punished?

The question that tugged at me even more was this one: How had Shannon managed to cross paths with the same person who had killed Amy and Page? In so many of the serial killer cases I'd either read about or covered, there'd been a *pattern* to each killer's choices. Victims were snatched when they were hitchhiking, for instance, or working as prostitutes, or had made the mistake of agreeing to help an

average-Joe-type guy—or average-Ted type, as in Bundy—
because he was feigning vulnerability with something like a
(fake) cast on his arm. In this situation, though, there didn't
appear to be any pattern. Shannon had either been jogging or
still at home when she was attacked, and Page and Amy had
come from a dive bar.

Maybe the killer had targeted Shannon for being a sinner
as well. If so, what in the world had her sin been?

CHAPTER 14

I WOKE THE NEXT MORNING TO THE SOUND OF RAIN COMING down in sheets, splattering across the parking lot and dripping hard from the narrow overhang above my unit.

The rain, I realized, was not only going to make shooting the video a bitch but was also going to make me look like a soaked yak on camera. I decided to hold off on washing and blowing out my hair until right before the shoot.

I threw on jeans, a pair of short boots, and a black leather jacket. The look was a little too biker chick for conducting interviews at St. Tim's, but it was my best shot at not being totally defeated by the weather.

After a quick breakfast in the village, I was back in my car by nine fifteen. I had a few minutes to kill before showing up at St. Tim's, and it seemed like a sane enough hour on a Sunday morning to try to reach Kayla for a follow-up conversation.

"How are you doing?" I asked when she finally answered. She sounded glum, though it didn't seem like I'd woken her.

"How do you *think*? I heard the news last night—that Amy's definitely dead. She was murdered by a fucking *serial killer*."

"Kayla. I'm so sorry. I know this must be a hard time to talk, but I was hoping to ask you a couple more questions."

"I'll do whatever it takes to find the madman who did this. Shoot."

"I went to the campground yesterday, and I saw what you meant. If Amy didn't like the outdoors, it's hard to imagine why she would have decided to spend two nights at that campsite. She never said anything that would explain it?"

"No, but I always assumed Page talked her into it. Page could talk her into anything."

Interesting. Maybe Page had convinced Amy to check out Muller's, too. And more.

"Kayla, please understand that I'm not passing any judgment with this next question. Do you think Page could have talked Amy into using drugs? Or even selling them?"

"No way *whatsoever*."

"Are you saying she wouldn't sell them or use them or both?"

"Both. Look, Amy wasn't a saint. She drank and she liked to party. But she hated drugs. A guy she was friends with had died from an OxyContin overdose and she steered clear of them. She never even smoked weed."

"Okay, I hear you." But Kayla might not have been clued in to everything there was to know about Amy. People using or dealing drugs became experts at keeping secrets from even their most intimate acquaintances.

After saying goodbye and promising to do what I could to find Amy's killer, I drove the short distance to the church. The parking lot—at least what I could see of it through the ribbons of rain—was about half full. I backed into an open spot, providing myself with a view not only of the front of the church but also of the side entrance, in case Nolan exited that way after mass. I cracked my window an inch to prevent the car from steaming up inside.

Over the next twenty minutes I watched a steady flow of cars arrive and a number of parishioners making a mad dash to the front of the church, dodging puddles and grasping the outer edges of their umbrellas to prevent them from flipping inside out.

The last car to arrive pulled in at seven after ten. The driver, a bald, middle-aged male, rushed for the steps with a newspaper over his head, cursing loud enough for me to hear him.

For all I knew, he could be the killer. Or it might have been any one of the other men I'd seen scurrying towards the church and who was now kneeling in prayer or standing with his voice raised in song. No one I'd seen today had appeared creepy to me, but that didn't mean anything. Serial killers often wore the so-called mask of sanity.

I was aware from the several Catholic weddings and funerals I'd attended that I had about an hour wait ahead of me, but that was fine. I'd brought a take-out cup of coffee from the café, as well as my notes to review for the video.

As I worked, the rain kept coming, at times drumming lightly on the roof of my Jeep and then suddenly accelerating, creating a frantic tattoo on the metal surface. The sound put me on edge, eager for action.

At just before eleven, the downpour abruptly stopped, as if someone had jerked a faucet closed. I peered outside. The sky was still overcast, but light was beginning to seep through the clouds, like a flashlight burning inside a paper bag. I stepped from the car, stretched my legs, and positioned myself a few yards from the church. I had to make sure that Nolan didn't escape before I could corner him.

At five to eleven the wooden doors of the church opened and people began to emerge, stepping tentatively at first with umbrellas half-cocked and then relaxing as they saw that the rainstorm was over.

To my surprise, Kelly and Doug Claiborne were among the parishioners. Some people found it difficult to be out in public right after a death in the family, particularly such a traumatic one, but perhaps Kelly had decided that any discomfort would be outweighed by the solace that came from attending mass. I was still eager for a chance to speak to her again, though Doug would surely shoo me away like he had the last time. I watched as he leaned in, one hand on his wife's elbow, spoke quickly to her, and then hurried down the steps alone. He must have offered to bring the car around to the front. Kelly, dressed in a black trench, stepped back against the stone wall of the church. This was my chance.

I took off like a bat, soaking my boots as I ran. As I neared the steps, a woman leaned in and murmured something to Kelly that looked to be words of comfort, and then moved on.

"Kelly, hello," I said, reaching the top of the steps. "Do you need a ride?" She looked tense and drained.

"Please don't tell me you came here for a quote. I've tried to be respectful of the press, but you guys go too far, you really do."

"No, I'm not looking for a quote. What I'm trying to do is find out anything that could aid the police in their inquiries."

She shook her head in dismay. Her hair, worn loose today, looked clean, as if she'd managed to summon enough stamina for a shampoo, but the only makeup she'd bothered with was a swipe of mauvy lip gloss.

"I'm sorry to be curt," she said. "But this has been hell on earth."

"I'm sure."

"How's my poor mother supposed to deal with this? First my father, then my cousin, and now *Shannon*."

"Like I said, I want to help expose the killer. And the more information I have, the better."

She sighed, her shoulders dropping, and I sensed she was taking me at my word.

"Okay, what is it you need to know?"

"The other day when I asked you if Shannon had ever been to the retreat center, you didn't have a chance to answer. Do you recall if she had?"

"Not that I'm aware of. But there's a four-year gap between us, and I was in college by the time Shannon entered high school. I didn't always know what she was up to."

"Did she ever talk to you about her decision to rejoin the church? Why she wanted to become involved again?"

"She didn't volunteer anything. It actually came as a surprise. I showed up at mass one Sunday and there she was."

Out of the blue. Just as J.J. had indicated.

"Any thoughts on what led her back here?"

Kelly turned her head slightly and stared into the middle distance, as if the answer might lie there. "Why does anyone come here? A yearning for spiritual guidance? A need for community? A desire to make amends? But what does it matter at this point?"

"I've been wondering if someone she came into contact with here this summer, someone who knew about the center at Sunset Bay, might have targeted her."

She narrowed her tired eyes.

"I can't imagine that. Besides, isn't it clear there's a predator at large? And that's what everyone should be focusing on."

Her gazed shifted again, this time to directly over my shoulder. "I need to go. My husband's pulled the car up."

"Thank you for your time," I said as she moved toward the steps, tightening the belt on her trench. There was still one more topic to explore in the seconds I had left. "I hope you have good friends you can turn to at a time like this."

"Fortunately, I'm blessed that way, yes."

"I spoke to Shannon's friend J.J. I take it she's been providing a lot of support at this time."

"*J.J.?*" She shrugged. "She was Shannon's friend, not someone I really know."

With that she hurried down the steps and ducked into the same SUV I'd seen Doug drive the other day.

What I didn't want to do was lose my shot at Nolan, and that meant beating it back to where I'd been standing earlier. But as I started to descend the steps, I caught sight of him in the foyer, chatting with an elderly male parishioner. I slipped inside and parked myself by the holy water font. The church smelled faintly of incense and lemony furniture polish, a combination both comforting and exotic. Nolan soon caught sight of me out of the corner of his eye. He nodded a few times to the parishioner and then touched him reassuringly on the shoulder.

The old man shuffled off, and Nolan made his way over to me. The misty weather had added a few more waves to his thick brown hair and one had formed into a little curl at the top of his forehead.

"Hello, Ms. Weggins," he said, friendly enough. "I'm sorry I didn't have a chance to return your call yet."

He looked like such a straight arrow, a guy who'd fought and survived a serious illness, who seemed more than eager to be of assistance to others. Was it a total stretch for me to consider that he was also a serial killer?

"No problem, I'm sure you've been really busy, but I did want the chance to chat again. Are you aware that I was one of the reporters who came across Shannon Blaine's body?"

His expression darkened. "Yes, the Claibornes told me. That must have been a dreadful experience for you."

"It was, yes. I'm not sure if you heard this detail or not, but I was tipped off to the retreat center by a phone call. I have reason to believe that the person on the other end saw me talking to you—either in the parking lot here or earlier that day at Dot's. Do you happen to recall anyone paying close attention to us at either location?"

He slowly shook his head. "No, I don't. As you can imagine, I had a lot on my mind, trying to help the Blaines and the Claibornes. Wh—?"

"Could you have mentioned the conversation to anyone?"

"Goodness, no. I don't believe so. . . . No, I'm sure I didn't. But what exactly did the caller say to make you think he saw us?"

"I'm sorry, but I'm not allowed to share that."

His brow furrowed, suggesting frustration.

I flashed a friendly smile, trying to look like I was on his side. "I wish I could, but the police made me promise not to divulge the details. . . . What can you tell me about the retreat center at Sunset Bay?"

Nolan sighed, suddenly looking preoccupied, perhaps with my comment about the caller having observed us. "Not much really. I was vaguely aware the center was there, but it closed down before I began serving as a deacon. And even if things had still been operational, I probably wouldn't have spent any time there."

"You don't get involved in retreats?"

"Well, I wouldn't have at that location. Our parish apparently used it for retreats on only rare occasions."

"Really? Why?"

"It wasn't much of a retreat setting for people who live near the lake year-round. From what I've been told, the center was reserved mostly by other parishes in the diocese. It would be a special treat for members of their congregations to spend a few days on the lake."

I hadn't ever thought of that, but I guessed it made sense.

"Did anyone from this parish ever work there, do you know?"

"Not that I'm aware of. It was really run by the diocese."

"Back to Shannon Blaine for a second. I know she'd been back at church for only a few months, but did you ever notice anything unusual? Someone paying too much attention to her?"

"You mean, was someone *obsessed* with her?"

"It doesn't have to be obsessed. Checking her out a little too closely, for instance. Overly curious."

"No, nothing like that. Of course, she was a beautiful woman, and people noticed her."

And was Nolan one of them? I wondered.

"It must be gratifying to have someone come back into the fold."

The muscles in his face sagged, leaving his face without expression, though his eyes were alert, as if he'd picked up a sound that was inaudible to me, like a border collie hearing a dog whistle.

"It *is* gratifying, yes," he said, "and we do what we can to support those people as best we can. Her death is a tragedy on many levels, including the loss it means for this community. Excuse me now. I see there's a couple of parishioners waiting to speak to me."

He strode across the foyer and out onto the top step of the church, where he struck up a conversation with two middle-aged women. I couldn't tell if one of them had tried to catch his eye, or he'd simply taken advantage of their presence to escape from me.

I scurried past the group and splashed my way back to my Jeep. I hadn't wanted to show up at the church with a pen and notebook in hand, but now I took the time to quickly scribble down what Kelly and Nolan had shared and then review their comments in my mind.

I'd managed to score only a couple of minutes with Shannon's sister, but the encounter had been enlightening on several fronts. First, there was the fact that Kelly didn't know why Shannon had come back to St. Tim's, which was interesting in itself. Based on what Matt Wong had revealed, there may have been a rift between them, even real antagonism.

I couldn't ignore Kelly's remark about people sometimes rejoining the church to make amends. Had there been a reason for Shannon to make amends to her sister?

There was also the revelation that Kelly didn't consider J.J. a friend. So, clearly Doug hadn't stopped by J.J.'s in order to receive succor from a good pal or return the platter for cold cuts that J.J. had dropped off earlier at the Claibornes'. I wondered if Shannon had learned of the affair or at the very least had developed an inkling.

Of course, in the big picture, none of this family drama probably mattered, and I couldn't allow myself to be sidetracked. But it *intrigued* me, and maybe, just maybe, it related in some way to Shannon's death. What if Shannon had felt guilty about a transgression she'd committed against her sister or about the friction in the family that had resulted from Cody's taking over at Baker Beverage? She might have returned to the church for spiritual guidance on how to reconnect with her sister and mentioned her own failings and/or moral shortcoming to someone in the congregation.

Which brought me back to the idea I'd toyed with last night: the killer might be a man hell-bent, so to speak, on punishing women who had sinned.

I wondered if Tom Nolan had a harsh view of female sinners.

It was almost eleven thirty by this point, and I was due back at the Breezy Point. Time to peel off my wet boots and pretty up for my video session, as much as I wasn't relishing it.

I stopped in the village to buy two slices of pizza to go and then headed north along Route 9N, consumed again by thoughts of the case. My attention was diverted briefly by a closed liquor store along the right side of the road. Damn. I'd promised Alice I'd arrive bearing wine, but I realized there wasn't going to be any way to buy it on a Sunday. I called her from the parking lot of the motel.

"Hey, hi," she said when she realized it was me. She sounded distracted.

"Everything okay?"

"Um, yeah. I've just been at my dining table all morning, glued to my laptop. I need to come up for air."

Her voice still sounded funny to me. I wondered if coming across the bodies had been weighing on her as well.

"You sure that's all there is to it?"

"Oh, you're good, Ms. Weggins. Okay, I may have stumbled onto something today."

My heart skipped.

"About the case?"

"Right. A clue. Buried in something online. And it's scary as hell."

CHAPTER 15

I LET OUT A BREATH, MY THOUGHTS RACING.

"About the killer?"

"Maybe."

"Can you tell me?" It was hard to believe Alice would be willing to share a big scoop, but I had to ask.

"No. I mean, yeah, I'd actually like to talk this over with you, but I want to see if I can gather some confirmation first. Let's discuss it over dinner and then decide how to proceed."

"You wanna give me a hint?"

"I'd better wait. I don't want to let a cat out of the bag if it's the wrong cat."

"Understood," I said, though my curiosity was going to be eating me alive until dinnertime, to say nothing of my professional frustration that Alice had a hot lead and I didn't.

I explained to her about the wine and asked if I could pick up a dessert instead.

"Don't worry, I'm covered on the wine front. And dessert, too. Like I told you, we're going to be carbo-loading."

As soon as I was off the phone, I took a fast shower, blew out my hair with an extra glob of styling gel, and then did my makeup, doubling up on both foundation and mascara. Considering I'd packed light for the trip and had never expected to be on camera, I didn't have a lot of outfit choices. I opted for a hot-pink short-sleeved sweater, black pencil skirt, and black knee-length boots.

At exactly noon, someone tapped on the unit door and after checking the peephole, I swung it open to find the videographer, Keith Windgate, standing there. He was probably in his late thirties, African-American, with dreadlocks and oversize black-framed glasses. He was dressed super stylishly in tight olive-green cargo pants, a cropped teal sweater, and a blue-and-green-plaid scarf double wrapped around his neck.

"Hey, Bailey, nice to meet you," he said, smiling. His gaze shifted to my left as he took in the room. "They're big spenders at *Crime Beat*, aren't they?"

"Yeah, it was between this and the Four Seasons, but I'm a sucker for deer antlers. Do you want to come in and talk over the plan?"

"If you're all set, why don't we chat in the car? Thank God the rain stopped so we can shoot outdoors." Keith used a finger to tug down his glasses and then peered over them. "What you're wearing is great, by the way. It'll look nice on camera."

"Good, since I didn't have many options. What location are you thinking of?"

"I drove up to Sunset Bay earlier and they've blocked off the road to the place where you found the bodies. So let's go for Wheeler Road, near where Shannon lived. We can use the woods for a backdrop."

"Sounds good. And once the camera's rolling, I'm just supposed to recap the story from my point of view, right?"

"Right. Keep it casual, like you're having a conversation with the viewer. When you're done, I'll ask you a series of questions so you'll have a chance to cover all your bases."

Once we were in Keith's SUV, I directed him to Wheeler Road and we drove along slowly, looking for a spot to set up. As we passed by the Blaine house, I noted that there were three cars in the driveway, suggesting that family or friends had come to help. There was a boy's bike lying in the well-landscaped yard, and my stomach twisted at the sight. It was essential to keep an emotional distance when reporting a story because otherwise the details could gnaw away at you, even clouding your judgment, but this case made it tough to do.

Finally Keith decided on a spot about two miles from the house. Stepping out of the car, I looked up to see big cumulus clouds nosing each other across the sky. More rain didn't appear imminent, but the sun vanished at moments, making the dense woods look even more foreboding.

I narrowed my eyes, peering through the trees. I had no clue if we were close to where the earbuds had been found, but if Shannon had indeed been nabbed while jogging, it was probably from a spot like this one, with no houses nearby. Surely Shannon would have tried to break free. She might have even made it a few yards into the woods before he caught up with her again and dragged her back to his vehicle.

The shoot went better than I'd anticipated, in large part because Keith was so easy to work with. I recapped the case, describing what had transpired from the moment Shannon was reported missing and ending with the revelation about Amy and Page. When we were finished, I reviewed a few minutes of video with him and was relieved to see I didn't look like I was speaking on a hostage tape.

"I'm sure Dodson will love this," Keith volunteered.

"You won't just put up the raw footage, will you?"

"No, no. I'll create a timeline and intersperse pieces of what we shot with other material, like snippets from the press conference and photos of Shannon. I'm gonna work like crazy to have it up later today."

I gave him a hand loading his equipment back into the SUV and then jumped into the passenger seat. My toes were damp and cold from standing in wet brush, but I was relieved to be done.

Keith dropped me off at the Breezy Point, where I noticed that the white Camry was still in its spot, though it now had a black Beemer cozied up next to it. Since management seemed to be spacing out guests in the nearly empty motel, I wondered if the jogger might have an afternoon visitor.

Back in my room, I stripped off my boots and set them to dry by the heating unit. I helped myself to the second slice of pizza, which I'd left congealing on the dresser, and began reviewing my notes in my composition book from earlier this morning. Something seemed to be tugging my attention back to them.

As I reread what I'd scribbled down, I realized what was

calling to me: a comment Kelly had made about all the recent deaths in her family—her father, her cousin, and now Shannon. J.J., I recalled, had mentioned the cousin, too. A guy named Destin, whom Shannon apparently had been very close to. I probably should have checked him out earlier.

I dragged my laptop to the center of the desk and typed "Destin," "Lake George," and "obituary" into the search bar. Within seconds, I found a link to an obituary for Destin Michaels, who had died last year, at the age of thirty-three. That would make his birth date right around Shannon's, and they'd probably bonded as kids, particularly if Shannon had never felt close to Kelly.

There was no cause of death listed. That could reflect the family's desire for privacy, but it could also be a red flag, an indication that the reason was not one they wanted to broadcast to the world.

It didn't take me long to unearth the truth, though. It was in the *Post Star*'s coverage, topped with the headline: "Police Investigating Apparent Drug Overdose Death in Lake George." Destin Michaels had died from an overdose of the prescription painkiller oxycodone, which was the generic name for OxyContin. The fourth such death so far that year, the paper pointed out.

For the next three seconds, I thought I finally had the link between Shannon and the two campers. Kayla had stressed that Amy didn't do drugs because she'd lost a friend to an Oxy overdose—maybe that friend had been *Destin*. I quickly realized how totally dumb I was being. Amy's friend had died more than ten years ago.

And yet there *was* a link of sorts, and one probably worth noting—as links so often were. My old buddy Buddy always adhered to what he liked to call "Einstein's Law of Two or More." If something turned up at least twice in the universe, it was begging for your attention and you were a fool not to take note.

This was the second time drugs had come up, the third if I counted what I'd read last night about the busts on Route 149. Maybe, despite everything Kayla believed, Amy and Page *had* been caught up in the drug world, and it was there that they'd crossed paths with their killer. A serious user. Or dealer. One who also happened to be a psychopathic murderer.

But then how did any of that tie in with Shannon? She was a mom of two who had little in common with young single women like Amy and Page, at least on the surface. I couldn't picture her ever setting foot in a shit hole like Muller's.

But, of course, over the past couple of decades, countless ordinary people had become addicted to painkillers and now bought them illegally or moved on to heroin. It was possible that Shannon had been prescribed painkillers for an injury, perhaps a running-related one, and had become dependent without either Cody or J.J. being aware. That could have led her on a search for illegal drugs, which in turn placed her into contact with the person who had killed Amy and Page.

I didn't have a hint of evidence, of course, so for now I tucked the idea into my back pocket.

Though it was a little early to write my post, I went ahead

anyway, since I had the time and I could always update it if news broke later. I wished I had more to say, but right now things were in a state of limbo. With any luck, the forensic examination of the three bodies would soon produce compelling evidence and law enforcement would begin to close in on the killer.

And that would mean I'd have plenty of reason to stick around Lake George.

I wasn't ready to leave, I realized. Yeah, I was kind of sick of antlers and birch bark and recycling the same clothes, but I loved being a daily reporter again, chasing leads and seeing what surprises might be waiting at the end. Finding the bodies had shaken me, but it had been gratifying to know that I had played a role in the discovery, that Shannon's family at least knew her fate and wouldn't have to spend the rest of their lives haunted by uncertainty. It even gave me a weird satisfaction to know that the killer had chosen me to share with.

There was one more reason I didn't want to pack up and leave. I still felt a burning need to know who had killed the three women. I glanced up at the flyer with Shannon's photo hanging above my desk. It had started to curl inward on both sides, almost obscuring her face. I snapped off a few pieces of tape and used them to make it hang straight again.

Just as I started to close my laptop, I spotted an email from Jessie. She would definitely be driving south on the Northway tomorrow and was hoping we were still on for lunch. "You bet," I wrote back, and suggested a restaurant with an outdoor deck I'd spotted in the village.

It was 6:20 and finally time to leave for Alice's. I threw

on my jacket and punched my feet into the slightly shrunken boots by the heater. I was looking forward to dinner, and I even caught myself humming as I slammed the unit door shut. Both the Camry and Beemer were gone from their spaces, but no sooner had I noted that fact than the Camry pulled into the parking lot and jerked to a stop. Two seconds later the blond jogger emerged from the car, dressed in jeans and a fitted brown leather coat. This time she caught sight of me and drew back in surprise. She definitely recognized me and seemed startled to find me twenty feet away from her.

"Hello again," I called out.

She assessed me warily. "You're staying at this motel?"

"Yes, I've been here all along." I took a couple of steps in her direction. "I'm sorry if I startled you the other day. I'm a reporter who's been covering the Shannon Blaine case—the woman I mentioned to you—and you looked like her from the back. It threw me."

Her shoulders relaxed. "I heard about that woman later," she said. "It's horrible."

"My name's Bailey Weggins, by the way. After I realized you weren't Shannon, I worried about you being out on that road alone. I even stopped by the motel you said you were staying at to make sure you made it back okay, but the owner said he didn't have any guests fitting your description."

"The Lake Shore? I was there. But my friend checked us in, and the owner hadn't seen me yet, I guess."

I'd edged over a few more feet and was now fairly close to her. She'd blown out her hair in long, pretty waves, and she was wearing about twenty-five minutes' worth of makeup, including enough lip gloss to slow down any vehicle attempting to cross from one side of her mouth to the other.

"Why'd you switch?" I asked, curious.

She shook her head in disgust. "I finally *did* meet the owner, and he gave me the creeps. Every time I came out of the room, he seemed to be staring out that plate-glass window, eyeing me."

I didn't like the sound of that. Dobbs had spent more than his fair share of time watching Shannon Blaine from the same spot. I made a mental note to ask Alice more about the guy since she was the one who had initially interviewed him for the *Post Star*.

"It was probably smart to trust your gut," I told her. "Especially in light of everything that's going on." I reached in my bag for a business card and handed it to her. "Just in case I can ever be of help."

This was the moment when she might have introduced herself, but she chose not to.

"Thanks, have a nice evening" was all she said. At the moment at least, she was an under-the-radar kind of girl. Well, that was fine by me. I was about to enjoy a night of blissful carbo-loading.

I started to say goodbye and caught myself. "Oh, by the way. The night you checked in, did you have any reason to stop near my door? Unit seven. I thought I heard someone out there."

"Uh, yes, sorry. When I got out of my car in front of my room, I thought I'd left the key in the office. I started to walk back there and was digging in my purse at the same time. I finally figured out I had the key all along."

So it sounded like the night manager's take had been right.

"Oh, okay, thanks. Have a nice evening, too."

The sun had set by now, but I found Alice's road easily enough, grateful for my car's GPS since the sign was partially obscured by a leafy branch. It turned out to be a dirt road, lined close to the edge with trees, not unlike the one leading to the retreat center in Sunset Bay. By this point, I'd let my curiosity unfurl about whatever Alice had stumbled on and deemed "scary."

I passed three homes as I bumped down the road, all of them tucked into the trees on the right. Finally Alice's house materialized at the very end. I wouldn't have called it a cabin as she had. It was a nice-size house, painted a rustic brown and sporting a peaked roof. The downstairs glowed with warm, amber-tinged light.

After parking my car next to the red MINI, I hurried up the short flagstone path. Once I was within a few yards of the house, I could see through the windows that the ground floor had an open design plan, with the kitchen and dining areas closer to the front and the living space at the back, facing the lake. There seemed to be a patio running along there, illuminated from lights attached above.

The dining table wasn't set, but I remembered that Alice had said we'd eat on the screened porch if the weather obliged. It was farther back on the left, I noticed, though Alice hadn't flicked those lights on yet.

Mounting the front steps, I heard music and smiled to myself. So Alice was a Brandi Carlile fan, too. I went to reach for the handle and discovered that the door was actually open several inches. Alice might be in the shower or getting dressed, I realized, and had left it open in case she didn't hear me from upstairs.

"Knock, knock," I called out, stepping into the kitchen area. There was nothing simmering or braising on the stovetop, but a dozen red potatoes rested on the counter, along with a luscious-looking homemade pie, which explained why the air was redolent with the smell of apples and cinnamon. It was slightly chilly inside, I noticed, probably from the door being left ajar. I pushed it closed behind me.

I shrugged off my jacket and hung it on a peg by the door.

"Alice?" I said, my voice raised. When she didn't answer, I lowered the volume on the iPod speakers on the counter and called her name again.

There was still no response, but a sound emanated suddenly from the front of the house, a whoosh and then a snap, like someone flapping a piece of wet laundry. I took two steps toward it but the sound ceased. Then started again. Stopped. Started *again*. What the hell?

I was halfway across the dining area when the source of the noise swooped above my head. A freaking *bat*.

"Shit," I yelled, ducking. The bat vanished back into the living area, only to sail through the room again seconds later, this time smacking into the window and dropping with a sad little thud to the ground.

I backed into the kitchen and jerked open the door to a narrow closet next to the fridge. There was a corn broom inside and I grabbed it, then flung open the kitchen door. Using the broom, I nudged the bat toward freedom. The second it reached the threshold, it unfurled its wings and went airborne again.

I slammed the door and spun around. "Alice," I yelled again, this time even louder than before. Had the bat freaked her out so that she'd hightailed it upstairs for cover?

After wandering into the living room, I spotted the enclosed staircase to the second floor and, leaning into it, called Alice's name twice more. Not a peep. My heart was beating a little faster than normal by this point. I pivoted toward the front of the house and peered out to the patio, which was aglow from the overhead lights. She had to be outside.

I opened the rear door and stepped onto a flagstone patio. Bordered in front by a low stone wall, it sat atop a small embankment and ran the width of the house. The lake stretched out below, black except for the shimmering reflection of light on the water closest to shore. Alice was nowhere to be seen, and the only sound was from the water lapping below.

I glanced to my right. A set of stone steps descended from the patio to the lake, illuminated by metal light fixtures with tops like mushroom caps. I took a step in that direction, and my eye caught sight of a stemless wineglass sitting on the ledge of the wall to the left of the steps. It still held a splash of white wine. Had Alice set it there and gone down to the lake?

My stomach tightened. Something was off.

I grabbed hold of the black wrought iron railing and began to descend the steps. I was halfway down when I heard a rustling noise from above me. I spun around, my heart ricocheting against my chest.

"Alice?" I called out.

No. The sound, I realized, was the wind shaking the tree leaves above me. I turned my attention back to the steps. Squinting, I saw that they ended about twenty feet below, though the only light, I realized, was coming from above. It was hard to imagine that Alice was down there in near darkness, and yet the wineglass suggested she might be.

I took two steps down. And two more.

And then I saw her. She was sprawled facedown on the dirt, a few feet from the start of a wooden dock. Her legs were splayed and her body inert. She was wearing dark pants and a thick burnt-orange sweater.

"Alice!" I yelled, and tore down the last steps.

I crouched beside her. With the little bit of light that reached us, I could see that the left side of her face was actually pointing out, toward the left. Her eye was closed. I laid my hand on her sweater and shuffled it back and forth, trying to rouse her.

"Alice, can you hear me?" I said, my mouth next to her ear.

No acknowledgment. I called her name again, twice, but she didn't move.

I slid my purse off my arm and dug frantically through the bag, finding my phone and switching on the flashlight. I trained the beam on Alice. Her neck, I could see now, was at a terrible, unnatural angle, her chin raised too high, like that of a deer killed by a car on the highway. I leaned closer again and listened for her breath. Nothing.

Please, I begged, don't let her be dead. Not Alice.

I focused on my phone and tapped 911. With the other hand I carefully grasped Alice's wrist.

"What is your emergency?" the operator asked. I blurted out the details, stumbling once as I tried to recall the exact address.

"Is the victim breathing?" the operator asked.

"Not from what I can tell," I said, my voice catching. "And I can't find a pulse. But . . . I can't be a hundred percent sure. Send an ambulance. And the police."

Because my gut was telling me it wasn't an accident.

The operator said she would stay on the call with me. I told her I couldn't hold, but would wait for the ambulance. I wanted the chance to investigate the situation with both hands free.

I rested my palm on Alice's back and jiggled again. No response.

"Alice, it's me, Bailey. Hold on, help is coming." But I was almost positive my words were pointless.

I trained the beam of light around her body again. There was no sign of blood, nothing to suggest she had bled from her head or anywhere else. My best guess was that her neck was broken. But not because she'd tripped on the stairs. She wouldn't have been heading down to the dock when she was supposed to be making me dinner—and without even flicking on the lights below? I thought of the kitchen door, left weirdly ajar on a cool night. Someone came to her house, I told myself. And then they pushed her.

I rose to a standing position and directed the beam around the ground, farther away from Alice this time. No scuff marks in the dirt, no indication of a struggle. The killer might have shoved her down the stairs so that she broke her neck in the fall.

Alice's words from this morning echoed in my head again. "A clue . . . And it's scary as hell." Had the murderer figured out that Alice was on to him?

I jerked the beam back toward Alice, dragging it down to her left hand and then her right. There was no sign of cut marks or anything resembling stigmata. I stared for a moment at her weathered fingers, remembering the ragged cuticles. A sob caught in my throat.

From far off on the lake came the roar of a motorboat gunning across the water, then fading. I was engulfed once again in silence. But then another sound broke through the night. Not the trees this time, though.

It was the sound of footsteps. Someone was walking across the patio, ten or so feet above me.

CHAPTER 16

I FROZE, STRAINING TO HEAR. ANOTHER SCRAPE, THE sound of a shoe or a boot on the patio. Someone was definitely up there, near the top of the stairs.

I backed up fast, into the shadows, and dropped onto my haunches, pressing my body tight against the embankment.

If Alice had been pushed, it seemed unlikely that the killer would still be on the property. Unless he'd come back. To make sure she was dead? To dispose of her body somehow? To *mark* it?

I stayed squatting, my eyes riveted to the steps. Another scrape. But farther away this time, I thought, as if the person was reversing direction.

After a minute, there were no other sounds from above and I sensed that whoever had been there was gone. I turned my gaze back to Alice and felt an urge to howl in despair.

Finally the whoop whoop of an ambulance pierced the night. I struggled out of my crouch and then charged up the steps, two at a time. As I reached the top, I spotted two male EMTs hurrying through the house.

"She's down below, at the base of the steps," I told them as I flung open the door. "I couldn't find a pulse but . . ."

"Okay, take a seat inside," one of them said. "The police should be here any minute."

I didn't like being banished indoors, but I needed to let the paramedics do their job. I watched as the two descended below, striving to hear their exchange. But their words were indistinguishable beneath the sound of the wind. I backed into the house and collapsed into an armchair next to a wood-burning stove, facing the patio.

I could smell the apple pie still, the scent mixed now with traces of wood smoke seeping from the stove next to me. Alice must have sat in this chair so many times, I realized—reading, savoring the view, talking with her husband when he was still alive.

My gaze fell on several framed photos on a small wooden end table. There was one of Alice leaning into a beaming, husky, gray-haired man, who must have been her late husband. And another photo of Alice, this time in her familiar car coat and linking arms with her son, Ben, whose picture she had showed me over dinner. I choked back tears.

I knew I needed to sit tight and not touch anything in the house, but I scanned the room with my eyes, looking for any sign of disturbance. The space was slightly rumpled in spots—a messy pile of books and a stack of *Post Star*s near the foot of the armchair; a mohair throw tossed haphazardly on the sofa; a vase full of mostly wilted flowers, but nothing suggesting an altercation.

On the far side of the room, an open doorway led to the screened-in porch. Though it was dark in there, I could make out the silhouettes of objects on the table, like a distant city skyline. There were wine and water glasses. And hurricane lamps. Alice had set the table for dinner.

I looked quickly back to the living space. There was no sign, I realized, of Alice's laptop. Maybe she used a home office upstairs. But no, she'd said on the phone that she was working at her table. I bent at the waist, leaning forward, and glanced toward the dining area. The only thing on it was a coffee mug.

If Alice *had* determined the killer's identity and he'd come here to silence her, he would have, of course, wanted her laptop. That's where she'd found the clue, after all.

A movement outside grabbed my attention. One of the EMTs was ascending the steps, speaking on his phone. I dashed back outside.

"Is she—?" I said, my voice pleading.

He placed a hand over the phone and shook his head, his expression somber. "I'm afraid she's dead. An autopsy will have to determine the exact cause."

I felt shell-shocked, unable to fully process the truth, though I'd had little doubt of it. I turned to see two uniformed officers, one a middle-aged male, the other a younger female. They were both with the state police.

"Please, miss, you need to wait inside," the female cop commanded.

I retreated back into the living area, observing as the EMT conferred with the officers. The male cop descended to the dock with the EMT while the woman joined me inside. She chose the chair directly across from me and pulled out a pen and notebook.

She asked me to take her through what had happened. After explaining that I was a journalist friend of Alice's, I spit out a quick recap of my experience tonight and then answered a round of questions—what time exactly had I arrived, had I noticed any sign of anyone besides hearing the footsteps, did the victim have any next of kin that I knew of?

This cop was aware, of course, that I might be responsible for Alice's death. Maybe we'd quarreled on the patio and things had turned ugly, leading to an overwrought moment when I'd given my so-called friend a fateful shove down the stairs. I couldn't let her become bogged down with that scenario.

"Can you ask that Sheriff Killian come by here tonight as soon as possible? It's very important that I speak to him about Ms. Hatfield's death."

The request seemed to take her aback.

"Sheriff Killian? The state police are perfectly equipped to handle this."

"Killian is overseeing the investigation into Shannon Blaine's murder, and I believe Alice's death is tied to it."

She nodded after a moment, her curiosity clearly aroused. "Let me check to see if that's possible."

She went outside and spoke to the other state police officer, who'd come back up the steps, and they were joined soon by reinforcements: a man who, based on his bag, appeared to be with the coroner's office, and members of the state police crime scene crew. A minute later, a guy of about seventy entered the house through the kitchen and charged into the room where I sat.

"What's going on?" he demanded. "Where's Alice?"

"Are you a friend?"

"A neighbor. I live up the road and saw the ambulance."

"I'm so sorry, but Alice is dead."

"Dear God, no." He swept both hands through his hair. "How?"

"I think she was attacked. So I'm sure the police will want to speak with you in case you saw anything."

"*Attacked?* Are you saying it was a burglary?"

"Not a burglary. Did you see anything? Or anybody around here?"

"No, but I came by twenty minutes or so ago to return a wrench. I saw her car and another one but no one seemed to be around. . . . I need to get home. My wife's alone there."

"You came out to the patio?"

"Yes, right."

"Do you know how we can reach her son, Ben?" I asked.

"Oh, that poor guy. I think my wife has a number for—"

The officer who'd interviewed me caught sight of the neighbor, hustled back into the house, and after determining that the man was not next of kin, asked him to return home, where the police would stop by and speak with him soon. Once he'd departed, she told me that they were reaching out to Killian, but she couldn't guarantee he would come.

I parked myself back in the armchair to wait. My emotions were in a jumble but I detached myself as best as I could and tried to create a timeline for Alice's movements during the second half of the day.

She and I had spoken right before noon. She'd found the clue by then but was seeking confirmation, which meant she'd continued to work for a while.

At some point she'd baked a pie and set the table on the porch. She washed the potatoes, but it didn't appear she'd had a chance to start the main meal yet.

I was still in my seat thirty minutes later when, thank God, Killian arrived. I spotted him in plain clothes, dark pants and a brown windbreaker, along the side of the house. He spoke briefly to the female officer and then descended the steps to the lake. Ten minutes later, he returned to the patio and entered the house.

My face must have betrayed my distress because he approached with what seemed like sympathy on his face.

"How are you doing, Ms. Weggins?"

"Holding up. I appreciate you coming. I asked the police to contact you because I don't think Alice's death was an accident. I'm worried someone pushed her. Or killed her and threw her down the stairs."

"Because?"

"She told me on the phone earlier that she'd come across what she believed was a clue to the murders. Something she found, quote, 'scary as hell.' She said she wanted to confirm it first and that she would tell me tonight over dinner, but obviously that never happened."

My voice caught as I spoke the last words. Killian kept his expression as neutral as possible, but I saw his eyes widen slightly.

"When you spoke on the phone, did she give any hint to what she'd come across?"

"No, only that she'd found it buried online. It's possible that she shared it with her boss or a coworker, though. What I *do* know is that she'd been looking for any references to missing or murdered women outside this immediate area. She also mentioned she was doing her research at the table, but there's no laptop there now. So if it isn't upstairs someplace, someone took it."

He lifted a small pad and pen from a pocket in his windbreaker and scribbled down a few notes.

"What time did you arrive?" he asked.

"Right at seven."

"One of the police officers mentioned that you heard noises on the patio when you were down below. You think someone was up there?"

I explained quickly that it had been the neighbor.

"Did you notice anything else that seemed out of the ordinary at the time?"

"Yes, actually, I was going to mention it. The kitchen door was open. At first I thought Alice had left it ajar for me because she was upstairs, but it was chilly inside, as if it had been opened for a while. And there was a bat in the house."

"A *bat*?"

"Yeah, flying around. It probably snuck in through the door. So now I'm thinking someone might have run out of the house with the laptop and didn't worry about closing it. Maybe Alice had a real lead on the killer, and he got wise to her digging. And came after her."

Killian lowered his gaze and flicked through a page or two of his notebook. When he glanced back at me, his mouth was half scrunched, the right side tugged up. I was expecting him to say something blunt and gruff, like "Let *us* do the police work, Ms. Weggins," which I'd heard more times than I liked in my lifetime.

"That's good to know about the door," he said instead, nodding slowly.

"One more observation I want to share. Alice made a pie—it's on the counter, and when I arrived at seven, it was still warm, which means she probably didn't take it out of the oven any earlier than five thirty or six. There are potatoes out, but she hadn't done anything with them yet. If she'd planned to roast them for our dinner, she would have started a little after six, I'd guess. All of this suggests to me that she died somewhere between five thirty and six thirty, at the latest."

This could have been another opportunity to tell me to back off and stop playing junior detective, but once again Killian nodded.

"I appreciate your input, Ms. Weggins," he said. "In fact, if we're looking at foul play here, on top of everything else that's happened, we're going to need to rely on every resource available. I think it would serve both our purposes for us to be collaborative going forward."

Okay, this was good. He wanted my help and seemed to hint that he'd give me access to certain information in return. It was a coup for my reporting, but at this exact moment all I really cared about was Alice.

"I agree," I said. "If someone murdered Alice, I want to do everything possible to make sure he's caught. . . . Her son, Ben. Who's going to—?"

"Don't worry, we'll take care of that."

Killian dropped the pad and pen back into his pocket, signaling that his questioning was done for now. He then escorted me through the house.

"In the vein of cooperation," Killian said as we reached the kitchen door, "is there anything else you want to share?"

"About?" Did he think I was holding back?

"Have you heard from your mystery caller again?"

"Absolutely not. I would have told you. But actually, there is something else I wanted to pass along." I explained what the jogger had told me about the owner of the Lake Shore Motel, and also the fact that he'd been interviewed by Alice.

"Interesting. And is this woman still at the Breezy Point?"

I nodded and gave him the unit number. Oh, Miss Under the Radar was going to be tickled pink that I'd tipped off the cops to her location.

Killian walked me to my car and temporarily detached the yellow police tape by the driveway so I could escape. There were several hangers-on around the fringe, neighbors probably, but a state police person was encouraging them to return home. The ambulance, I noticed, had departed, though I hadn't seen anyone bring up Alice's body yet. The thought of her eventually lying on a table in the morgue made my heart hurt.

"Drive carefully, Ms. Weggins," Killian said, opening my car door for me.

"Please call me Bailey."

"Thank you, I will."

I bumped along the road I'd driven down several hours earlier in such a different frame of mind, so eager then for home cooking and the chance to spend an evening in Alice's company. Someone had probably come down here not long before I had, intent on killing Alice, making sure she couldn't report what she found—either in the *Post Star* or to the police. What the hell had the clue been?

I couldn't bear the idea of being back in my motel room alone, so I headed south on Route 9 to the village. The place was nearly dead, not unexpected for a Sunday night, but at least Jake's was open. I parked, nearly staggered to a seat at the end of the bar, and ordered a bowl of French onion soup and a glass of red wine. The bartender smiled empathetically as she quickly assessed me. I had a feeling she thought I'd been dumped on my ass by a guy only minutes earlier.

Speaking of guys, I felt a sudden, desperate need to speak with Beau. I checked my watch. Since it was one hour earlier in Bogotá, the worst I would be doing is interrupting his dinner plans. I tapped his name in Favorites. The phone rang six times and then went to voice mail.

"Hey, babe," I said. "Can you call me? I just need to talk to you."

As I waited for the soup, I pressed the heels of my hands into my eye sockets, trying to force my thoughts to quiet, instead of ricocheting crazily around my brain like a flying squirrel with its tail on fire.

How had the killer been tipped off to Alice's discovery earlier in the day? Perhaps, in seeking confirmation of her revelation, she'd begun making inquiries, and word of those inquiries had made its way back to him. She might have even reviewed information with him without realizing what she was giving away.

Had the killer surprised her in the kitchen? And had she run out to the patio, fearing for her life? There had been no sign of commotion, of Alice trying to fight someone off, but it could have happened quickly enough not to leave any evidence.

I thought suddenly of the wineglass on the ledge of the stone wall. In my frazzled state, I'd forgotten to mention this detail to Killian—though, of course the police would make note of the glass when they saw it.

Perhaps, after making the pie and setting the table, Alice had taken a short break, treating herself to some white wine and a contemplation of the lake from the patio before darkness descended. She'd been wearing that heavy sweater, after all. Someone could have come through the house and caught her unawares. And then shoved her down the stairs.

Something about that scenario didn't fit, though. If a stranger had snuck up behind her, catching her off guard, she would have jumped up in fear and the glass would have probably dropped and shattered. Or it would have flown from her hand when she was trying to fight the person off. It seemed to me that she'd had time to look up, rise, take a few steps, and set the glass carefully on the ledge.

Perhaps she'd heard a sound emanating from the house before she'd set eyes on anyone.

Or perhaps she *knew* the person and assumed she had nothing to worry about. Or she might have known she had something to worry about but urged herself to remain calm.

Yes, I told myself with no real proof other than what my gut was telling me. She *knew* whoever it was.

Maybe I was getting too far ahead of things. The fall *could* have been an accident, though right now the chances of that seemed slim, especially if the laptop was missing. Regardless, Alice had found a detail online that had alarmed her, a clue about the case, and I needed to know what it was. If I had any hope of figuring it out—and then determining who had murdered her—I was going to have to follow her digital footprints as best as I could.

The soup arrived, and I managed only a couple of bites. It tasted weirdly smoky to me, like it had been flavored with bits of charred firewood. Even the wine seemed off.

I ordered the bill and a coffee to go. As I dug out my wallet, I overheard someone at the far end of the bar utter the name "Alice." I jerked my head in that direction. A middle-aged man, his expression stricken, was speaking to the bartender as she clasped her hands to her face in unhappy surprise.

It looked like word of Alice's death might be starting to spread. Had her son been informed yet? I wondered. The thought of him hearing the news was unbearably sad.

I had little interest in being alone at the Breezy Point with my thoughts, but I was eager to start my own online search.

The four-mile drive seemed even more forlorn tonight, with so many darkened motels and shops along the route. The office light was burning when I pulled into the motel lot, and so was a lamp in the jogger's unit, though her Camry was without its BMW sidekick tonight.

As soon as I was inside, I tore off my jacket, grabbed my laptop, and set to work at the desk. My plan was to use the same approach Alice had—starting not far from the area and working my way out. I found state police sites listing missing persons in New York State and Vermont and began making note of any cases involving young and youngish women within a radius of two hundred miles. I turned up ten or so, and though I knew most were probably runaways, I tracked down local news coverage of each case just to be sure. None of the cases seemed to bear any relation to the ones here.

Around midnight, I peeled off my clothes, set the alarm on my phone for six thirty, and crawled into bed, torn up inside. Part of me wanted to keep working, but tomorrow was going to require all the energy I could muster. I briefly wondered if I should email Jessie, canceling lunch—it would take time from my research—but I decided not to. I was in desperate need of a friend right now.

I dozed off quickly from sheer exhaustion, but moments later my ringtone roused me with a start. I shot a hand out in the darkness and fumbled for the phone on the bedside table. My heart skipped as I brought it close enough to read the screen.

Sheriff Killian.

"Did I wake you?" he asked as I used my free elbow to help me scoot up in bed.

"Um, yeah, but that's okay."

"There's no sign of Alice's laptop. She definitely told you she was working at home?"

"Yes. God, somebody's taken it then."

"We didn't come across any notes or files about the case, either, so those must have been grabbed as well. And though I can't go into detail at this time—and this has to stay between you and me—there were indications at the scene that Alice's death was not an accident."

"Have you managed to reach her son yet?"

"Yes, he's been notified. He's planning to arrive tomorrow."

"Would it be possible for me to get his cell number from you?"

"You know I can't give out that kind of information."

"Okay."

"But I'm very appreciative of your cooperation. Is there anything more you can tell us? Any hint that Ms. Hatfield might have dropped about what she'd been researching?"

I wondered if I should reveal what Alice knew about the stigmata, but I'd given my word that I'd protect her source, and it didn't seem to be the line of inquiry she'd been pursuing over the weekend, anyway.

"No, nothing more. I've started to search myself. If I find anything at all, I'll let you know."

A pause. Hard to tell if he was weighing my words or winding up for a comment.

"Ms. Weggins," Killian said finally. "The person who

called you the other day was most likely the killer. And it's possible he thinks Alice shared what she knew with you. You need to be extremely cautious."

I swallowed hard.

"I will be."

After hanging up, I considered Killian's warning. I knew he was right, that I might indeed be in danger now. The killer was surely reading my *Crime Beat* posts, keeping tabs, and so he knew that Alice was with me at Sunset Bay, that I must have told her about the phone call before bringing her along to the retreat center. And he might assume we'd swapped additional information over the next few days. In his eyes, therefore, I was no longer a harmless messenger for him. I was a potential threat.

Would he call me again? Killian probably hoped he would, because it might prove fruitful. Yet I was growing doubtful. He'd wanted his handiwork discovered, that much was clear, but Alice's murder proved he had no interest in being apprehended. It seemed unlikely he'd take the risk of phoning me another time.

I realized suddenly how utterly silent the room was. There weren't any sounds from outside either, no cars whizzing down Route 9N, not even the muted whoosh of the wind.

I threw back the duvet, jumped from the bed, and dragged the old wooden dresser against the door. It would hardly offer much protection, but it made me feel better.

First thing tomorrow, I decided, I was going to find a new place to stay, a motel where I'd feel less exposed, or perhaps a hotel instead.

After slipping back between the sheets, I flicked off the

light and lay with my eyes wide open, summoning the killer in my mind.

You think you're so smart, don't you? I thought. Spreading out your murders over the years. Using a voice adapter. Silencing a reporter who was on to you. But I'm going to find the clue that Alice came across. And then I'm going to know who you are.

CHAPTER 17

ISTIRRED AWAKE JUST BEFORE SIX THE NEXT MORNING AT
the sound of voices directly outside my door.

"You can't put anyone in fourteen," a male voice murmured. "The drain's still clogged in there."

"Okay, okay," a female replied. "It's not like we don't have
space."

I unstuck my eyes to half-mast. The first thing my gaze
landed on was the dresser shoved up against the door, and in
a split second everything came crashing back—Alice's death,
Killian's call, the missing laptop. I moaned, my stomach
churning from the memory.

After dragging myself out of bed, I checked the *Post Star*
online. There was a short news item on the home page
announcing Alice's death. Though the piece offered scant
details, it pointed out that the police were considering foul
play. No mention of me. It looked like Killian was trying to
protect me, hiding the fact that I'd been on the premises.

The article included a link to an obit of Alice, which detailed her long career as a reporter, first in Massachusetts and then here for many years. She was survived, it said, by a son, Ben Hatfield of Chicago. Was he already at O'Hare by now, I wondered, beginning his sad journey here?

With a heavy heart, I made a reservation online for a room at the Courtyard by Marriott in the center of Lake George village, which had a check-in time of three. I'd feel safer there than at the Breezy Point, and hopefully more people would be hanging around. If Dodson flinched at springing for the upgrade, I'd cover the difference myself.

After a quick run to a nearby general store for take-out coffee—checking more than once over my shoulder—I settled back at the desk in the room. I composed a short update to last night's post, announcing Alice's death. For now, I included nothing about my role in finding her, though I shot an email to Dodson filling him in, confidentially, about the situation.

With the update out of the way, I plotted my moves for the morning. My top priority was continuing my online research in the hope of lighting on Alice's discovery. I also wanted to track down her son. I'd suggested to Killian that Alice might have shared the information with a colleague at the paper, but I'd also begun to wonder if she'd run it by Ben since they were clearly close. If he were taking a morning flight from Chicago, he'd arrive at the Albany airport by midday and in Lake George about an hour later.

In addition, I wanted to talk to Cody. My gut was still telling me that Alice had been familiar with her killer, and I wondered if Cody might have any theories. He knew who'd been hanging around the volunteer center and might have seen Alice interacting with people. It was a long shot, but long shots were all I had at the moment.

There was another subject matter I wanted to raise with him—the question of drugs—and though I knew he wouldn't like it, I was going to go there anyway.

I spent the next two hours glued to my laptop, widening the radius of my search even further. People were missing, that was for sure, all over the state and New England, too, many more than I would have imagined, and the stories made you ache for the relatives, lovers, and friends who'd been left searching and yearning. But I found no cases of missing women that seemed relevant.

My phone rang. I wasn't surprised to see Matt Wong's name on the screen. He would have caught wind of Alice's death by now and would be on the prowl for details.

"You know, I assume?" he said, barely giving me time to mutter hello.

"About Alice Hatfield? Yes."

"They're hinting at foul play. Do you think it has anything to do with the case? Or was it just some spat that got out of hand?"

"*Spat?*"

"You know, a personal issue—with a kid or neighbor. I doubt it's a lover's quarrel gone wrong. She wasn't what you'd call a looker."

"I don't think Alice cared about being a *looker*," I said, wishing he'd just shut the fuck up. "She was too busy being a good journalist."

"Sorry, didn't mean to be rude. I know Alice was good. I've followed some of her stuff since I've been up here."

"Matt, can I call you back?" I wasn't in the mood for him.

"Yeah, okay, but we talked about having a drink. Does tonight work for you?"

"Maybe. Let me see how the day goes, okay?"

After I'd signed off, I double-checked my phone for texts in case Beau had tried to make contact and I hadn't heard the ping. Nothing. I knew his cell service was spotty, but I felt a burning need to talk to him, to share about Alice. It would have to wait. At least I was going to see Jessie.

Checkout at the Breezy Point was at eleven, so at ten minutes before the hour I stuffed my clothes and boots into my duffel bag and work gear into my tote and then lugged everything outside. The white Camry, which had been parked in the lot when I'd made my coffee run earlier, was now gone. I hoped the jogger hadn't checked out. Killian had said he'd follow up with her, and the easier she was to locate, the better.

A woman I didn't recognize, middle-aged with a friendly, open face, was at the front desk of the motel. After paying my bill, I gushed disingenuously about my stay.

"Glad you enjoyed it, sweetheart," she said. "You should come back when the pool's open next summer. We keep it heated."

"I definitely will. By the way, I noticed my new friend in unit eleven isn't here at the moment. She didn't check out yet, did she?"

"No, they're still around. Guess they must have gone for food. You gotta eat, as they say."

It was spoken with more of a chuckle than a snicker, but her tone definitely suggested that the jogger and the owner of the Beemer had been keeping carnal company over the past couple of days. Clearly they hadn't come to the area simply to relish the limpid blue lake water and scent of wood smoke in the air. But why travel in separate cars? I wondered. Maybe they resided in different areas and met up here periodically. Maybe one of them—or both—was married, and they were here for a clandestine fling, which would explain why the jogger had been trying to keep a low profile.

At least she was still here and Killian would have a shot at speaking with her soon.

Two minutes later I pulled out of the lot and aimed my Jeep north toward the Lake Shore Motel rather than south toward town. I knew Killian would be speaking to Terry Dobbs today, and I was sure he wouldn't like me tramping on this turf and possibly eliminating his element-of-surprise card with the motel owner. But the morning had left me so frustrated that I felt the need to do *something*. I'd decided on the spur of the moment to take a crack at him myself.

I would be careful, though. I'd avoid any mention of Alice, and would instead chat with Dobbs about Shannon again to see how he responded.

The parking lot of the Lake Shore looked as forlorn as the Breezy Point's. Though the temperature had warmed up again, a light breeze was blowing, snapping the tarp that protected the heating unit of the pool.

Dobbs was on duty, as I'd expected. Through the window I saw him glance up curiously from the counter as soon as I'd emerged from the Jeep, and then drop his gaze back to a newspaper until I stepped into the office. His steel-gray tufts of hair were now combed into submission, proof perhaps that he'd been roused from a nap the last time I was here.

"Morning," he said. It was a few seconds before he recognized me, and I watched his guard go up an inch.

"I'm Bailey Weggins. We met the other day."

"Sure. I remember." Friendly enough.

"I wondered if you had a couple more minutes."

"I can spare a few, but I'm afraid that's about all," he said, which was funny. Based on the apparent activity level at the motel, he seemed as busy as a bee in the Arctic tundra.

"I appreciate that. I have a few follow-up questions about Shannon Blaine."

"I reckon you heard they already found that poor young lady."

"Yes, and now I'm actually doing a profile of her. I'm interested in anything else you can share about her."

"Don't know what more I could tell you than what I said the other day. I saw her run by every morning, but I didn't know her enough to say boo to."

"But you knew she went to church each week."

He twisted his chubby lips. "Wouldn't take a genius to figure that out. She stopped running on Sundays and I saw her drive by instead—around ten to ten each time. Figured she was heading to St. Tim's."

"How'd you guess that? I mean the St. Tim's part."

"St. Tim's is the only church with a ten o'clock service. When you run a motel, you gotta have that kind of stuff at your disposal. Guests ask you for it."

Was I supposed to believe that Dobbs was the kind of considerate motel owner who rounded up details like this for his customers? Or had he simply been *way* too curious about Shannon's comings and goings?

"Do you go to St. Tim's yourself?"

"Nope, not my thing. But I never fault anyone else for travelin' that road if it makes them feel good." He glanced down at the counter at something out of my view. "Now since there's really nothing more for me to contribute, would you mind letting me attend to some business?"

"Of course, thanks for your help."

Driving south afterward, I assessed Dobbs as a suspect. He gave off a creepy vibe for sure, and it was clear he'd seemed a bit fixated on Shannon and her routines. I'd seen him hanging out at the volunteer center, including on the day I'd chatted with Nolan. He was familiar with Alice because she'd interviewed him for the paper following Shannon's disappearance. And last, but hardly least, I'd given him my cell number on the day I'd arrived.

But if he was the killer and Alice had figured it out, I had no clue what she could have possibly found online to point her in his direction. I would have to be on the alert for anything else I came across about him or the motel.

I didn't expect to check in to the Courtyard until at least three, but they ended up having a room ready. It was spare, done mostly in grays and beiges, a far cry from the funky decor of the Breezy Point, but I already felt safer. I set up shop at the desk in the room and resumed my Internet search, but again without any luck. "*Alice*," I pleaded out loud. "What did you *find*?" Was the clue so subtle that I was missing it? It couldn't be if it had alarmed her that much.

Of course, Alice had been very familiar with the area and knew a ton of people, so it was entirely possible that a piece of info that had spelled *clue* to her seemed utterly insignificant to me.

It was time for my lunch with Jessie. I was not only dying to see her but also eager for a break from the Internet. I hoped that an hour or so away would allow me to return to the research with a fresh eye.

The restaurant was only a short distance from the hotel so I set out on foot, checking a couple of times over my shoulder. All I noticed were people who appeared to be off-season tourists or locals in a hurry, dashing out to lunch themselves or running errands during the workday.

I was the first to arrive. I was glad I'd requested a table outside because the sky above was bright and cloudless, and the soft breeze felt good on my skin. The lake was speckled with sailboats and powerboats, and off in the distance I saw bunches of people filing up the ramp of the *Minne Ha Ha*.

Two minutes later, Jessie came striding across the weathered wooden deck. Her glossy brown hair flowed around her shoulders and bounced as she walked. Several male diners glanced in her direction, not bothering to disguise their positive assessment.

"Hey, hey," she called out in greeting. I jumped up from the table and we embraced in a hug.

"Forgive the cliché, but you're a sight for sore eyes."

"Ditto." She plopped into a chair across from me, beaming. "Wow, what a view. I see why people dig coming here."

"I know. I'd love to come back one day when I have more time to enjoy it."

"Isn't there a scene in *The Last of the Mohicans* that takes place at Lake George?"

I nodded toward the rise at the end of the lake. "Yeah, the fort was up there. No sign of Hawkeye these days, however. I could sure use his help at the moment."

She hooked a leg around a spare chair at the table, dragged it closer, and propped one of her booted feet on the seat.

"Tell me more about this crazy story you're covering. I've been reading your posts and I'm completely hooked."

"It got even crazier as of last night," I said. "And sadder, too."

I filled her in on Alice's death, knowing that since she'd been in her car part of the morning, she probably hadn't viewed the latest post yet.

"Oh Bailey, that's horrible," she said. "And what about you? Aren't you scared?"

"Yeah, a little bit. But as long as the killer doesn't think I've been tipped off to his identity, I should be okay."

We took a moment to each order a Cobb salad and an iced tea, and then Jessie eyed me intensely.

"Have you told Beau yet? He's not going to like this new development."

"Actually, Beau's been much better about the job risk issue since we talked it over this summer. The irony is that he's in Colombia right now, and he's been hard to reach, which has been frustrating the hell out of me."

"Columbia, South Carolina?"

"No, *South America*."

"God, isn't that the country where people get kidnapped by drug cartels?"

"Yes, in the past, but it's supposed to be pretty safe now. He's been having issues with cell service, though."

I didn't really think that Beau had been kidnapped, but her comment had stirred my unease. I pushed it from my mind, knowing that it was useless to fret.

The waiter returned with our drinks and I seized the opportunity to shift topics.

"So how was the weekend with Jason?" I asked.

"It was really nice, especially considering I hate fishing and don't eat trout. I guess that means I must be wild for him."

"I'm really happy for you, Jessie. He seems like such a great person." Her last boyfriend had cheated and lied, and I was glad she'd found a stand-up guy to replace him.

"What about you and Beau? Is he still dropping hints about marriage?"

"He told me he's giving me time to get used to the idea before he raises it again. I'm not skittish about Beau. I just feel so gun-shy about being *married* again. My first one turned into such a disaster."

Our salads arrived and we discussed her next assignment,

as well as several former colleagues from *Buzz* who were attempting, like us, to navigate the upheaval in the media landscape. It should have been fun to catch up—it had been a few weeks since we'd seen each other—but I could feel my attention constantly being tugged away and my mood turning seriously gloomy. I kept picturing Alice lying dead on her dock, her full, vibrant life wiped out in an instant. And I was thinking about the killer, too, wondering if he'd read my post and convinced himself that I knew more than I was letting on.

"Bailey, are you okay?" Jessie asked.

"Yeah, sorry. I guess I'm pretty shaken up about Alice."

And I was, I realized. Not only had I felt a connection with her because of our harrowing experience at Sunset Bay but also I'd really grown to like her as a person—her passion for reporting, her wry sense of humor, her down-to-earth, bushy-brows-and-black-beret style. We probably would have stayed in touch.

"I don't blame you, Bailey. It's such a loss."

"And it makes me sick that her killer is out there, probably right in this town. I've been going crazy trying to determine what clue Alice stumbled on, but I'm not having any luck."

"You'll figure it out. Maybe you have to do that thing you always do, look at it from a totally different angle—backward or sideways or whatever."

I smiled in spite of my mood.

"I told you I do that?"

"Not in so many words. But I've listened to you discuss stories before and that always seems to be your strategy. You write it all down in one of those composition books of yours and then stand it on its head, seeing what it tells you."

"Well, this time, unfortunately, that isn't working."

Following lunch, I walked Jessie to her car and we hugged goodbye. She begged me to keep her posted on developments, how I was faring, and when Beau turned up.

Hurrying back to the hotel, I checked the time. There was a good chance that Ben Hatfield had arrived in town by now. Rather than head upstairs to my room, I decided to swing by Alice's place in the hope of finding him ensconced there. If the house hadn't been cleared yet or Ben wasn't there, I would look for the neighbor who'd told me that his wife had Ben's number.

As I was reaching for my car key, my phone rang. Cody Blaine returning my call.

"You left a message saying you had something important to talk about," he said. "About Alice Hatfield."

"I'm sure you've heard that she was killed."

"The paper's saying it might be foul play. Do you think that's true?"

"I do, and I suspect the person responsible murdered Shannon, too. And the campers who went missing."

"But—if she was murdered, how does that connect with Shannon?" His voice sounded ragged with both concern and frustration.

"I think she figured out a clue to the killer's identity, and he went after her. Which means it's definitely someone in our midst, someone you might even be acquainted with."

"My god."

"I know I've asked you before if anyone's aroused your suspicions, but let me get more specific. Can you think of anyone who was hanging around the volunteer center, maybe more than he should have, and also knew Alice? And who Shannon might have been familiar with from St. Timothy's?"

He sighed.

"I only stopped by the center now and then. Mostly I was working with the search teams. And when I *was* there, I was too much of a zombie to notice anyone hanging around."

"What about the guy who owns the Lake Shore, at the end of your road? He told Alice he always used to see Shannon run by the motel. Do you know him?"

"I've never met the guy, but I've seen him around. Wait, are you thinking he could have done this? Do the cops—?"

"I don't have any specific reason to suspect him other than the fact that he seemed to keep tabs on Shannon, but I've told the police and they're going to talk to him again."

"You say Hatfield interviewed him. Could he have let something slip at the time?"

"I don't think that's what happened. She found something online, probably yesterday morning when she was working at home."

The call went deadly still.

"Cody?"

"Okay, this might mean something."

"What?" I asked, my heart skipping.

"Alice Hatfield called me yesterday with a question. Maybe it relates to the clue you're talking about."

CHAPTER 18

T ELL ME," I DEMANDED.

"I've already mentioned it to Killian, so I assume I'm not out of line telling you," Cody replied. "Right?"

"Right." Killian would hardly endorse Cody spilling the beans to me, but advising him not to blab wasn't in my job description.

"And this needs to stay off the record. I don't know what Killian plans to do with it."

"Of course."

"She left a message for me on my home phone around one, but I didn't call her back. I assumed she was angling for a quote, and needless to say, I had more important things to focus on. It's been a nightmare dealing with the press, by the way, but I don't want to change my number while the investigation is active and someone might call with a tip."

Please, I thought. I don't need all the backstory. Just tell me what the fuck Alice said.

"But you eventually talked to her?"

"She called again, and I decided if I didn't respond, she'd only keep hounding me. She asked if I could confirm that Shannon had gone on retreat at the Sunset Bay center the summer she was fifteen."

My breath caught. So Shannon had once stayed in the very location where the killer dumped her body. It was possible that she'd crossed paths there with the person who would murder her years later.

"Do you think Alice had this on good authority?"

"It seemed that way, but like I told you the other day, Shannon had never mentioned anything about the place to me."

"Did Alice say where she'd learned this piece of information?"

"No, she refused to tell me. Said it was confidential. I would have pressed her—what right does she have to keep that kind of detail all to herself?—but I was dealing with my kids."

"Kelly seemed fairly sure that Shannon hadn't ever been there, but I'm wondering—has anyone asked your mother-in-law?"

"I don't know and, frankly, I doubt it'd do much good. She's so loaded up on Xanax, she can barely remember her own name right now."

The mention of drugs was the prompt I needed for my next point of discussion. In the background I heard a child's voice. The words were indistinguishable, but the tone implied an urgent request, which meant my time was running short.

"I really need to go," Cody said.

"Please, one more second. Is there any chance—and I ask this only because I want to help find the truth—that Shannon had developed a reliance on drugs this past year, like painkillers for an injury?"

"*What?* Absolutely *not.*" I could feel his anger spike through the phone. "What the hell are you basing that on?"

"Initially there were rumors that the two campers might have been dealing drugs or at the very least buying."

"Not Shannon. Ever."

"Sometimes a person—"

"I said not Shannon, *ever*. I better not see even a *hint* of that on your website."

The child's questioning tone had morphed quickly into a wail.

"I was simply—"

But he'd already hung up.

I paced the dull gray carpet, raking my hands through my hair as I digested his revelation. Who could have told Alice that Shannon Blaine had spent time at the Sunset Bay Retreat Center? And was *this* the alarming clue she'd turned up?

In and of itself, this tidbit hardly seemed worthy of the word "scary." It would have piqued her interest, as it had mine, but not rattled her. And it was tough to imagine how she'd found it online. I'd already come up empty searching the Internet about the retreat center. Perhaps Alice had come across an old photo from there that had included Shannon.

And perhaps this detail had led to another revelation, a

fact that *was* truly scary. Shannon might have befriended one of her fellow attendees—or even an employee—while on retreat, a guy who became fixated on her. The person could have known about the basement storage area in the outbuilding. Perhaps the fixation burned off over the years, only to become reactivated when the two of them recently became reacquainted. At church?

I needed to bag the missing-woman Internet search, at least for now, and follow this new thread.

Shannon's mother might be too doped up to talk to me, but there was a chance Kelly could coax the information out of her on my behalf. Surely Killian would be trying to follow up on Alice's question, but I had no guarantee he would share any findings with me.

I grabbed my phone and tapped the number for Kelly. Voice mail. Her words from earlier echoed in my head: "I've tried to be respectful of the press, but you guys go too far." I bet there was little chance I'd hear back from her.

But I had to find a way to convince her to ask her mother about Shannon staying at Sunset Bay, and whom she might have met there. My best option, it seemed, was to pay Kelly a visit at home. I knew where the Claibornes lived—I'd looked up their address in the white pages last week in case I needed it—and if she wasn't home, I'd wait until she showed.

Unlike the Blaines, Kelly and her family didn't live in Lake George. They were farther south, in Queensbury, and I was there in less than twenty minutes. Though the parts of the town I'd seen before had featured mostly commercial buildings, today I found myself in an attractive residential section filled with fairly upscale-looking homes, probably forty or fifty years old.

The Claiborne house, the smallest on Linden Lane, wasn't in the same league as the Blaines' place, but it was attractive and spiffy looking, a center hall colonial painted white and accented with black shutters. The yard was bordered by a white picket fence, which looked freshly painted. There were no cars in the driveway and both doors on the double garage were down, so I couldn't tell at a glance if anyone was home. I parked in front, swung open the gate, and after stepping under the portico, rapped on the door with the brass lion-head knocker.

No one responded. I peered through one of the windows that framed the door, wondering if Kelly might simply be ignoring uninvited visitors, but there was no sign of movement through the sheer white curtains. Had she returned to her job? If that was the case, her work as a reading specialist was probably tied to school hours and she would be home soon. And then there was the young daughter. In light of Shannon's murder, Kelly would want to be home when the girl returned for the day.

I waited for well over an hour without seeing anyone enter the house. After a quick bathroom break and coffee stop, I returned and knocked again, but still nothing. Another thirty minutes passed. My iPod had already shuffled through most of its songs and was now into repeats. But there was no way I was leaving.

Finally, at about four, the family SUV crept into my rear-view mirror and pulled into the driveway to my rear. I was relieved to see Kelly, not Doug, emerge from the driver's seat. Dressed in the same black trench as yesterday, she assisted her mother out of the car. Mrs. Baker moved unsteadily and seemed to have aged ten years since the first press conference. Kelly grasped the woman's elbow and guided her slowly indoors.

I gave them about ten minutes to settle in, hoping to keep the annoyance quotient of my visit to a minimum, and then jumped from the Jeep, retraced my steps up the walk, and knocked again. The curtain in one of the front windows twitched, and seconds later Kelly swung open the door. I was anticipating exasperation, but her expression betrayed only weariness.

"Yes, what is it now?" she asked.

"Kelly, I'm not sure if you heard my message yet, but I think there's a chance that the reporter Alice Hatfield's death is related to Shannon's. Can we speak for a moment?"

She took a couple of beats before nodding, her mouth set in a grim line.

"All right, come in," she said. She led me down the center hall into the mutely toned living room. The large coffee table was strewn with newspapers, half-full coffee mugs, used paper plates, a couple of wineglasses, two apple cores, and an old pizza box, reflecting the chaos of the Claibornes' lives over the past days.

Kelly was wearing dark pants and a turtleneck sweater in burgundy, a color that to my knowledge had never flattered anyone. I was struck again by the contrast between her and Shannon, or at the least the dazzling, luminescent Shannon I'd seen in photos. It couldn't have been easy having a gorgeous younger sibling. If Kelly *had* felt jealous or resentful of her sister, her grief was probably now mixing with guilt in a strange, awful brew.

Frowning, Kelly perched on the edge of an armchair and motioned for me to sit across from her.

"From what I read, Alice Hatfield's death bore no resemblance to the others," Kelly said. "Or are you saying she was murdered because she *knew* something?"

"I believe the latter. The other day, you said you weren't sure whether Shannon had ever been to the center at Sunset Bay, but Alice had reason to think Shannon *had* been on retreat there. When she was fifteen."

Kelly rose from the chair, apparently too restless to sit.

"Okay, but if she had, how could that be anything more than a coincidence? It would have been close to twenty years ago."

"It could be significant in a way that we don't understand yet. I know your mother must be suffering terribly right now, but would you be willing to ask her about this?"

She pursed her lips together as she weighed my request.

"All right, give me a moment," she said finally.

When she returned five minutes later, she didn't bother taking a seat again.

"According to my mother, my sister never spent any time there," she announced. "Apparently Shannon asked once about a retreat—she doesn't recall if it was Sunset Bay or elsewhere—but my mom wouldn't let her go. She had heard that kids snuck into each other's rooms at those things and ended up having sex."

"Okay, so Alice's tip had been incorrect. But I still think she managed to discover something about your sister's killer, and the guy found out she was on to him and killed her, too. I have a hunch it was a person she knew, and very possibly your sister was acquainted with him as well."

"And so we might know him, too. God, that's chilling."

"Perhaps from church."

"Are you back to that? I don't want to be dismissive of leads, but I already told you that I couldn't imagine anyone we're familiar with from the church murdering her. And Shannon had been back in the congregation for only a few months."

"Has anyone from the parish ever struck you as hyper-religious? For instance, talking about sinners needing to be punished?"

"No . . . no one." She seemed distracted suddenly, as if a thought had begun to skirt around the edges of her mind.

"Kelly? Did you think of something?"

"No, it's just all too much to bear. And besides, I need to pick up my niece and nephew in a little while."

"Okay."

She extended an arm indicating she would see me out and began to move toward the hall.

"How are they coping?" I asked, following her to the front door.

"They're too young and shell-shocked to have fully absorbed it yet, but when they do, it's going to be utterly devastating. Shannon was so involved in every single aspect of their lives, twenty-four/seven."

The remark could have been taken as a compliment—like the unicorn-colored cupcake comment the other day—but her tone once again gave off a whiff of criticism, as if Shannon's involvement with her children had been of the smothering variety.

We'd arrived at the front door, and Kelly reached for the handle.

"I'm really grateful for your time," I said. "And again, I'm so sorry for your loss."

"Thank you. And I hope you won't take this the wrong way, but I'd really appreciate it if you left us alone from now on. I've tried to be helpful, and there's nothing more I can contribute."

"I'm sure dealing with the press hasn't been easy," I said, not making any promises. There was every chance I'd want to circle back to Kelly in the next days, but I'd simply have to cross that bridge when I reached it.

I stepped back to let Kelly swing open the door, and as I did, my gaze fell onto the surface of the small hall table. Tucked under the base of a lamp was a bright red-and-white business card with the words *Cunningham Real Estate*, along with the agent's name, Janice Talbot. I made a quick mental note of the information as I stepped onto the portico and felt the door close firmly behind me.

Back in my car, I tried to regroup. By itself, the revelation from Cody about Alice's query hadn't given me anything much to work with, but I'd convinced myself that if I followed this particular thread, I'd end up *somewhere*. Yet, it was looking now as if Shannon had never been on retreat, and Alice might have even determined this before she died.

What I needed to do now was get back to my computer, continuing to retrace what I hoped were Alice's digital footsteps. Perhaps I'd missed a critical detail and needed to review areas I'd already covered.

I drained the lukewarm remains of my coffee and stared back at the Claiborne house. There were a couple of things about the visit that gnawed at me. For one, Kelly's comment about Shannon's 24-7 involvement as a mother. Shannon was supposedly kicking her career back into gear, working as a marketer for Baker Beverage, but Kelly's comment seemed to indicate she wasn't aware of that. Maybe Shannon, hoping to avoid judgment on Kelly's part, had decided not to let her in on the news.

Poor Shannon. She'd probably never been able to win with her older sister, who considered her too involved with herself one minute and too involved with the kids the next. That was one of the problems with being both beautiful and talented. People overscrutinized you for flaws and when they couldn't find any, they blew up a momentary error into a deficiency. Or they trivialized your accomplishments—like J.J. had done by categorizing Shannon's work at Baker as simply "giving herself something to do."

I was also thinking about the real estate agent's business card. One of the Claibornes might have tucked it under the lamp or a real estate agent could have left it there after showing the house to a prospective buyer. I googled the number for the agency and talked to someone at the office who gave me Janice Talbot's cell number.

"This is Janice," she said when I reached her a minute later.

I introduced myself, and inquired if the house on Linden Lane was on the market.

"Um, yes and no. I *had* been showing it, but for personal reasons the sellers recently decided to take it off the market temporarily. But I have some fabulous properties I could show you that are very comparable in style and price."

"Let me think about it, all right? I was in that house once for a baby shower, and I loved it, so maybe I'll wait until it's available again. Why are the owners thinking of selling, do you know?"

A pause before the answer as she chose the right words.

"They love the house, but I think they're looking to downsize. Why don't you give me your contact info so when it does come back on the market, I can reach you?"

I told her I'd prefer to be the one reaching out and signed off. I didn't buy her explanation for the sale. The daughter was still around five years away from college or moving out.

The decision to sell could relate to their marital issues. Kelly might have suspected that Doug was cheating—or had even discovered it—and had decided they should split. Shannon's disappearance and death would have surely put that plan on hold.

I had better things to think about at the moment, though. It was time to see if I could track down Ben Hatfield.

My heart was pounding before I even reached Alice's road and by the time I made the turn, I could hear it in my ears. God, it was so damn sad to be there. I imagined her

bumping along the road in her MINI every morning, itching
to tackle her next assignment, and then returning late in the
day, eager for a glass of wine and the sight of a moonrise over
the lake. No more.

I caught a brief glimpse of a movement through the trees.
Was it Ben? Reporters inspecting the scene? Once I pulled
closer, though, I saw that it was simply a piece of yellow crime
scene tape that had broken off and was flapping like a kite tail
in the wind.

Interestingly, Alice's car was missing from the driveway,
which suggested Ben had already arrived and was currently
using it. More than likely, the crime scene unit had declared
the premises cleared by now, and Ben had been given access.

I didn't want to occupy the driveway in case Ben returned while I was there, so I parked along the side of the
road against a cluster of fir trees. As I reached for the door
handle, my phone rang. *Killian.*

"You doing okay?" he asked.

"Yes, thanks." I wondered what he'd think if he knew I
was currently outside of Alice's house. "Anything new?"

"Unfortunately, and I'm speaking totally off the record
here, we have nothing pointing to the assailant's identity. We
won't have DNA results for days, of course."

Expected but still totally frustrating.

"What about the autopsy?"

"Scheduled for tomorrow. But as I mentioned to you, we
have good reason to believe her death wasn't accidental. The
bottom line, Bailey, is that I want you to remain extremely
careful."

"Yes, of course. By the way, I talked to Cody Blaine today. He mentioned Alice's call and the information she wanted him to confirm."

Killian might be annoyed at Blaine for revealing the call to me but that wasn't my problem.

"That Shannon stayed at the Sunset Bay center years ago? That actually doesn't appear to be true. The parish had only a handful of retreats at that location, and didn't save records, but the diocese did. There's no evidence Shannon was ever there."

So I'd staked out Kelly's house for nothing.

"How do you think Alice ended up with that idea?"

"Don't know, but it was clearly bad information. I'm sure you've had your share of false leads and tips."

"Oh yeah. That happens even to us fancy pants."

He chuckled. "I need to sign off, but let's stay in touch."

So I was still in his good graces. Which meant he might continue to share developments with me, and frankly, it was nice to know he had my safety in mind.

"Just one last thing," I said, my memory jogged. "Did you have any luck finding that woman at the motel?"

"One of my deputies is looking into that. I'm waiting to hear from him."

As I'd been speaking with Killian, I'd felt Alice's house exerting a force field–like pull on me. With the call concluded, I climbed out of the Jeep and strode in that direction, my stomach knotting. The curtains on both floors had been pulled shut, so it was impossible to tell if Ben was inside, but I thought not. The place seemed utterly empty and forlorn.

After stepping over a strewn length of crime tape in the yard, I walked up to the kitchen door and knocked a few times, not expecting an answer and not receiving one, either. Ben might not even be planning to stay at the house, I realized, given how creepy it would surely feel. After fishing in my purse for a slip of paper and pen, I scrawled a note for him—introducing myself as a friend of Alice's and asking him to call me—and wedged it into the crack between the kitchen door and the frame. Even if he didn't intend to sleep here during his trip, he'd hopefully come by the house again at some point.

Before leaving, I made my way around to the other side of the building and stepped onto the patio. Whatever crime scene tape had been around the patio had been removed. I let my gaze run down the steps to the dock and rest on the spot below where Alice had lain. My eyes welled with tears but I quickly brushed them away.

I still had one more task to tackle. In case Ben didn't see the note, I needed to wrangle his cell number. I spent the next twenty minutes knocking on doors of the other houses along the road, in the hope of finding the neighbor—or any neighbor for that matter—who had Ben's contact info. Not one person was home.

My frustration mounted. Maybe I could at least convince Killian to give Ben a message from me.

I trudged back to the Jeep. It was nearly six o'clock by now, and the daylight had begun to fade. My cell phone rang the second I closed the door. With a jolt I saw "blocked number" on the screen.

"Yes?" I asked, keeping my voice steady. Was it the killer again?

I heard a sharp intake of breath, but no one spoke.

"Who's calling, please?"

"Is this Bailey Weggins?" A woman's voice.

"Yes, speaking."

"This is Lisa," she whispered hoarsely, her tone desperate. "Lisa Mannix."

The name meant nothing to me.

"Lis—?"

"The woman at the motel."

"Right. What—?"

"You said I could call you. You have to help me. Someone's after me—and he's out there now."

CHAPTER 19

"Out where?" I said. "Outside the motel? Is that what you mean?"

"Yes, God . . ."

"Is your door bolted?"

"Yeah, but . . . this is freaking me out."

"Uh, where's the guy who comes to see you? The one with the BMW."

It might actually be him she was freaking out about, I realized. An abusive boyfriend who was now scaring the crap out of her.

She hesitated, perhaps caught off guard that I'd noticed her paramour's car.

"I—I can't reach him," she said after a few seconds. "It's going to voice mail."

"When you say someone's out there, who do you mean exactly? A man? Can you describe him?"

"I'm not sure who it is. But a white SUV has been tailing me this afternoon. I thought I'd lost it, but as I pulled in here, I saw it shoot past me, going farther north. It may have turned around."

"Do you see anyone out there now?"

"Not from the window. And I'm too scared to go outside."

"If you think you're in danger, you should call 911. Right now."

There was such a long silence that I wondered if the call had been dropped.

"You still there, Lisa?"

"I—I can't call 911."

"Why not?"

"I don't want any cops involved."

Hmm, now that was curious.

"Well, at least call the front desk. Ask if they see anyone hanging around."

"And then the clerk'll end up getting the police here."

"Okay—" I gave myself a second to think. "Why don't I drive up there and see what's going on. You're in unit eleven?"

"Yeah, okay. Thanks. I don't mean to seem like a baby, but I swear someone's after me."

"I'm staying in the village now, so give me fifteen minutes. If anything happens before then, you *have* to call 911."

Seconds later, I was on my way. What was my plan? At the moment, I didn't have one. There was a chance Lisa Mannix—if that truly was her name—had allowed her imagination to go rogue. And it wasn't hard to see why. I'd stopped her mid-jog and warned her about women disappearing in broad daylight, a skeevy motel owner had subjected her to his lecherous stares, and a serial killer appeared to be at large in the area.

But what if she wasn't simply conjuring up boogeymen? What if Terry Dobbs actually *was* the killer, had figured out Lisa was now ensconced at the Breezy Point, and had begun to stalk her? It seemed odd, though, that he would make himself that obvious. I'd check out the situation and, if necessary, urge her again to call the cops. Lisa wanted to leave the police out of it, but she didn't know that I'd already alerted Killian to her existence.

When I pulled into the Breezy Point there was no white SUV, but also no Camry. The only car near any of the rooms was a muddy four-door Honda, in front of unit one—a new guest, I assumed.

I jumped from the Jeep and pounded on the door of unit eleven. No response. Maybe she had simply cleared out after her call to me rather than wait for my arrival. Or in the time it had taken me to get here, Beemer man had finally come to her rescue and the couple had split simultaneously, but in separate cars. And without her bothering to notify me.

And there was also the chance that something bad had gone down.

I hustled to the front office and shoved open the door. The woman I'd chatted with earlier in the day was still on duty, and she smiled in recognition.

"You forget something, hon?"

"No, I wanted to see if my friend was around, Lisa, the woman in eleven. No one's answering her door, and I don't see her car."

"Her car's not there? That's funny, because when I went out back a minute ago, I thought I saw her walking down toward the lake."

All the hairs on the back of my neck shot up at once.

"Was anyone with her?"

"She seemed to be alone."

"And what's down there anyway?"

"We've got a swimming dock with a few chairs on it. I assumed she wanted to sit outside for a bit, enjoy the view."

Fifteen minutes ago, Lisa had been too scared to open the door of her unit, and now she was taking a scenic stroll? And where the hell was her car?

"Is there a path behind the motel?"

"Yes, it's about a ten-minute walk to the lake. You'll see a couple of camps to your right, but keep going till you spot the dock."

I turned to bolt, then stopped and swung back to the clerk.

"You haven't seen a white SUV around here, have you?"

"White? Actually, I have. One pulled in earlier today but then pulled right out again."

"What about a few minutes ago?"

"Afraid not. Were you expecting someone?"

"No, but thanks."

After exiting, I quickly rounded the building and located the path, which descended toward the lake through an area fairly thick with firs, maples, and poplars. It wasn't seven yet but the sun was sinking behind me, veiled by a filmy layer of pink and yellow clouds.

It didn't make sense that Lisa would have gone out here on her own, and I wondered if the desk clerk was mistaken. Perhaps Lisa had darted behind the building to hide and then circled back to the front once Beemer man called her to report he'd arrived. That didn't explain her missing car, however.

I started down. As much as I didn't relish being on the path alone, I needed to make sure she wasn't in any trouble.

On the right, I spotted the first camp the clerk had referenced, boarded up for the season. But no sign of Lisa. The only sounds were the tremble of leaves high in the trees and the steady, urgent chirping of a solitary bird.

I kept moving, past the second camp, also closed, and finally, through the trees, I saw a sliver of lake. I could hear the water, too, lapping lightly and methodically against the shore. If Lisa was at the dock, I was close. I picked up speed, following the path along a large, shaggy outcropping of rock.

As it rounded the rock, I saw her, smack in the middle of the dirt path, her hair tucked up into a baseball cap and her back to me.

But it wasn't Lisa. I realized that this woman, dressed in jeans and a quilted navy jacket, had darker hair flowing from beneath her baseball cap. At the sound of my footsteps, she spun halfway around and looked at me. To my complete shock, it was J. J. Rimes.

And she had a black gun in her hand. Pointed now in my direction. I didn't know a whole lot about firearms, but I was pretty sure it was a mini Glock.

My breath froze in my chest and fear shot through me

fast as the snap of a whip. "J.J.," I said, trying to keep my voice calm. "What are you doing here?"

"What the fuck are *you* doing here?"

"I stayed at this motel for a few nights, and I—I'm looking for someone I met here. Are you in trouble?"

She didn't answer. Instead, she swiveled her body so it was square again with the area behind the outcropping and swept the Glock through the air so that it pointed in front of her. There was someone behind the rock, I realized. Someone she'd been aiming at before I arrived. I slowly shifted my hand until it reached my shoulder bag, ready to dig for my phone.

"Let me help, okay?" I said.

She scoffed, looking back at me. "What are you going to do? Make me a star on the *Crime Beat* website?"

As her gaze flicked away from me again, I dragged one foot slightly forward, and then the other, shifting my position enough to see around the bend. Holy cow.

Doug Claiborne, dressed in a sport jacket and collared shirt, was standing on the other side of the rock, mouth agape, hands fisted. His eyes darted over and met mine. This was clearly some kind of showdown between the two of them, but how had they ended up *here*? I let my eyes roam the area, hoping someone might spot us, but we seemed to have these woods to ourselves.

"Why don't you put the gun away and tell me what happened?" I said as low-key as I could manage.

"What *happened*?" she barked. "This worthless dick was two-timing me. It takes a pretty big fucking ego to two-time the person you're having an *affair* with."

"J.J., please," Doug pleaded, his voice husky with fear. "I thought you wanted to cool things with me. I don't care about her; I don't."

"You expect me to believe that? You were holed up with that bitch for hours yesterday."

Okay, pieces were speed-clicking into place, forming a story line that finally made rough sense. Doug was the guy with the Beemer who was sleeping with Lisa, and J.J. had figured it out. She was probably the one who'd been tailing Lisa around town. But where was Lisa now?

I knew I had to do something and do it fast. There was no way I'd have time to grab my phone without J.J. noticing. And it would be utterly stupid to try to wrestle the gun from her or knock her off her feet. My only recourse: try to talk her off the ledge.

"J.J., don't do something you'll end up regretting for the rest of your life," I told her. "Please put the gun away."

She snickered, bobbing the gun at Doug. "Trust me, I wouldn't regret shooting him for a second. I'd sit in prison with a smile on my face every single minute of the day."

"Prison is horrible," I told her. "You wouldn't want to be there."

She shook her head slowly, my words not seeming to register.

"Listen to me, J.J.," Doug said into the vacuum. "You know I'm crazy about you. I want to make this work."

You freaking idiot, I thought. She'd have to have a brain the size of a fever blister to believe that crock of shit.

J.J. shook her head again and raised her arm so that the gun was directly aimed at Claiborne's head. My panic was storming the barriers now. There was a chance she would take the shot, then turn the gun on me.

"J.J., you have to consider your kids," I said, desperately playing one last card. "Think about what it would be like for them to have you in jail. All because of a loser like this."

With utter relief, I watched her arm start to sag, and finally she lowered the gun to her side.

"She's right. You aren't worth the fucking bullet, Doug. Get the fuck out of my face."

He backed away, slowly at first. Then, reversing direction, he bolted down the path toward the lake, soon disappearing from view. Maybe the jerk thought he could wave down the *Minne Ha Ha* twilight cruise and plead for rescue, but thirty seconds later we heard him crashing through the woods to our right, scrambling uphill like a herd of deer on the run. So much for chivalry. The guy was going to save his own ass and leave me here with an unhinged and armed woman.

But J.J. was already unzipping her shoulder bag and stuffing the gun inside. I let out the long, ragged breath that had been trapped inside my chest.

"You think he's going to call the cops?" she asked me.

"I don't know," I said truthfully. "What about Lisa? Is she okay?"

"She's fine. I saw her take off in her car a little while ago, like a bat out of hell."

"Then he might not call them. He won't want to open that can of worms if he doesn't have to."

"And what about you? Are you going to blast this all over the Internet?"

"No." That was the truth, too, at least for now. "I write about homicides, and as far as I know, you haven't committed one."

J.J., I noticed, had begun to tremble, and I could sense her rage quickly retreating, leaving behind only the ugly muck of regret.

"Where's your car?" I asked.

"Behind the leather outlet on the far side of the motel."

"Why don't I walk you over there, make sure you're all right."

I was betting on the fact that she didn't have any fight left in her and even if she did, she wasn't going to direct it at me.

She nodded, looking stunned, as if what she'd done was finally sinking in. I took her arm and led her back up the hill. As we rounded the building, it occurred to me that there could be cops pulling into the lot at that very moment. Doug Claiborne might want to keep his bad behavior under wraps, but he probably also cared about his family's safety, at least more than he did for mine.

If the cops were coming, though, they were taking their time. J.J. and I trooped the short distance to the outlet, where the bright white SUV was parked all by its lonesome in the lot. As she climbed into the driver's seat, I opened the passenger door and slid in beside her. This was my chance to snag the backstory, which I figured she'd cough up simply to discourage *me* from going to the cops.

It was going to take some coaxing, though. She had her face in her hands now and was rocking back and forth. This had to be a rare sight, I realized—J.J. not being the boss of the moment.

"Are you going to be okay going home?" I asked. "I could drive you myself and take a cab back for my Jeep."

Nothing. Just the rocking.

"J.J.?"

"No, I can drive. I need a minute, though."

"Will anybody be home when you get there?"

I wasn't exactly worried she'd harm her kids, but she still seemed agitated, and I didn't like the idea of her being alone with them tonight.

"No, my kids are overnighting with my ex."

"And what about the gun? Is it yours?"

"Yes. I bought it for protection after my divorce."

I considered asking her to turn it over, but I had little experience with firearms, and I wouldn't feel the least bit comfortable with this one in my possession.

"Do you have a safe place to store it?"

"Yes—and don't worry. I'm not going to hurt anyone. I just wanted to scare that dirtbag, make him wet his friggin' pants."

She dropped her hands into her lap and looked up. Though it was cool in the car, she had a film of sweat on her face and black mascara had smudged like bruises under her eyes.

"Of course, I'm the *real* asshole, for ever falling for him."

"When did it start?" I asked gently.

"About six months ago. I'd never socialized with either him or Kelly, but he and I went to the same gym. We had a fucking smoothie together after a workout and one thing led to another. How rich is that?"

"How did you learn there was someone else?"

"Remember me telling you that I was supposed to have company that Monday I was in the Adirondacks? That was Doug. Originally we were going to meet on Sunday—he'd signed up for this three-day professional workshop or conference-thingy in Lake Placid, so he had an excuse to go up there—but at the last minute I had to change to Monday. He said he'd keep his hotel room Sunday night because if he started switching the plan around, it might raise a red flag with Kelly.

"Once I was already up at the cabin, he totally blew me off, said his whiny daughter was having a meltdown over school stuff and he had to bag the entire trip to Lake Placid. But after I was back in town and started reading everything about Shannon's disappearance, I saw a quote from Kelly about needing Shannon's help because Doug was out of town Sunday night. That's when I first smelled a rat."

"You figured he must have been with someone else that evening?"

"Exactly. When I finally reached him on the phone and called him on it, he rushed over to my house with a totally lame explanation, like I was an idiot. So the next day I followed him. After going to church with Kelly, he drove home, switched cars, and drove up to the Breezy Point for a couple of hours. About twenty minutes after he left, I saw the blonde sashay out of the room."

"You started following her after that?"

"Yeah, I wanted to know what her story was since I could tell by her plates that she wasn't local. Doug was here earlier today, and I was hoping he'd come back tonight so I could finally confront the two of them together."

"How did you and Doug end up down by the lake?"

"It's a long, boring story."

"I've got time."

"After the blonde bolted, I was about to take off when I noticed Doug's BMW show up. But he parked it across the road, in the lot for the taxidermist, and he sat for a while as if he was casing the place."

I could now make a good guess as to what had transpired. Lisa had grown antsy waiting for my arrival and split. Doug, having finally heard Lisa's voice mail about the stalker, had sped over here, but gutless and yellow-bellied, he pulled in across the street to assess the situation from a safe distance.

"He eventually crossed the road and let himself into the room," J.J. continued. "When he came out a minute later, I saw him tiptoe around to the back—probably wondering where she was. I followed him."

"He hadn't noticed your SUV so close to the motel?"

"I don't think he ever realized it was mine—everybody drives an SUV up here—and I kept my head down. You should have seen the look on his face after he saw me on the path."

She exhaled loudly and slapped her hands on her face.

"Look, I need to go home and pour myself a glass of wine. Plus, if he *did* call the police, I don't want to be here when they show. Let 'em come find me."

For a moment I thought Flinty Girl might be back, ready to kick ass and take names.

"I need to repeat myself, J.J. You have two kids. Don't jeopardize everything by getting into it with Doug again."

"I won't, I won't. I'm done with him."

"One more question. Do you think Shannon had any idea you were carrying on with her brother-in-law?"

She pinched her lips together and nodded. "Yeah, maybe."

"Why?"

"Remember when I talked to you that first time and I told you about my call to Shan, how she was on the phone?"

"You mean about her voice sounding odd?"

"Yeah. I started to think a little more about it. I'd called that day to say I was definitely going to the cabin and now that I know Kelly told her that Doug was in Lake Placid, I wonder if she put two and two together. Even in the weeks before, I think she sensed I might be seeing someone on the sly. That was the thing with Shan. She had a way of reading people."

"Is that why you played it down the next time we spoke?"

"Yeah, I certainly wasn't going to confess my new theory to *you*."

"Did—?"

"Look, I need to go. I can't stand to be here one more second."

I nodded and reached for the door handle. I told her to phone me if she ran into any issues—which I hoped translated as "If you feel the urge to whip out your Glock again and point it at someone's head"—and she even muttered a thank-you as I slid out of the vehicle. I waited for her to exit the parking lot and then scurried back to my Jeep. She had a good head start, but I drove quickly and before long, I was only one car length behind her.

I used the first red light in the village to try Lisa. I was inclined to believe that J.J. hadn't harmed her, but I had no proof. Reaching voice mail, I asked her to call me back pronto. I was relieved a minute later to see J.J. take the right-hand turn that led to her home.

Back at the Courtyard I made a beeline for the bar and ordered a glass of red wine—J.J. wasn't the only one in need of vino therapy at the moment. As I reached for the glass, I realized that my shoulders were still somewhere up near my ears, rock-hard with tension. The experience had really rattled me. There'd been a moment when I'd been almost certain that she was going to shoot Doug, and that I'd end up as collateral damage.

But what, I wondered, did all this *Real Housewives of Lake George* stuff matter in terms of the case? J.J. had been sleeping with Doug. Doug and Kelly had briefly put their house on the market. Doug had ditched J.J. the week of Shannon's murder in order to sleep with another woman, one who looked vaguely like Shannon. And there was a chance Shannon had picked up a whiff of what her BFF and Doug had been up to. It was a hot mess of a family drama, but in the end I couldn't see how it was related to the murders.

I paid my tab and grabbed my glass, which was still half full. As I crossed the lobby toward the elevator bank, I heard my name. I knew even before I swung around that Matt Wong was paging me.

"Wait, I thought you were going to have a drink with me tonight," he said, his tone petulant.

"I am, promise," I said, though it had totally slipped my mind. "I'm just taking this to my room for now."

"You're here at the Courtyard? Why haven't I seen you?"

"This is my first day at this location. Why are you staying here? Can't you drive back and forth to Albany each day?"

"Usually I do, but I decided to book a room for a couple of days. There's a ton of reporters and TV producers around here. You're not the only one who'd like to be on the tube one day."

"For the record, Matt, I have absolutely zero interest in being on TV. My boss insisted on me doing the video."

"It might be smart to *learn* to like it. It's all going to pivot to video in the future."

"Wow, aren't you the trend guru. . . . Sorry, but I really need to head upstairs for a bit."

"And what about the drink?"

"Later, okay?"

"Nine at the bar here?"

"Um, yeah, okay." I didn't really have the energy to deflect him another time, plus as annoying as I found the guy, he was correct about the necessity of mingling. Who knew what you might learn at the bar.

Back in my room, I took another gulp of the wine, which unfortunately had a vague aftertaste of cherry cough medicine. Probably because my stomach was still churning from this afternoon's showdown. Once again I warned myself not to let it distract me. I needed to return to what mattered.

I shrugged out of my jacket and changed into a new shirt since the one I'd been wearing was still damp with perspiration. As I reached for my laptop, my gaze fell on the composition book I'd been using over the past week. Jessie had said over lunch that I had a skill for seeing information from fresh and different angles, and if that was true—which I liked to think it was—the credit lay in part to my endless composition books. On more than one occasion, I'd had a eureka moment simply from rereading my notes.

I'd been good about scanning each day's notes before turning in, but I hadn't gone over them from start to finish. Maybe it was time to do that.

I opened the book to the beginning and began to read. On one of the earliest pages, I lighted on the rough timeline I'd sketched out for Shannon once I'd gathered bits of information. I'd been hopeful that if I kept fleshing that out, it might eventually point to a place or time where she'd intersected with her killer, but nothing had even whispered to me.

I stared at the points on the timeline: her cousin's death last September, her return to work in March, her reinvolvement in the church midsummer. Not exactly much to work with.

Staring at the page, I was reminded of something Keith Windgate had mentioned when he shot the video. He worked with timelines, too, he'd told me. He would create one for each video he was doing and plug in various clips at points where he thought they would have the most impact.

Something began to tug at my memory, but it stayed stubbornly out of reach, as if I were patting around inside a desk drawer for an item I needed—an envelope, or a note card, or a take-out menu—but couldn't put my hands on it, or even recall what I was looking for.

And then I realized what it was. I had Shannon's timeline wrong. When I'd met with Riley at Baker, she'd mentioned that Shannon had been working at home for a period, which meant I had the wrong date for when she'd appeared regularly at the main office. During the interview with Riley I'd been so caught up in the significance of Shannon restarting her career that I'd neglected to adjust the timeline. It was probably insignificant, but I wanted to be sure I had everything right in my mind.

I snatched my phone from the bed where I'd tossed it and called Cody. To my surprise he picked right up.

"Is there news about Alice Hatfield?" he asked bluntly.

"No, not that I'm aware of. I have a question on another subject, though. I heard that when Shannon started working for Baker back in March, she did it mostly from home for the first few months. Can you confirm that for me?"

"Look, I'm trying to clock a few hours at my desk this afternoon because I haven't shown my face here in days. I don't see how this is relevant."

"I've been trying to create a timeline for the last months of Shannon's life, see if it points me anywhere."

"Uh, okay. She began helping me around March. And yes, she worked from home at first—developing a batch of marketing materials."

"And when did she start coming to the office several days a week?"

"Jeez, I don't know. June maybe. Yeah, June. The kids had just started camp."

I used my free hand to pencil in the new detail on the timeline.

"It's probably nothing, but I've always wondered if the killer could have targeted her, that he might have crossed paths with her in the weeks or months before her death. I'd been thinking she started at your office in March, but I realize I had that wrong. Could one of the workers have become fixated on her?"

"You mean like one of the loaders or drivers? I don't see—"

A pause.

"What?" I prodded.

"We actually had a couple of new drivers come on for the summer. But they're good guys. Both of them."

My heart skipped. Alice had theorized that the killer could be a trucker.

"Just out of curiosity, how far away do you end up delivering?"

"We cover three counties right now, though we plan to expand eventually."

Not enough to fit with Alice's long-haul trucker theory. So maybe my revised timeline wasn't going to tell me a freaking thing.

A call came through on the other line and I was about to send it to voice mail when I saw that it was a Chicago number.

"I need to take this, Cody, but thanks for your time."

I clicked to the other call.

"Bailey Weggins."

"It's Ben, Alice Hatfield's son. I found your note."

My heart squeezed at the sound of his voice.

"Thanks very much for calling, Ben. I'm so sorry for your loss."

"I appreciate that. Look, I need to talk to you. It's important."

"Yes, I'm eager to speak with you as well." I glanced at my watch. It was now after eight. "I could meet you first thing tomorrow, even for breakfast."

"No, this can't wait. Can you meet me right now?"

CHAPTER 20

HIS VOICE SOUNDED TINGED WITH URGENCY AS MUCH AS grief. Maybe Alice *had* told him something.

I said yes, of course, I could meet tonight. He asked where I was staying and after hearing my location, he said he'd meet me in the hotel bar in twenty minutes.

I used the little bit of time I had to freshen up. According to the mirror, I looked drained and fish-belly pale, possibly the aftereffects of staring down the barrel of a Glock. The mascara and lip gloss I swiped on barely helped.

Before dashing from the room, I placed one more call to Lisa Mannix, still perturbed that I hadn't heard back from her. Based on my read of J.J. when we parted, I was betting Lisa was okay and was probably stonewalling me, regretful for having dragged me into her sordid little drama. And yet I wanted to be sure. Once again, the call went to voice mail.

I also sent another text to Beau. I knew he was having cell service issues, but it had now been two days since I'd heard from him and I was starting to fret.

When I arrived at the bar, it was bursting at the seams with reporters, producers, and crew members, and ripe with the smell of people hyped up and ready for action. Luckily I was able to snag a fairly private table tucked in a corner and kept my eye trained on the entrance for Ben, whom I was pretty sure I'd recognize from his photo.

And I did. He appeared two minutes later, dressed in dark jeans, a blue button-down shirt open at the collar, and a brown tweed sports jacket, looking the part of the college professor Alice had been so proud of. I waved him over to the table and rose as he approached.

"Ben, so good to meet you," I said as he settled into a seat across from me. He was a nice-looking guy, most likely in his early thirties, bearded, and possessing the same thick, coarse hair as his mother. His hazel eyes were just like hers as well, and I found myself wincing inside at the resemblance. "I had the chance to get to know your mother a little and I liked her so much. This must be such a horrible time for you."

He sighed, visibly distressed. "Thanks . . . to be honest, it hasn't totally sunk in yet. I feel like I'm operating more or less on autopilot."

"I can only imagine. Have you had a chance to speak to Sheriff Killian?"

"Yes, a little while ago. They haven't done an autopsy yet, but he told me that, based on some evidence at the scene, they think she was strangled and shoved down the stairs." He pressed the tips of his fingers into his forehead and rubbed back and forth. "How could someone *do* that to her? My mother never hurt anyone in her life."

The waitress sidled over, interrupting us for our order, and we quickly requested drinks—beer for Ben, another glass of wine for me.

"Ben," I said once we were alone again. "I don't have any proof yet, but I think your mother was murdered because she'd figured out an important clue about the Shannon Blaine case. Have you been following that story at all?"

He nodded dully. "Yes, I've been reading my mom's coverage online. And Killian asked me if my mom had told me anything about the case."

"*Did* she?"

To my dismay, he shook his head.

"The last time I spoke to her was Saturday, in the early evening, like we always do—*did*—and though the murders came up, she didn't mention any leads she was following or anything like that."

He could clearly read the disappointment in my eyes.

"I'm sorry," he said. "It was mostly a catch-up on personal stuff."

"Don't be sorry," I told him, though I felt like kicking the table in frustration. "Since you asked to meet right away, I was hoping that you might know something."

"I wanted to hear what *you* knew. Killian said that you were the one who discovered her."

"Yes, she'd invited me for dinner, and when she didn't answer the door, I checked outside."

"Did you see anything? Anything that might tell you what happened?"

I let my eyes briefly roam the bar area, making sure no one at the other tables was close enough to hear me.

"Nothing that would point to the identity of the killer. But as Killian probably told you, her laptop is missing. Over the weekend your mom told me she was doing online research and on Sunday morning she said she'd found a scary piece of information that she wanted to confirm before telling me. I think she somehow tipped off the killer and he came after her."

"God," he muttered, through fingers clasped to his mouth. His cuticles were ragged like Alice's.

Our drinks arrived and Ben took a big slug of beer directly from the bottle.

"Are you going to be staying at the house?" I asked.

"No. I went by with a friend to pick up my mom's car, but I can't bear the idea of sleeping there. I'm staying with an old high school friend of mine."

So Ben still kept up with people in the area. This wasn't the right moment to dig, but he might prove to be a good source as I continued my research.

"I'm glad you have a friend to be with. I'm going to do everything I can to find the killer, but if I can help in any other way, will you let me know?"

"Thanks, Bailey. Just so you know, my mom mentioned you on the phone when she called on Saturday."

"You're kidding."

"Yeah, she laughed and said that I wasn't the only one with hip, feisty thirtysomething female friends. She seemed to really like you."

"I appreciate you sharing that. As I said, the feeling was mutual."

He shot the cuff of his sports jacket and checked his watch.

"I'm afraid I can't stay long. My girlfriend's flying in tomorrow, and I need to make arrangements for her to be picked up at the airport."

He reached in his back pocket for a wallet.

"I've got this," I said. "I'm going to be meeting another reporter for a drink in a few minutes, and I'll add it to the tab."

"I wish I had something of value to offer. When my mom called me, it was a bit earlier than we usually talked and I had a few papers to finish grading. I feel awful about it now, but I kind of rushed her off the phone."

My brain, always a sucker for discrepancies, zeroed in.

"Did she explain why she was calling earlier than usual? Was she on her way somewhere later, perhaps?"

"She didn't say," he said glumly.

"Please don't beat yourself up about the call. From what your mom told me, she made her discovery on Sunday morning, so even if you'd had more time to talk on Saturday, she wouldn't have had anything to share. But do me a favor. If you think of anything else that's odd, will you let me know? Even something that seems inconsequential."

"Will do." He rose from the table.

"And when you finalize plans for her service, would you mind letting me know the details?"

"Yes, of course. Good night, Bailey."

As he trudged through the bar, his head lowered, my heart ached. Because of my father's death, I knew something about the kind of loss he was experiencing, the feeling of being thrown overboard and trying desperately to keep your head above the waves. But Ben had now lost both parents, and one of them under horrible circumstances.

As I waited for Matt Wong to show, I nursed my wine and wasn't surprised when he ended up being ten minutes late. After spotting me, he strode toward the table like a guy who owned the room. He was wearing a tight cotton plaid shirt half-tucked—intentionally—over a pair of slim-fit rust-colored chinos, the kind that were sold broken-in.

"Good, you started without me," he said, nodding toward my wineglass. "Something important came up and I *had* to deal with it."

He let it hang there, hoping perhaps that I'd assume he was following a red-hot lead or had been short-listed for a Pulitzer.

"Who's been in tonight?" he asked once he'd ordered a Heineken.

"Who's been *in*? I don't know what you mean, Matt."

"What other *reporters*?"

I told him I had no idea, and from there he launched back into his theory from earlier—the fact that video was *everything* now and he needed a sizzle reel that could totally showcase his talents. I briefly humored him and then directed the conversation back toward the case.

"How long do you think all these reporters are going to be buzzing around?" I asked.

"Not much longer. From what I hear, the cops have squat from the retreat center, and you know as well as I do that these kinds of cases can go for years without being solved. If there's nothing to report, the press will go on to the next big thing."

"Who told you the cops had squat?"

"Now, now, Bailey, you can't expect me to share my sources. That would be unprofessional of me."

"I'm not asking for the nuclear codes, Matt."

"Well, if you were less stingy with your own info, I might be more willing to share."

"I gave you that tip yesterday—about Page's boyfriend lying when he said she wanted to split."

He rolled his eyes. "Please, that didn't lead *anywhere*. Maybe the dude did embellish the truth, but the cops had other reasons for thinking those girls had left of their own accord. For one, they never found Amy's car. Plus, Page had taken two grand out of her savings account the day before."

Okay, how had he managed to unearth *that* nugget?

"Is that so?" I said, trying to keep my tone light. Matt was the kind of guy who could pick up the scent of a too-eager beaver from *waaay* across the pond. "Why wasn't that mentioned in the papers?"

"Who knows? Bad local reporting? But trust me, it's true."

Two thousand dollars. Since it now seemed pretty clear Page and Amy *hadn't* intended to blow town, what was the money for? Buying drugs? As much as I'd been brooding over Alice's death, I hadn't lost track of the idea that if Amy and

Page had begun dabbling in the drug world—despite Kayla's protests to the contrary—they might have intersected with the killer there.

And that raised the question again about Shannon. Had *she* taken a step into that world?

If so, it didn't mean she'd been a user. She'd been haunted by her cousin's death and it was possible, I suddenly realized, that she wanted to learn who his dealer was. She could have started asking questions, maybe of the wrong person. She might have even stumbled on unknown details about Amy's and Page's deaths.

Before I followed this thread any further, though, I needed to confirm Page's two-thousand-dollar withdrawal.

When I disentangled myself from my thoughts, I discovered that Matt was droning on once again about his TV prospects. Please, I thought, spare me. There were a lot of things I could say about the guy, but "He could be the next Anderson Cooper" wasn't one of them. I glanced at my watch, faked surprise, and told him I needed to take a call from my editor at *Crime Beat*. I tossed more than enough cash on the table to cover my drink and Ben's and said good night.

As soon as I was in my room, I dug out the business card Hank Coulter had given me, and despite the fact that it was nearly ten o'clock, dialed his number. I still didn't have a read on how sincere he'd been about me reaching out anytime, but he was probably my best shot at confirming Wong's revelation.

He answered on the third ring, his voice husky, as if he'd been quiet for a stretch.

"Chief Coulter, hi, it's Bailey Weggins. I'm sorry to call

so late, but I had a couple of questions. Do you have a minute now?"

He paused before answering. "How can I help?"

"I'm interested in learning more about the initial investigation into the disappearance of Amy Hunt and Page Cramer. Can you—?"

"Let me stop you right there, Ms. Weggins. I can understand your interest, and I *was* involved in that investigation, but as I've stressed previously, it's not appropriate for me to be taking questions on law enforcement issues. The case has been reopened and there are other people in charge now."

"What if I rely on you only as a deep background source? Meaning I won't even quote you anonymously. I'll simply use what you say to help me clarify my thinking."

"Is this going to be about the authorities not trying hard enough to find those young women?"

"No, it isn't. Because I know you had your reasons for believing they'd simply left town."

Another pause.

"All right, deep background only."

"Thank you. I learned from a source tonight that Page had withdrawn a fairly substantial amount of cash—two grand—before the camping trip. Is that true?"

"Yes, it's true. And that factor contributed to our theory."

"Okay, so we know now that they weren't necessarily planning to leave town. What are the chances, do you think, that Amy and Page were using or dealing drugs?"

"There were definitely rumors on that front. Not so much about Amy but Page. The Oxy epidemic had kicked off with a bang around here, and we thought she might be trying to score a piece of the action. She had made a number of calls to a burner phone, one we couldn't trace."

"Drugs could explain how they ended up in Fort Ann."

"Could."

"So my next question is whether you think Shannon might have stumbled into that world, too."

"No way," he said, having barely let me spit out the full question. "Shannon was a total straight arrow."

"I know this is crazy, but—but what if she was snooping around in order to figure out what happened to her cousin Destin, the one who overdosed? She might have heard rumors about the dealer, someone possibly right here in Lake George. And then ended up intersecting with the killer that way."

"Shannon wouldn't have intentionally exposed herself to drug dealers. She was too devoted a mother to have put herself at that kind of risk."

"I—"

"Look, Ms. Weggins, you seem like a smart lady, and I can see why you'd want to explore different theories. And it *could* be that Page withdrew that money exactly as you suggest—to buy drugs and begin selling them. But I'm sure you've read enough about serial killers—in fact, probably covered a few in your day—to know that they generally pick their victims at random. The average victim is someone they see walking along a street at night or crossing a deserted parking lot on her way to her car. It often comes down to being in the wrong place at the wrong time."

Yes, I thought, but as I'd already reminded myself, there was often a pattern with serial killers. The women were all prostitutes or all brunettes. It made sense that Alice's death didn't resemble the others, though. The killer had wanted nothing more than to silence her and might have even hoped her death might appear to be an accident. As for the other three women, there had to be something linking them. I simply wasn't seeing it.

"I appreciate your input," I told him. Clearly I'd be beating a dead horse if I tried to pursue it with him any further. "I'd love to circle back if anything else crosses my mind."

"Please do. Good night."

I was desperate for a bath, but I was afraid I'd pass out from fatigue in the tub, so I opted for a shower instead. I tried to savor the sensation of the hot water on my weary limbs, hoping it would relax me, but my jangled nerves refused to calm. I felt dogged by so many questions I couldn't find answers to, including why the hell Lisa Mannix wasn't calling me back.

Toweling off, I heard my phone ring, and I scrambled for it, hoping first and foremost that it was Beau.

But the caller turned out to be the elusive Lisa.

"You're safe?" I asked.

"Safe? Yes. I'm back in Rochester, thank *God*. That's why I didn't have the chance to call you until now. I appreciate what you did. Doug told me that you came to the motel and helped defuse things."

Ha-ha. I bet he *hadn't* told her that he'd acted like a complete weenie and had left me behind to fend for myself.

"Why did you take off after pleading with me to help you?"

"I'm so sorry I didn't wait for you, but I was really freaking out, and when the coast looked clear, I jumped in my car and just *drove*. By the time Doug heard my message and showed up at the motel, I was already gone. My car wasn't there, of course, but he found some of my toiletries still in the room and got scared, so he started looking for me behind the building. And that woman followed him."

"Did he tell you about her?"

"She's apparently someone he used to see, who became obsessed with him. Like Glenn Close in *Fatal Attraction*."

Oh, J.J. would love hearing herself pegged as a bunny boiler. She'd have the Glock back out in no time.

"You live in Rochester? How did you and Doug meet?"

"At a conference for chiropractors about four months ago. It was nothing more than a fling, the kind of thing they make conferences *for*, but the sex was good and Doug convinced me to come to the area for a week so he could sneak over every day to see me. It was supposed to be a nice diversion, but the next thing I know women start turning up dead. And then I end up being stalked by a crazy chick. You couldn't pay me to go near Lake George again."

"When I stopped you on the road, you didn't seem to know that Shannon Blaine had gone missing."

"I didn't. It was only when I mentioned what you said to Doug that he filled me in."

"That sounds weird. She was his *sister-in-law*. And he was supposed to be helping search for her."

"Look, I understand now that the guy's an asshole. I wish I hadn't used up a week of vacation days on him. Do you know he actually came by the motel a couple of times when I think he was supposed to be passing out flyers? I saw boxes of them in his back seat."

"Did he ever explain why he didn't tell you about Shannon right away?"

"Oh, sure, he had his excuses. He claimed that when I arrived Monday afternoon, no one knew she was gone yet. After that he supposedly didn't want to burden me with the news because it might, quote, 'spoil the mood.'"

I started searching my memory. J.J. had told me that Doug had bagged the Lake Placid workshops and it was obviously so he could be with Lisa rather than her; Kelly had stated for the record that Doug was out of town Sunday night. But now Lisa was saying that she and Doug hadn't met up until Monday afternoon.

"You still there?" Lisa asked.

"Yeah. Just to clarify: The first time you saw Doug was Monday afternoon?"

"Right."

"So where was Doug the night before you arrived?"

"Where? I have no idea and I don't really care, either. I came here to have sex with him, not be his hall monitor."

It might not matter to her but it mattered to me—not Sunday night, specifically, but Monday morning, the last time Shannon was seen alive. What, I wondered, had he told the cops about his whereabouts?

I signed off and further pondered the information she'd

let drop. Was it possible Doug had murdered Shannon—and that he'd done the same to the two campers ten years earlier? A few details about him certainly jibed with what I'd concluded about the killer: he was from the area, he could have easily seen me shortstopping Tom Nolan after the press conference that day, and he could have put his hands on my cell number in a cinch. Plus, he was a parishioner at St. Tim's.

Had he gone to Shannon's house that morning and overpowered her? He would have been at a disadvantage on her home turf, however—and there probably would have been signs of a struggle when she realized what he was doing. Perhaps, instead, he'd waited until she was jogging and pulled his car up alongside her, frantically announcing that, let's say, her mother had been rushed to the hospital. He might have offered to drive her back to the house so she could pick up her own car.

If he *had* murdered Shannon, and the campers as well, it meant he was a psychopathic serial killer, one posing as a Ken doll–like chiropractor with a wife and kid.

I decided that tomorrow I would give the spineless Doug a call. Maybe I'd even try a game of hardball with him, hinting that I'd keep his infidelity under wraps in exchange for a full explanation of his whereabouts the morning Shannon vanished.

I tossed the wet towel back in the bathroom, slipped into a T-shirt, and peeled back the covers. It was a relief to be at the Courtyard, to know that there were other guests on the floor, and a desk clerk downstairs.

After turning off the light, I burrowed under the covers.

A brisk autumn wind was blowing tonight, surprising after such a mellow day, and it rattled the window, as if someone was tapping his fingers against the glass. I needed sleep, and I needed it badly. Despite how disturbed I felt over Alice's death, Beau's incommunicado state, and the endless questions churning in my head, I was banking on sheer exhaustion to send me quickly into a state of oblivion.

I'd barely closed my eyes when my phone rang on the nightstand. Please, I thought, let this finally be Beau.

I was already saying hello by the time my mind processed the words on the screen. It read, "Caller unknown." My heart lurched.

"Good evening." It was *him*. Using the adapter again so that his words quivered.

"Hello," I managed, hearing my voice catch in my throat.

"You've been busy. Bravo."

"Have you been reading my posts?"

"Of course. Why wouldn't I?"

Silence. I needed to engage him, bait him even.

"Why did you kill Alice Hatfield? Did she figure out who you were?"

"Now, now. Let's not get into that."

"You told me about Sunset Bay. I'd love to hear more."

"I really only called to say good night."

"But—"

"Enjoy your new digs at the Courtyard. . . . And don't forget to say your prayers tonight."

CHAPTER 21

THE CALLER DISCONNECTED, AND I EXHALED A CHOPPY breath into the darkness.

After struggling to find the switch for the lamp, I leaped out of bed, grabbed a pen, and quickly transcribed the brief exchange. Then I phoned Killian. To my dismay the call went to voice mail, but he rang back two minutes later. I read him my notes, pointing out that I'd changed hotels and the killer was aware of that fact.

"Christ, what's his game?" Killian asked. "Why's he toying with you this way?"

"I wish I knew."

"And he gave nothing more away? No hints this time?"

"No, though I think the prayer comment is significant. Another indication of a religious fixation."

As far as Killian was concerned, I didn't know anything about the stigmata marks, only the weird references to Shannon's Catholicism the killer had made, and though I briefly considered telling him that I'd been clued in, I decided that protecting Alice's confidence was still important.

"I'll have the call checked out right away, but I'm sure it was from a burner phone, like the last one," Killian said. "Would you consider changing hotels again?"

I sighed, conflicted.

"I hate that he knows my whereabouts, but I doubt it would do any good to switch. If he has me under surveillance, he'll know as soon as I relocate again."

"Then you need to be more cautious than ever, Bailey. The guy may be unraveling. I'm going to send a car over there now and have the hotel watched tonight."

"Thanks, that makes me feel better."

It did, alongside the fact the caller hadn't given any indication that he thought I knew his identity, that I'd been tipped off by Alice.

"And please, don't post anything about this on the *Crime Beat* website yet," Killian said. "I want to keep it under wraps while we try to learn more."

"I'm sorry, I appreciate what you're up against, but I can't have my hands tied as a reporter."

"Just give me tomorrow to investigate, okay?"

I agreed. Though I hated being muzzled, I needed Killian on my side.

After signing off, I rang the front desk and asked the clerk if anyone had made inquiries tonight—by phone or in person—about whether I was a guest at the hotel. He told me no, not that he was aware of, and even if someone *had*, the information would not have been divulged. Somehow, however, the killer had traced me here. As the clerk ran through a brief spiel about guest privacy being a priority, I parted the curtains and peered down to the street three stories below. It looked like a ghost town out there.

I crawled back into bed, knowing that falling asleep would be near impossible now. For the next few hours I twisted in the sheets, endlessly replaying the call in my head. Each time I came close to drifting off, I was startled awake by a noise—the window rattling, the drip of water from the showerhead, the churn of the ice machine down the corridor. Around five I finally managed to surrender to sleep.

I woke with a jolt the next morning. My heart was still pounding, as if I hadn't been able to let go of the call even in slumber. This experience scared me far more than the first contact with the killer, because I now knew what the guy was capable of, what wretched evils he could inflict on another human being. I tried to remind myself that he *needed* me, though, that I was still his messenger.

And yet, as Killian had pointed out last night, the caller had provided no new information this time. It felt as if my role had shifted slightly, like a car drifting over the centerline of a highway.

As wigged out as the call had left me—compounded by the fact that I still hadn't heard from Beau—I still intended to do everything possible to find this guy, first and foremost for Alice's sake. That meant, for starters, having a nice little chat with Doug Claiborne as soon as he arrived at the office. It also meant reactivating my attempt to follow in Alice's digital footsteps—to uncover the clue that had cost her her life.

I threw off the covers and trudged to the bathroom. As my feet hit the floor, I noticed that my head was pounding, too, as if there were a little kid in there banging a pot with a spoon. In the midst of trying to dissuade J.J. from shooting Doug, meeting unexpectedly with Ben, and being forced to play sounding board to Matt Wong's career fantasies, I'd managed to consume nothing but red wine last night.

After starting the coffeemaker on the counter, I ordered eggs to go from the restaurant on the ground floor since the hotel didn't offer room service. Next, I tracked down a number online for Claiborne's chiropractic business, the Back Wellness Center in Queensbury, which opened at nine.

I also checked my email, and saw that a message from Dodson Crowe had come in past eleven last night.

"Fantastic job," he wrote. "I couldn't be happier."

Well, at least things were working out on *that* front. The next line, however, caused a flutter in my chest.

"We're getting excellent traffic on the video, so we should do another. I want you to shoot one today."

I should have expected as much, but I didn't love the idea. With the killer's eyes on me, it seemed stupid to engage in an activity that would make me feel even more exposed.

Dodson went on to write that Keith would meet me in the lobby today at two forty-five unless I indicated otherwise. He also said that he wanted to touch base with me and that he'd give me a call later this morning.

I was careful when I left the room to pick up my food, making sure no one was skulking around on the floor. I also hung the "Do Not Disturb" sign on the doorknob, having decided to handle my own housekeeping and not provide anyone access to my room.

After grabbing my breakfast and heading back upstairs, I drafted notes for the video. And at nine on the nose, I phoned the Back Wellness Center, asking to speak to Dr. Claiborne.

"I'm afraid he's not available to take a call right now," the receptionist told me in the kind of fake cheery tone suggesting that she secretly relished blocking access to him. "Are you a patient?"

"No, not a patient. Could you ask him to call Bailey Weggins, please?"

"Dr. Claiborne has a very busy day ahead. May I be of assistance somehow?"

"No, I'm a friend. It's a personal matter."

"If this is regarding his sister-in-law, Dr. Claiborne is asking people to communicate by email or leave a message on the funeral home website. I can give—"

"No, it's not about that. I'm calling in regard to another matter entirely."

"All right then." She didn't sound pleased, but I knew she'd sensed something was up—and she would be smart enough to inform her boss. I bet this was hardly the first call she'd fielded from a mystery female with an edge in her voice.

For the next few hours, I trolled the Internet again, continuing the missing-woman search I'd set aside a day ago and widening my hunt even more—to New Jersey, Pennsylvania, and Ohio, as well as Canada. Nothing showed any promise.

Weary, I leaned back in my chair and massaged my scalp. I knew Alice's discovery was from an Internet search—she'd *said* so—but I was beginning to wonder if it might not have been from the one she described to me. It was entirely possible that she'd moved on to a new area of research.

Finally, around one o'clock, Claiborne made contact.

"I'm glad you got in touch, Ms. Weggins," he said, oozing unctuous charm. "I owe you a big thank-you for yesterday, but unfortunately I had no way to reach you."

"*Really?*" I said. "Kelly has my number."

"I wasn't aware of that."

"And so does Lisa. Surely you knew *that.*"

"Lisa—Lisa and I aren't in contact any longer."

Was this stuff about my cell number all bullshit? If he *was* the killer, he wouldn't want me to know he had it.

"Well, you have it now and we need to chat. Where were you a week ago Sunday?"

"Pardon me?"

"A week ago Sunday. Your wife said you'd gone out of town, but you weren't with Lisa and you weren't with J.J., either."

"I—I was in Lake Placid. Staying at the Crowne Plaza. I had an early breakfast meeting the next morning. Originally I'd planned to attend a three-day program up there, and though I ended up canceling, I kept some of the appointments I'd made."

"Why did you need to spend the night at the hotel when it's barely over an hour away from your home?"

"Well, I had a dinner scheduled up there for Sunday night as well. It didn't make sense to go up and back and then up again. I—I honestly don't see why my personal life is any business of yours."

"You don't? Your girlfriend calls me screaming for help and when I show up, your *other* girlfriend waves a gun in my face. So your personal life became my business whether I wanted it to or not. Now back to your schedule. Who did you have breakfast with that Monday morning?"

"Breakfast? Why—? I don't believe this. You can't possibly think I had anything to do with Shannon's death."

"Just tell me who you had breakfast with."

"Another chiropractor I've been thinking of opening a branch with."

"Is that right?"

"You think I'm lying?"

"Well, you're not exactly a paragon of honesty."

"Ask the sheriff if you have to. He inquired as to my whereabouts for that time period and I not only told him where I was, but I also turned over my receipts. I'm sure he's verified the information."

Something told me that this time, at least, Claiborne was telling the truth. Because if this hadn't all checked out, Killian would have been all over him.

"Good. I'll follow up with him."

"You're not going to say anything to Kelly about this,

are you? Things have been shaky with us and I don't want to make it worse. Not with everything she's going through."

"I'll tell you what. Take my call the next time I need info from you, and it'll stay between the two of us."

I hung up before he had time to respond.

The phone was still in my hand when Dodson rang.

"You're all set for the video, right?" he said.

"Yes, thanks, all set. I—"

"And then what do you think?"

"About what?"

"About where we are with the story. Maybe it's time to close up shop in that location and handle any additional reporting from the city."

"*Close up shop?*" He'd caught me totally by surprise. "Dodson, this doesn't seem like the right moment to do that. What I was about to tell you is that the killer called me again last night."

I recapped the exchange, stressing that it had to be kept quiet for now.

"That's really disturbing. I hate the fact that he's got eyes on you."

"The sheriff has a car watching my hotel."

"If you were back in the city, we wouldn't have to worry about your safety. And after all, the guy has your number. He can still make contact."

"But there's still a lot cooking here."

"Do you have reason to believe the cops are close to an arrest?"

"No, but they're clearly still waiting for forensic test results.

Alice Hatfield's autopsy is happening today, and something may turn up from that. . . . Is it a money issue?"

"It's partly a money issue, because my budget is tight. We're a new operation, as you know. But the bigger factor is the case itself. It's in limbo, wouldn't you say? They may never even catch this guy."

Despite the fact that I'd been semi-expecting this conversation, and that Dodson's suggestion made sense on one level, I found myself incredibly irritated. I had to warn myself not to sound bitchy.

"But they *might* catch him," I said. "And he may be prepared to kill again."

"Right on both counts. And if they arrest this guy, or another woman ends up dead, we'll send you right back up there. In the meantime, you can still interview people by phone and post updates every day, which we'll pay you for. There just doesn't seem to be a need for you to be in Lake George at the moment."

I could certainly stay in touch with the locals by phone. I had a pipeline to Killian, which I'd be able to take advantage of from Manhattan. But if I was going to find Alice's killer, I needed to be *here*. Unfortunately, that argument wouldn't carry much weight with Dodson. In his eyes I was a reporter, not a member of the sheriff's department.

"Can we see what the rest of the day brings and decide later?" I asked, bargaining for more time, as Killian had done with me last night.

"Okay, sure, why not? Let's speak around seven, after I have your post for the day."

I tossed the phone on the bed. As frustrated as I felt, I had to admit that the case did seem to have stalled—at least on my end. Every lead I was currently following was vague, and in some instances dubious, amounting to nothing but a list of *maybes*. Maybe Page had begun dabbling in the drug trade, exposing Amy and herself to a serial killer; maybe Shannon had made contact with a few dealers, hoping to find the person responsible for her cousin's death, and had inadvertently put herself in contact with that same killer; maybe a new driver at Baker Beverage had become obsessed with Shannon and later abducted her; maybe the killer was someone from the parish, even the local deacon himself, who'd targeted Shannon because she was Catholic, blond, and beautiful; maybe the creepy motel owner did it.

Maybe, maybe, maybe.

Still, I had no intention of hitting the road with Alice's killer still at large. I would pay room and board myself if it came down to it.

I ordered more food for a late lunch and returned to the Internet search. Rather than hunting any farther afield this time, I reviewed the missing-persons cases I'd found earlier, but once again decided that they didn't seem relevant. By the time I was due to dress for the video, I was almost certain that Alice must have abandoned her research about missing women and moved on to a new area of inquiry—and it was there that she found her clue.

Without her computer, though, it was impossible to have even a hint of her discovery.

Sorting through a ball of limp, already worn clothes, I

managed to find another top that looked video-worthy, as long as the camera didn't pick up a dried marinara stain. I threw it on with a pair of jeans and did the best job I could with my hair and makeup, which amounted to nothing more than turning a sow's ear into a slightly *perkier* sow's ear.

Keith was already in the lobby, studying his phone, when I disembarked from the elevator. I told him about the call last night, convinced I could trust him to keep it confidential, and my fear that the killer might be watching me. He suggested pulling his vehicle up to the back of the hotel and having me jump in there. The back lot was empty and as we drove away, I twisted in my seat, surveying the area behind us. We had the side street to ourselves.

"So where do you want to shoot this one?" I asked.

"Dodson wants us to set up in front of Alice Hatfield's house."

I flinched at the prospect of returning there.

"Keith, we can't trespass," I told him. "That would be out of line."

"I don't mean on her property. I checked the place out earlier today and there's a spot on the road right before you turn into her driveway. We wouldn't be trespassing, and yet you can still see the house from there."

What choice did I have? I couldn't allow my personal feelings about Alice to interfere with the way the story was presented.

As expected, the cabin looked deserted. Though the sun was shining brightly today, the air was crisp. I stripped off my jacket when it came time to shoot, fighting off a shiver.

I went through my remarks as best as possible, but I hated standing there with Alice's house looming in the background, talking about her death and knowing that many viewers would be titillated by the details. I kept wondering, too, if the killer would be watching. Of course he would.

"You okay?" Keith asked after we'd wrapped.

"Yeah, sorry. You've probably met rice cakes with more charisma than I managed today. But it's been such a crazy week."

"I hear you. It must be really tough at times to do what you do. Covering gruesome stuff like this."

"Yeah, it can be."

But that wasn't really true. Yes, I cared about victims, and was saddened for their families and friends, but my job had never seemed *tough* to me before. I loved it. Loved chasing down leads and digging for clues, and, when possible, ripping truths out from beneath the rocks they liked to hide under. And yet there was no denying that at the present moment, I couldn't relish any part of it.

Keith dropped me behind the hotel and I hightailed it directly to the small café right off the lobby in search of caffeine.

Now what? I thought, staring out the window and waiting for my cappuccino to arrive. From where I was sitting I could see a slice of the lake. The water was a sparkling blue today, mocking my dreary mood. I felt a desperate urge to take action but had no clue what to do.

The waitress had just brought my drink when, to my surprise, I spotted Ben Hatfield striding purposefully across the room in my direction.

Oh God, I hoped he hadn't been tipped off that we'd

been shooting video near his mom's house. He might have taken it as a real affront, and I wouldn't have blamed him.

"Hey, there you are," he said, reaching me. "I tried your phone a bunch of times but it kept going to voice mail."

"So sorry," I said, realizing I'd switched my phone to vibrate while Keith was recording and hadn't readjusted it. "How are you coping?"

"Not great, I have to admit." He sounded anxious rather than miffed. "Can you spare a minute?"

"Of course, please sit down. How about some coffee?"

"No, thanks. I'm already over my limit. I've been thinking about what you asked—about my last conversation with my mom. You said I should call you even if I remembered something small."

A chill raced through me. Do *not* get your hopes up, I warned myself.

"Yes, please. Tell me."

"It's so minor, I'm sure it's meaningless." He scraped a couple of times at the cuticle of his right thumb.

"But maybe it isn't."

"Like I told you, my mom and I spoke on Saturday, like we usually did. Our normal routine was for me to call her in the early evening, generally before my girlfriend and I made dinner or went out for the night, but this time she ended up calling me. At around five."

It was the same discrepancy my mind had snagged on last night. I took a sip of my cappuccino, thinking.

"So it was pretty out of the ordinary?" I asked, setting the cup down.

"Well, not hugely so. Once in a while she'd initiate a call if she wasn't going to be around at our normal time, but it'd been a while since that happened. My mom used to say there were too many crazies on the road on Saturday night and she preferred to stay in with Netflix and a glass of chardonnay."

Perhaps Alice had become apprehensive about her discovery, and, eager for the comfort of Ben's voice, had called him earlier than usual. But no, that couldn't be it. She hadn't turned up the detail that scared her until Sunday morning.

"There's one more thing," Ben said. "Again, it's probably nothing."

"Go ahead."

"Like I told you, she didn't mention any leads she had on the murders, but when I was lying in bed last night, I remembered something she'd asked about a guy I'd gone to high school with. She'd heard that he'd once worked at Baker Beverage and she wanted to know if it was true."

"*Who?*"

"Tom Nolan."

My stomach tightened.

"And he did," Ben added. "Work at Baker, I mean. Tom was in sales there."

"Was this recently?"

"No, I'd say somewhere around six or seven years ago. The poor guy ended up with cancer and had to stop working for a while. But he's fully recovered now. From what I hear, he works for one of the hotels."

Okay, I could see why Alice's curiosity had been aroused.

And yet his connection to Baker went back years ago, so that hardly pointed to anything.

"Did your mom say how she found this out? Could it have been online?"

"No, it sounded as if someone told her, though I can't recall the exact words she used."

"And how did she react when you confirmed it?"

"She just said something like, 'Hmm, okay, thanks.' I'm sorry not to have mentioned this last night. She'd been so nonchalant, I didn't even think of it until after you and I spoke."

I pressed my hands to my lips, thinking. This couldn't be the scary clue Alice had stumbled on. Besides the fact that she hadn't turned it up online, she would have already known that Nolan and Shannon were acquainted through the parish, and so why would it have mattered that they might have crossed paths when Nolan worked for her father's company?

And yet it was possible that Alice had followed the thread and it led her someplace truly disturbing. Maybe Nolan had developed a desperate obsession with Shannon while he was at Baker but let it subside during his cancer treatment, only to fan the flames again once Shannon began attending mass in July.

"I'm just glad you told me now," I said finally. "I'm not sure it's of any significance, but it's worth checking out, and I'm going to do that."

"By the way, the memorial service is going to be on Thursday. I'd love for you to be there."

"Ben, I'd be so honored to attend. Will you text me the details?"

He promised he would and excused himself, saying he needed to meet up with his girlfriend.

Back in my room, I tried the parish house, hoping to reach Nolan there, but I ended up with the outgoing voice-mail message, which told me the hours were between nine and four.

I glanced at my watch: 5:24. There was a slim chance Baker Beverage might still be open. I tried the main number, hoping to speak to either Riley or Cody, but the outgoing voice-mail message relayed that business hours ran only until five. I had no luck reaching Cody on his cell, either.

One option, I decided, was to simply show up at Baker. Even if Cody wasn't there, Riley might be hanging around, still playing catch-up, and she could fill me in on Tom Nolan's employment history with the company.

When I pulled up near the front of the building twenty minutes later, I was relieved to see a light on in the reception area. I parked in the same spot I'd used the other day and hurried toward the building, but before I even had a chance to ring the bell, two men emerged through the doorway, zipping their jackets in unison as one regaled the other with an anecdote. They both wore khaki pants and collared shirts, open at the neck. Sales guys, I figured.

"Can I help you?" one of the men inquired.

"Yes, hi, thanks. I'm here to see Riley," I said, stretching the truth.

"You know where she sits?"

"Yes, thanks." It looked like I was in luck.

He held the door for me, and I made my way down the

long hall to the bullpen area. There was a sweet, syrupy smell to the air today, which I assumed was emanating from the bottling plant.

Riley was at her desk, eyes glued to her computer screen, and I could see Cody through the glass wall of his office, talking on his landline with the glass door closed and his back to the main room. There was only one other person in the cubicle area, an older woman with long, wavy gray hair, buttoning a red sweater coat. The overhead fluorescent lights were off, which gave the place a slightly more inviting vibe today, though it had to be tough to work someplace without windows.

Riley looked startled when she eventually caught sight of me, and she rose quickly from her chair. Her glossy hair was pinned in a sloppy bun today, and she was wearing more makeup than she'd bothered with on Saturday. Pretty but professional.

"How did you get in here?" she demanded.

"Oh, sorry, someone was nice enough to let me inside. I hope you don't mind, but I had a follow-up question."

"Is there a problem?" She glanced quickly toward Cody's office, and, perhaps sensing my presence, he swiveled his chair in my direction and raised his free hand in a half wave.

"Not a problem, no. But I discovered a piece of information that I wanted to run by you. It might be important."

"Um, sure. We want to help, of course." Rather than make me sit on the filing cabinet this time, she pulled a desk chair over from another cube.

"I understand that Tom Nolan worked here six or seven years ago," I said, taking the seat. "Did you know him then?"

"You mean the deacon?" She turned away briefly to wish

the departing female staffer good night. "I believe he worked here once, but that was before my time. I only know him because he's been helping Cody with funeral arrangements."

"Would Cody be able to spare a moment so I can ask him?"

"He's probably going to be on this call for a while longer. He's trying to find a counselor for the kids. But, um, why don't I check."

Since he'd first spotted me, Cody had turned his attention mostly back to his phone call, listening intently it seemed, but I sensed him keeping an eye on Riley and me. As she stepped into his office, closing the door behind her, he placed a hand over the phone, gesturing for her to speak. She apparently filled him in and I saw him nod.

Riley returned to her desk. "He can answer your questions once he's done with the call, but it's going to be a few more minutes."

"No problem."

"Do you mind waiting on your own, though? I'm on dinner duty tonight."

"No, please, go ahead."

Riley took a minute to straighten the piles on her clean, spare desk, shut off her computer, and throw a nubby brown jacket over her sweater. As she wished me goodbye, a guy in a shirt sporting the Baker Beverage logo emerged from the door at the rear. It was my first glimpse of the bottling area—lots of stainless steel and a long U-shaped conveyor. The guy gave Cody a thumbs-up through the glass wall of his office.

"You headed home now, Riley?" the man called out, turning his attention to her. "I'll walk out with you."

After they were gone, I dug my phone from my bag. I'd flown out of the hotel in such a hurry, I hadn't checked to see what might surface online about Nolan and Baker Beverage.

I clicked on my Safari button and typed "Tom Nolan sales Baker Beverage Distributors Lake George New York" into the search bar. Not much turned up. A link to Nolan as the deacon at St. Timothy's. And a ghost link to the "About" page of Baker from six and a half years ago, featuring Nolan's short profile from the time he worked there. And then a link to an article from an online site called the *Lake George Bulletin*, written around the same time. I clicked on it.

Cody, then the sales manager at Baker, had won a huge award from the main soda company they did business with. In an interview with the *Lake George Bulletin* site, he spread the wealth around, mentioning a few members of his sales team, including Nolan.

I kept reading. Cody sounded like the golden boy, and he addressed how lucky he'd been to be mentored by Shannon's father.

Blaine hailed from Texas, the item noted, and hadn't been to the area until marrying Shannon Baker. "But I knew about the region," Cody told the interviewer. "An army pal of mine had grown up here and he talked about it—how beautiful the lake was. And the Adirondacks, too."

At that moment I heard a sound in my head as piercing as a car alarm. He'd been familiar with the area before moving here.

Something didn't feel right.

CHAPTER 22

I BIT MY LIP, MY MIND RACING. CODY HAD BEEN IN AF-
ghanistan ten years ago. Thousands of miles away from
here. But he'd learned about the area back when he was in the
army. Did that mean anything?

And if it did, had Alice discovered it? Over the weekend, she'd confirmed with Ben that Nolan had worked at
Baker. And she probably turned to Google next, as I had,
and would have soon lighted on the article in the *Lake George
Bulletin*. Surely she read Cody's comment about his army pal.
So when Alice called Cody on Sunday, she probably would
have asked him to confirm that.

But according to Cody, Alice had simply asked whether
Shannon had stayed at the retreat center as a teen.

I needed to raise both topics and see how he reacted.

I suddenly sensed a presence to my right, and when I
twisted my head, I realized Cody Blaine was two feet away
from me. I'd been so lost in thought that I hadn't heard him
emerge from his office.

"Must be interesting," he said.

"Pardon me?"

He was dressed fairly spiffily—navy chinos, an untucked jean shirt, and an olive-green unstructured blazer—but his handsome face was drawn and his eyes were bloodshot. Was that from fatigue? Or had he turned to booze to drown his sorrows?

"Whatever you're reading."

"Oh, just emails." I rose so I wasn't craning my neck and staring up at him, like a staffer talking to the boss. "I was catching up while I waited."

"Riley said you had a question about Tom Nolan."

"Yes, right, thanks for taking the time. I heard he was in sales here at one point. I was hoping you could fill me in on his employment."

"What specifically?"

"How long he worked here. Why he moved on."

He narrowed his eyes, curious. "Tom was here for a couple of years, and left, I'd say, about five, maybe four, years ago. He was a terrific sales guy, but after a bout with cancer, he was looking for a job that didn't involve so much coming and going during the day."

"Would he have had much contact with Shannon when he worked here?"

"*Shannon?* Whoa. If I didn't know better, I'd think you were eyeing him as a suspect. Tom has been totally focused on fighting his illness and staying healthy in the last few years. He couldn't have had anything to do with what happened to Shannon—or those two other women."

"I appreciate the insight. I'm sure you're eager to split, so only a few more questions." I could feel my pulse quicken—because of where I was headed next. "When Alice called you on Sunday, did she happen to ask about Tom?"

Cody parted his lips and looked off, as if trying to recall.

"Nope."

Wouldn't she have been curious like me, wondering if Nolan's employment here was significant in any way? And wouldn't she have queried Cody about his familiarity with the area before meeting Shannon? That definitely would have stopped her, like it did me.

"Everything okay?" he asked.

"Um, yes, just thinking. Did she ask you about anything else? Besides, of course, Shannon attending a retreat. Shannon hadn't, by the way. Attended a retreat. Kelly checked with her mother for me."

"No, nothing else. Now, if you don't mind, I really need to turn out the lights, lock up, and go home to my kids."

This was my chance. I had to take the plunge, prick him a little.

"She didn't ask if you knew anything about Lake George before meeting Shannon?"

"No, why would she? But the answer would have been yes. Believe it or not, they teach you about the French and Indian War even in Texas."

"But hadn't an army friend told you about this place? Back when you were in Afghanistan together?"

He leveled his gaze at me and held my eyes with his.

"That's right," he said. "Dirk. He was from around these parts."

"What a coincidence. Then you met Shannon."

"I guess you could call it that. I heard her mention Lake George at work one day, so I struck up a conversation."

"Do you and Dirk still stay in touch?"

"Nope, sad to say, but he didn't make it out of there. He ended up dying a few feet away from me."

My gut was now flashing a yellow caution light. Cody had met a guy from this area. Had he described places here? Told him stories from here? Stories about two missing girls?

"I'm sorry to hear that," I said. My voice sounded stupidly squeaky to me, stress playing havoc with my vocal cords. "It must have been hard for you."

"Very."

His eyes left mine, and I watched as they scanned the area behind me. Oh shit, he was checking to see if anyone was still hanging around the office.

Adrenaline pumped through my body. There was something wrong about Cody and the army pal, and I needed to get the hell out. I faked a check of my watch.

"Well, you need to head home to your kids," I said. "And I'm due to meet another reporter for a drink at the hotel. I'm probably pushing off for the city tomorrow."

Lies, of course. But I had to make him think someone was waiting for me, and that I'd soon be long gone from these parts.

"Sorry to see you go. Again, I appreciate what you did— finding Shannon."

"Thanks, Cody. Good luck with everything. Do I go out the way I came in?"

"Yes. Out the front."

I hitched my bag up on my shoulder and shot him a smile that I hoped didn't seem as phony as it was. I pivoted and began to walk past the deserted gray workstations toward the hall that led to reception. My heart was hammering hard enough for me to hear it in my ears.

He was letting me leave, though. Maybe he hadn't managed to read my mind, or if he had, he realized I had no proof of anything. Or maybe I was worried for nothing. But something about this whole thing scared me. I would call Killian the second I was out of there.

It was when I reached the turn in the hallway that I heard him behind me.

"Bailey, wait a minute."

Panic gripped me. Don't look scared, I warned myself. I slowed my gait and turned to face him.

"There's one other thing," he said. He'd caught up with me and moved a little ahead, his eyes nearly black and shiny. He took one more step, now fully blocking my path to the door.

"Yes?"

"It was a mistake, wasn't it?" He flashed a small, rueful smile.

"What was?"

"Mentioning Dirk in that article. I knew it the second I saw it online. I should have kept that to myself."

He had killed Shannon, I realized. I knew it now in my bones.

"Oh, don't worry about it," I said stupidly. I could feel the fear in my legs, dissolving them into jelly.

He shot out his arm and tried to grab me, but I jerked back fast, and he caught the strap of my purse instead, dragging it to the floor with a thud. I backed up, and without even thinking, reached for a rolling desk chair in the workstation to my right, then frantically shoved it toward him. The force wasn't much but it caught him just right, pitching him forward against the arm.

My only way out was through the factory, I realized. There would be exits inside, there had to be.

I swung around and bolted toward the back wall, practically flinging myself at the door and yanking it open. The lights were still blazing in the cavernous space, though it seemed empty of people. I took off down the middle, between two motionless conveyor belts. I desperately scanned the room for exits, but the belts blocked my view of the sides of the building.

I couldn't hear Blaine behind me. Had he raced outside, I wondered, planning to cut me off in the parking lot? But then seconds later he exploded through the door behind me.

I ran harder and faster, straight ahead, the effort searing my lungs. If he caught me, he would kill me, just as he'd surely killed Alice.

I reached a wide passageway at the end of the factory and barreled through it. I was now in the warehouse, loaded with rack after rack of sodas and beer. I flew by them, cartons and bottles all in a blur. At last, up ahead, on the left, I spotted an emergency door. Blaine was directly behind me now, and I felt the whoosh as his arm shot out again, trying to snatch me. I dodged to the right. He missed, and as I glanced back I saw him stumble a little. I darted toward the racks again, where I grabbed one of the liters of soda, throwing it hard at his head. He took the bottle in the face, yelped, and staggered back.

"You bitch," he yelled.

I grabbed another and hurled that, too, but this one simply glanced off the side of his skull.

I spun around and ran, my lungs on fire. Finally I reached the door and lunged for the crash bar. It flew open, and I spilled into the parking lot, with the alarm blaring behind me.

I'd exited at the very rear of the building onto a tarmac illuminated by security floodlights. My freaking car key, I realized, was in my bag, which was lying on the floor of the office. I would have to make for the road and flag down a passing vehicle. I gasped for air and took off past the loading docks toward the front of the building.

The sound of a car engine cut through the night, coming from the other side of the building and drowning out the alarm. Was it *him*? Before I could decide what to do, a dark car rounded the back of the building. I moved even faster, a stitch stabbing at my side. I could hear the car coming up behind me. If it was Cody, I was sure he'd plow right into me.

But the car slowed, and I turned to see Riley sitting in the front seat, her window half down. Relief flooded through me like water gushing through a hose.

"What's going on?" she called out, bringing the car to a stop.

"I need to get in, okay?" I said, nearly breathless.

"But what's the matter?"

"Please," I begged.

"All right. Yes, get in."

I raced around the front of her car, threw open the door, and nearly dove into the passenger seat.

"We need to leave—right this second," I told her.

"What?"

"Please, it's an emergency. I'll explain afterward."

"You didn't drive here?"

"I did, but I'm missing my key."

I craned my neck and peered out the rear window. There was still no sign of Cody. "Hurry," I urged.

In frustration, Riley made a tsk sound with her tongue against the roof of her mouth, but she did as I'd instructed, accelerating the Audi and aiming for the road.

"I wish you'd tell me."

"Please, Riley, I promise to in a minute." I worried that Blaine had reversed direction in the building and raced to the main exit, hoping to head me off. But no one burst through the front door as we neared the road.

"Which way do you usually turn to go home? Right?"

"Yes."

"Go left instead. And then drive straight to the municipal center, to the sheriff's office. You know where that is?"

"Um, yeah, I think so."

Again, she followed orders, picking up speed even more after she took the turn. I was desperate to call Killian and alert him to the fact that I was coming, but my cell, with his number programmed into it, was also in my purse.

I twisted around in my seat but didn't detect any car beams behind us. Maybe Cody hadn't seen Riley come to my rescue and was searching for me on foot.

I still wasn't sure what the hell was really going on. My gut told me Cody had killed his wife, but I had no clue why or how the campers figured into it. He wasn't even in the country when they'd disappeared.

So . . . so maybe this guy Dirk had murdered Page and Amy and confessed to Cody when he lay dying. Even told him where he'd hidden the bodies. And when Cody had decided, for reasons unknown, to murder his lovely wife, he'd left her in the same place, making it appear like the work of a deranged serial killer.

I'd been looking for connections between the lives of the victims—and so had Alice—but maybe the only connection was the dark, forlorn basement where their remains had been dumped.

"I'm so lucky you came," I said, turning back around and looking over at Riley. "You hadn't left yet?"

"No. My husband and I ended up in a fight on the phone while I was walking to my car, and I needed to chill for a minute. And then I heard the door alarm go off. What *happened* back there?"

"Cody came after me."

"What?"

"It was because of something I asked him. About the reporter who died, Alice Hatfield."

"Maybe he's sick of going over the same ground again and again. No one seems to appreciate the hell he's been through."

"Riley, I know it sounds crazy, but I'm almost positive he murdered Shannon."

Her mouth dropped open in disbelief.

"And Alice Hatfield, too."

"That's ridiculous," she said. "Why would he do that?" Her eyes were focused straight ahead and both hands gripped the wheel. This stretch of the road was far less populated than the part I'd traveled earlier, with only a few scattered houses set far back under tall, leafy trees. And no streetlamps.

"I think she figured out he'd killed Shannon. She called him and asked a couple of questions that made him see she was getting close. And then he showed up at her house."

Riley's eyes left the road for only a split second, but long enough for me to see the anger flashing in them.

"For starters, Cody couldn't have killed Shannon," she said. "I saw him before he took off to look at a piece of property and we talked on the phone a little while later. He seemed perfectly normal."

"He's slick, a sales guy. He knows how to put on a front. And he may have been planning it for a while, so he had plenty of time to work out all the kinks."

"But he *loved* Shannon," Riley said. "Why would he have killed her?"

I massaged my scalp, pulling my thoughts together.

"I don't know. Could he have been having an affair?"

"No way. And what about those other women?" Her irritation seemed to be intensifying. It was going to be tough to convince her.

"I think someone else committed those murders. Someone Cody met in the army—he called him Dirk tonight."

"You *are* crazy," Riley said. For the first time I thought I heard fear in her voice. Was I finally getting through to her?

"I'm sorry, this has to be hard for you." I swiveled again and peered through the back window. Far, far back on the road, two high beams penetrated the darkness, like disembodied torchlights.

"Shit, that may be him behind us," I said, keeping my eyes on the lights. "Can you speed up?"

The view behind me suddenly slid out of view, and I realized Riley was hanging a sharp right. But not onto another road. As I faced forward again, I saw that she was pulling into a parking lot. The sign at the entrance read "Pine Grove Tennis and Swim Club."

"Riley, what—?"

"I missed the turn for the municipal center. I never come this way."

She took her foot off the gas and eased into the lot.

"But Cody might be tailing us. Look, we better call 911. Can I use your phone?"

"Are you going to turn Cody in?" she said.

God, was she so devoted to the guy she couldn't wrap her mind around the idea of him being a killer?

"I'm going to explain to the sheriff that we might be in danger, and the police can sort it out from there. If Cody didn't do anything wrong, he won't be in any trouble."

"All right."

She shifted into park.

"Riley, we shouldn't stop. Give me your phone and I'll call."

"Fine."

She grabbed her bag from the floor by my feet and fished around inside it.

But it wasn't a phone she pulled out. It was a gun. Small and black with wood on the handle. She pointed it directly at my torso.

Panic flooded through me all over again.

"Riley, please, if he's innocent, he has nothing to worry about."

"You don't get it, do you?"

Oh wow, maybe I did. They were lovers. I'd been right to wonder about them.

"You're—you're having an affair with him?"

She said nothing.

"Riley, please, don't ruin your life. If Cody killed Shannon to be with—"

"Cody's not my lover," she snapped. "He's my business partner. And I'm not going to let you turn him in."

"Your *business* partner? What do you mean?"

She scoffed and the gun jiggled a little in her hand. "What does it matter to you?"

"What have you got going at Baker?"

Wait. The answer had been whispering to me for days.

"It's drugs, isn't it? Are you moving drugs in the Baker delivery trucks?"

If she was in on it, her husband must be, too. I thought of the boat in their driveway, the big TV.

No reply. She stuffed her free hand in her purse and rooted around again. Hunting for her phone, no doubt. She was going to call Blaine and tell him where to find us. I had to keep her talking instead.

"Did Shannon find out?"

"You know what the problem with Shannon was? She had *everything*. A huge house and a condo in Florida and all the nice clothes she wanted, and she didn't have to lift a *finger* for any of it. But she wasn't satisfied. She had to start butting into our business."

Riley was nearly stabbing the contents of her purse now, trying to find the damn phone without taking her eyes off me.

"What tipped her off?"

"Who the hell knows? She just announced one day that she wanted to give us a hand at Baker, and Cody had to say yes—because she was *Daddy's girl*. She was real sneaky about it, going slow at first, working from home, and then the next thing you know she showed up there. She started snooping around from the moment she arrived, like she knew something was up."

"And she found proof?"

"Oh yeah, she turned out to be a great little detective. Cody tried to reason with her. Begged her not to blow up their lives."

"And it didn't work?"

"At first he thought he'd managed to get through to her, but he finally realized she was actually going to tell on him. Betray her own *husband.* Send him to prison so he couldn't be with his kids. She didn't leave him any choice."

Finally she yanked the phone from her purse. With her eyes flicking between me and the screen, she jabbed at it a couple of times and pressed it to her ear.

The call was answered instantly, and someone barked on the other end.

"It's okay, I've got her," Riley announced.

A pause as she listened. My heart was pounding so hard it felt like it could burst from my chest.

"In my car," she said. "In the parking lot of that tennis and swim place, the one— Okay." She disconnected and let the phone fall to her lap.

Though Riley's tone had suggested firm control of the situation, even in the dark I could make out the sheen of perspiration on her face. Could I manage to distract her, see if I could bolt out of the car fast enough so she couldn't shoot me in the back of the head? Because I had only min- utes before Cody arrived.

"So he had the perfect way to make it seem like a serial killing, didn't he? Did he say he was going to do that—leave Shannon there and confuse everybody?"

"I didn't know anything about the other bodies until you found them. He told me he had a plan and to insist that I'd seen him first thing that morning and that we'd talked on the phone a couple of times right after that."

"And why exactly did Alice have to die?"

"Like you said, she called and was totally nosing around. She knew Dirk's name. Cody could sense she was putting it together."

"Dirk killed the women?"

"Not him. But he was drugged out of his mind one night and he was with this guy, Sean something, who did it. It was supposed to be a drug deal, but one of the women had no idea what was supposed to go down. She lost her shit, and Sean ended up strangling both of them and then slashing at their hands and feet. Sean told Dirk he'd implicate him if he didn't help him hide the bodies and get rid of their car."

"And Dirk told Cody in Afghanistan?"

"When he was dying. Cody never knew whether to believe him, but he went there one day finally and saw for himself."

"He wanted me to find the bodies so that everyone would think Shannon had been murdered by a serial killer."

"You should have been happy. You got your little scoop." With one eye still on me, she craned her neck to peer anxiously through the back window, desperate for Cody's arrival. "Now just shut the fuck up."

Could I scare her, make her see what the stakes were?

"Riley, even if Cody kills me, the cops are still going to find out the truth. You have a chance right now to turn yourself in and strike a deal with the police. To protect yourself and your husband."

"The cops don't have a clue."

"Oh, but they do," I lied. "Sheriff Killian knows Cody

was lying about why Alice Hatfield called him Sunday. I just beat him to the punch by coming here tonight."

I could hear that her breathing had quickened, so I knew I'd hit a nerve. She shook her head, without speaking, as if she was telling herself no, not to buy what I was saying. My only choice was to leap out of the car and pray she didn't have the nerve to shoot.

Riley flicked her eyes away to check the rearview mirror, and with her attention briefly diverted, I tiptoed my fingers toward the door, hunting for the handle. I willed my hand to stop trembling.

A vehicle swung into the parking lot, its high beams flooding the car. He was here. It was now or never.

I grabbed the handle and shoved open the door. In one quick move I spilled into the night, scooted around to the other side of the door, and shoved it closed. I crawled for a few feet and then sprang up, aiming for a dumpster at the edge of the lot.

I heard a door fling open and the sound of booted feet landing on the asphalt.

"Hold it right there," a male voice shouted. But it wasn't Blaine's.

I twisted around far enough to see. Hank Coulter was standing in front of his pickup truck, legs astride and holding a gun himself. God, was he in on this, too?

"You're working with them?" I called out, frozen in place.

"No, I'm not working with them," he yelled back. "I'm here to save your butt."

CHAPTER 23

THERE WAS NO WAY I COULD BE SURE, BUT SOMETHING told me to trust him. Besides, it wasn't like I had a boatload of butt-saving options.

"Look out, she's got a gun," I shouted. "It's Riley, Cody's assistant. And he's headed here."

"What's going on?"

"Cody killed Shannon. And Alice, too. Riley knows all about it."

"Okay, jump in my truck. But stay low."

I crouch-ran to the truck and flung myself into the passenger seat with Coulter covering me.

Once I was safely inside, he stepped backward, gun still raised, until he reached the driver's side door and let himself into the cab of the truck.

"You okay?" he asked, flicking his gaze in my direction.

"Yeah, just rattled. They—"

"Hold that for now. You said Cody was nearby. Was he coming from Baker?"

"From around there. He should have been here by now."

"I heard a car go by a second ago. He might have seen she wasn't alone and driven past."

Hank transferred the gun to his left hand and with his right, reached behind him and began patting. I twisted a little to see what he was up to. There was a very narrow seat behind us, wide enough for a dog but in this case cluttered with car parts, a stack of Missing flyers with Shannon's photos on them—and a length of rope.

My breath froze. *He's going to tie me up.*

But after a brief fumble, he grabbed an object I couldn't make out and lifted it into the front seat.

Bless his heart; it was a bullhorn.

"Sit tight," he commanded, and stepped cautiously from the vehicle again. Two seconds later, his booming voice cut through the night.

"Step out and away from the vehicle," he commanded. "Keep your weapon lowered and lay it on the ground." A bird, apparently roused from a nearby tree by the noise, responded with a startled shriek and flap of wings.

I peered through the windshield. No sign of movement from Riley's Audi. I lowered the window a crack so I could hear.

"I said step out and away—" Hank barked, trying once more. Before he could finish this time, the driver's door eased open. Riley slowly emerged with both arms by her side and the gun drooping from her right hand.

"All right, all right," she shouted. Her voice was high-pitched and frantic by now. She set the gun on the ground, and I could see that she was shaking.

"Is that your only weapon?"

"Yes . . . I'm not responsible for what happened to Shannon. You have to know that."

"Mrs. Hickok, law enforcement will be here shortly. I advise you to say nothing. Now toss your phone and car key on the ground along with your weapon and get back into your vehicle."

Again, she did as instructed. Her phone and key hit the ground, one right after the other, and she stumbled back into the car.

Hank reentered the cab, tossed the bullhorn into the back, and made a phone call. I heard him request help, lots of it.

Once he was done, I quickly recounted what had happened to me at Baker and in the car with Riley.

"Good God," Coulter said, his anger palpable.

"How in the world did you end up here?" I asked. It all seemed so improbable.

"It was because of your call last night. Asking about drugs."

"Yeah?"

"I heard something weird this past winter. A rumor about Baker Beverage and drug trafficking. Cody's always been a little slick for my liking, but I was glad Stan had found someone to entrust the business to and I didn't want to believe it. Still, I made a few discreet inquiries . . ."

"And?"

"Nothing about drugs turned up, but I did hear that Baker might be struggling. Another distributor had been poaching their business and they hadn't figured out how to rebound. Plus Cody is reportedly a big spender. When Shannon disappeared, I decided to stay close, keep an eye on Cody. Once the other bodies were found, it seemed like he was off the hook, but your question made me wonder again if something dirty was going on."

"Did you follow me to Baker?"

"No, but I parked near there this morning and watched the trucks roll out with a pair of binoculars, not even sure what I was looking for. I went back again tonight, and saw your Jeep arrive, and then all of a sudden I saw you tear out of there and hop into that car. And a minute later Blaine comes barreling out and jumps in *his*, heads off in a different direction. It took me a minute to catch up to you guys, but I finally saw the Audi turn off the road. I knew you must be in some kind of trouble."

"I can't thank you enough, Chief. If you hadn't come, I might be dead by now."

"I'm just glad you called me last night." There was little joy in his tone, and I suspected that he was beating himself up. If he'd been able to learn the truth about Baker when he'd snooped around several months ago and reported it to his contacts in law enforcement, Shannon might still be alive.

Before I could say another word, we heard vehicles pulling in behind us and saw the windshield dancing with the reflection of pulsing red and white lights.

Backup was here. I could only make out Riley's silhouette

in her car, but she appeared to have her head in her hands. Cody had taken everyone in, even her.

About thirty minutes later, after the police had assessed the scene and taken a brief statement from me, they drove me to the municipal center to make a fuller statement and to speak with Killian directly. When the sheriff finally arrived, along with a few state police colleagues, he handed me my purse—and a good news bulletin.

"Cody Blaine was apprehended north of here a few minutes ago," Killian said. "It's possible he was making his way to the Canadian border."

I felt a rush of relief, but also a wave of sadness. Those poor Blaine kids. No amount of resiliency would help them handle what life had dealt to them.

"And what about this guy Sean? I told the police about him at the tennis club."

"Yes, we're on that. Now why don't you start from the beginning about what happened tonight."

I went through the story again for Killian. He seemed warmer than he had the first time I'd sat across from him, but I could sense he was irritated by my having taken matters into my own hands. He and the others pelleted me with questions, trying to be sure they had everything Riley had revealed to me.

When I'd finally been wrung dry of answers, Killian leaned back in his tan metal chair and exhaled deeply.

"You realize, don't you, that you put yourself in tremendous danger tonight? And as far as you knew, you were thwarting our own efforts."

"I know, I see that. But I'd only driven there with a quick question about Tom Nolan and then everything unfolded so quickly. . . . Had you begun to figure it out?"

"We had our suspicions. Blaine was one of the people Alice Hatfield had called the day she died."

"Yeah, I feel dumb about that now. He told me she'd just called him with a question about Sunset Bay. And I was not initially suspicious of that."

"He had a lot of people fooled, Bailey. I wouldn't take it personally."

"Do you have any idea how Alice put it all together? She knew—most likely from reading the same article I did—that Cody had an army friend who'd come from the area. I wonder how she figured out his name."

"One of the other calls she made on Sunday was to a contact of hers with the county veterans' affairs office. She asked him for the names of area men who'd served in Afghanistan just under ten years ago, and even though it was Sunday, he went through digital records for her and tracked down a list of names. He supplied us with that list, but since she'd never mentioned any suspicions to him, we assumed she simply wanted to interview people who served with Blaine."

"She obviously saw Dirk's name on the list and knew it was significant for some reason—and probably mentioned the guy to Blaine."

"And then he figured she was close."

Killian made a movement to suggest we were done.

"Once you sign your statement, you're free to leave. We'll have someone drop you off at your vehicle."

"Are you going to call Ben Hatfield?" I asked as he started to rise.

"Yes. Please leave that to us."

When I set foot in the Courtyard an hour later, the lobby and bar were both buzzing with press who'd clearly heard the news and were waiting for updates. Under other circumstances I might have wanted to revel in the moment, but I had a big post to churn out, and I wasn't in the mood. Besides, now that I had my phone in hand, I could see that I still hadn't heard from Beau. And it was making me nuts.

As soon as I was in my room I ordered food to pick up later from the café, updated Dodson via email, and dashed off my post. Due to mental fatigue, it was hardly my finest hour prosewise, but considering the news I was sharing, it didn't matter much. Within minutes Dodson shot me an email congratulating me on my efforts.

A little while later, having picked up my meal, I sat at the desk, my mind churning. Once Alice had the list of names from the veterans' office, she must have searched to see if one of them surfaced anyplace else. I popped open my laptop and began scrolling one more time through every article the *Post Star* had run about the campers. And then there it was, buried deep in a follow-up story about the disappearance: a quote from a guy named Dirk Hagen. Somehow Alice's colleague Luke Orsini had learned that Hagen, a resident of Fort Ann, had been in Muller's the night Page and Amy vanished and had cornered him for a quote.

"Those girls? They left around seven, I'd say," were Hagen's words. Alice must have realized that Hagen had been involved in the murders and had shared his story with Cody Blaine.

I immediately called Killian, alerting him to my discovery. He explained that they'd figured this out, too, having found Dirk on the list of veterans from Fort Ann. He also shared that a search of Cody's car had turned up a voice adapter.

So it *was* the killer who'd called me.

I thanked him and said good night. Bone-tired, but still reeling, I flopped down on the bed, phone in hand, and stared at the dull white ceiling. Cody had been captured, the police were looking for Sean-whatever-the-monster's-name-was, the pieces of truth were all coming together, and yet I still felt heavy with residual dread. If Blaine had caught up to me at Baker or arrived at the tennis and swim club before Coulter had, he would have killed me. With a gun. Or even his bare hands, as he'd done to Shannon and Alice.

The phone pinged in my hand.

I brought it to eye level, expecting to see a text from another reporter eager for details. But it was Beau. I moaned in relief.

Bailey, so sorry. On board flight home. Someone on
crew was hit by car. Ok now but nightmare.

Can you talk?

Making me turn off phone. Tomorrow. Love you.

Thank God. Knowing finally that Beau was okay and
hadn't been abducted by a resurrected arm of the Cali cartel, I
succumbed to the sleep of the dead. When I woke shortly before
six, I was thrilled to see another text from Beau announcing that
he'd landed safely at JFK and would call me later.

After racing through media coverage of the case and
answering a few of the emails that had blown up my phone,
I ate breakfast in the hotel café, grateful to be in public
without having to constantly check over my shoulder.

At nine Dodson called me, over the moon about both my
efforts and the traffic for last night's post, and determined for
me to tape another video with Keith. Natch, he wanted to
shoot on the road in front of Baker Beverage.

Keith arrived several hours later. Returning to that location didn't pack the same emotional wallop for me as being
back at Alice's house, but it still made my stomach flip. I
couldn't forget the rage in Cody's eyes, and running so hard
for my life that I'd thought my lungs would burst.

As soon as Keith and I finished, I took my phone off
silent and was surprised to see a missed call from Kelly.

"I'd like to talk in person," she said soberly when I reached
her. "Do you have time today?"

"Of course. Where and when?"

"At my house, as soon as possible. Come around to the porch on the back."

The only hitch: I would have to return to the hotel to retrieve my car, and then drive all the way back in this direction to meet with her.

"Do you have Uber around here?" I asked.

"What? Uh, yes."

"Okay, I'll be there in ten."

I had Keith drop me off at the Claiborne house instead of the hotel, and I made my way around the side of the house, shuffling through the first drop of dried leaves from a big maple in the yard. Kelly was where she'd promised to be—the screened porch, leaning into a white wicker couch with lightly faded floral cushions.

"Thanks for coming," Kelly said. She rose in greeting and indicated with an outreached arm that I should take the matching chair across from her. She was wearing a pair of dark jeans and the burgundy turtleneck I'd seen her in two days ago. "I hear I owe you another thank-you."

"You don't owe me anything, Kelly. I'm just glad we finally know the truth now."

She nodded listlessly in response.

I settled onto the chair. "I'm curious. When your sister went missing, was your first instinct that Cody might be responsible?"

"Yes and no. The whole vanishing-into-thin-air thing seemed improbable to me, but I hadn't noticed any red flags when it came to the marriage. Though I never warmed up to Cody, he seemed crazy about my sister, and unlike my loser husband, he reportedly kept it in his pants. Besides, once the other bodies were discovered, it let him off the hook. The fucking monster."

"My sentiments exactly."

"There's another reason I called, though, something I need to ask you about." I noticed her swallow hard. "Killian said that Shannon learned about the drugs because she went to work at Baker and started poking around there. Is that true?"

"According to Riley, yes. Shannon was helping with marketing initiatives. Quote, 'restarting her career.' You weren't aware your sister was working there again?"

"One of her kids said something to me about her helping Daddy, and when I quizzed Shannon, she said she was lending a hand now and then. I figured it had to do with people on the administrative staff taking summer vacations."

"She gave the same impression to J.J. I've been mulling it over and my guess is that she didn't want to draw attention to what she was really up to. Maybe she *would* have restarted her career one day, but in this case it was mostly a front, I think, for getting in the door again at Baker."

"So she could snoop?"

"Right. She probably knew if she offered to assist with paperwork or man the phones, Cody would have insisted they didn't need the help. I'm sure he didn't want her anywhere near the place. But when she suggested doing marketing work, it was hard for him to refuse."

"And she came across evidence of the drug trafficking?"

"Yes, apparently."

"How?"

"Riley never spelled it out to me, though Killian may be able to extract more from her. I also don't know what aroused Shannon's suspicions to begin with. I mean, she clearly thought something was up at Baker, but I don't know what gave her that idea."

Kelly pressed a fist against her mouth, appearing stricken. More so, I realized, than she had at the press conference the day after Shannon's body had been identified.

"What is it, Kelly?" I asked. "Do *you* know?"

"I think it was something I said."

I held my breath, no idea what was coming next.

"It was the day after Christmas, right before Shannon and her family were leaving for Belize on vacation. Oh, sure, they had the condo in the Keys but they wanted an *adventure* this time. I made some fairly cutting comments to Shannon about how the Blaines seemed to be the beneficiaries of far more fruits from Baker Beverage than the rest of the family, particularly at a time when a competitor was eating our lunch. Shannon defended Cody, pointing out, per usual, that he also pulled down a salary as president, but—"

The fist was back against her mouth, smothering a sob this time.

"Are you thinking your comment began to weigh on her? And she decided to investigate."

"Sure sounds that way. I should have looked into it myself or hired someone to do it. I was too busy trying to figure out who my husband was banging."

"You can't blame yourself, Kelly. Sooner or later, Shannon would have probably wondered why they were living so large and started prying without that prompt from you."

"You think he killed her simply because she found out the truth?"

"No, not simply that. Riley said Cody tried to convince Shannon to stay quiet, and if she had, he wouldn't have hurt her. But he realized she was going to turn him in. It must have been an agonizing decision for her, and it's probably why she started going to mass again. She was searching for spiritual guidance."

"She would *never* have tolerated Cody trafficking in drugs."

"Because of your cousin?"

"That but also because of my father and what he built. Man, I can't believe any of this. And those poor little kids."

"Are you going to take them?"

"Yes. Though I'll be raising them on my own. Doug and I are over."

She collapsed against the back cushion, and I sensed that she needed time alone. She might not have been close to her sister—and she may have always envied her—but she had hardly wished her harm. I said goodbye softly and saw myself out.

When I reached the hotel in an Uber, it was late afternoon, and I kept my eyes lowered as I trudged through the lobby, loathe to the idea of chatting.

Still, there was no way to miss him. His face was like a beacon—the hawkish nose, those mysterious dark brown eyes taking me in from his perch on the orange sectional. *Beau Regan.*

"Omigod," I said, rushing toward him. "Wait, what are you doing here?"

"I know, sneaky of me. I couldn't wait any longer to see you, so I drove up as soon as I'd dumped the equipment at my studio."

I kissed him and then collapsed into a hug. It was intoxicating to feel his arms around me and take in the musky scent of his cologne.

"I've been so worried about you," I murmured into his sweater.

"I'm really sorry. It was all a bit of a nightmare down there."

"Why don't we go upstairs and talk?"

As soon as we were in the room, we flopped on the bed, and I tucked my head into the crook of Beau's shoulder.

"I read your last couple of posts in the cab from the airport early this morning," he said. "Any major developments since then?"

"A few, but you first. What the hell happened down there?"

The good news, it turned out, was that Beau had managed to shoot almost everything he'd been commissioned to include in the documentary, and even a bit extra for color. But the day before they were going to wrap, a crew member was hit by a car, and Beau had to negotiate the best medical care while miles away from a decent-seeming hospital. And the cell service had sucked, of course. Beau had spent hours with the guy at the hospital and then taken a torturous bus ride back to Bogotá.

Eventually I sensed that the subject was exhausting him, plus, he was clearly eager to hear more about my situation. I relayed my conversation with Kelly, as well as the details Killian had discouraged me from including in my posts.

"Okay, just so I have it straight," Beau said. "As of this moment, Sean, the guy who apparently murdered the two girls, hasn't been located."

"Right, though now that the cops have Dirk Hagen's name, they can probably figure out who he is and *where* he is."

"And this Sean guy must have a religious fixation, right?"

"It looks that way, though maybe it had less to do with an experience during his upbringing than the crazy state his brain was in when he was high on drugs. Clearly Dirk described the wounds to Cody and he replicated them on Shannon's body so there'd be a connection."

"Do you think Cody killed her at home?"

I shrugged, still unsure.

"I'm torn about that. In one sense it might have seemed safer to murder her at home, but a neighbor could have reported seeing his car pull into the driveway again. And Shannon might have been able to put up a decent fight on her own turf. So I'm thinking he drove around till he found her jogging on a deserted stretch of road and made up an excuse for why she needed to come with him—like one of the kids was in the ER. And he strangled her right in the car."

"But would he have made the stigmata marks there, too?"

"No, it would have left blood in the car. Plus, he's probably smart enough to know that you only have a short window before a body leaves a scent that a cadaver dog can pick up. I bet he drove her body to Sunset Bay as fast as possible and cut her before putting her body in the contractor bag."

"Is he the one who called you?"

"Well, they found a voice adapter on him. I don't think you need those for bottling beer and soda."

"Why do you think he picked you to call and drop the clue to?"

"That was a fluke, I'd say. He wanted the bodies found fairly soon so people would blame a serial killer. He must have spotted me talking to the deacon and realized that by calling me and referencing Shannon's Catholicism, he could make the religious angle even stronger."

"So Shannon's going back to church didn't really play a role in everything, right?"

"Not directly. I pursued that line pretty aggressively, but I guess you could say my theory was right church/wrong pew, if you'll excuse the expression. Shannon didn't cross paths with the killer at church, as I'd originally speculated, but I bet she started going to mass again because she'd discovered her husband was a criminal and found herself in a terrible moral dilemma."

I sat up, scooted to the edge of the bed, and kicked off my boots.

"You want a water?" I asked.

"Sure."

As I grabbed us each a bottle, I could feel Beau's eyes on

me, watching intently. Maybe after days apart, he found me fetching in a top that I'd worn three times in a row without washing, though I suspected there was something else on his mind.

"Last night must have been terrifying for you, Bailey," he said finally. "You going to cough up more details?"

"Sure," I said, plopping on the edge of the bed. I fleshed out the situation for him, without obfuscation. More than once a little voice in my head whispered that because of the red-hot—and to some degree, self-engendered—danger I'd placed myself in, I was going to badly rock the delicate truce we'd established about my job.

When I was finished, Beau sat up himself and put an arm around me.

"I'm so glad you're okay."

"And?"

"You mean, am I upset?"

"Yeah."

"I admit, this is tough to hear. But I made a promise to not rag on you about your job—and I'm trying to honor it. Besides, I'm hoping for a conjugal visit, and I don't want to do anything to piss you off."

I smiled. "Request for conjugal visit accepted. And, Beau, I really appreciate your understanding. More so now than ever. When I didn't hear from you for so long, it freaked me out a little, and I had a taste of what you must go through when I'm working on a story."

"Ahh, my plan worked."

"And if it's any consolation, I learned from last night. I should have handled a few things differently."

We ended up eating dinner south of Lake George, at a restaurant that was basically a huge log cabin, with not another reporter in sight. Some of my tension and angst melted away, and I managed to leave all the crap behind me until I fell asleep in Beau's arms that evening.

Beau had to leave by nine the next morning, but I was staying—for the arraignments of Cody, Riley, and her husband, and of course, for Alice's service. And hopefully for the return of a man named Sean Castle, last seen living in Vermont. The authorities had determined that he was the person Dirk had referenced and they were now scouring New England for him. Dodson and I had agreed that I'd depart for the city on Friday but return down the line if necessary.

"You okay?" Beau asked over breakfast at the hotel.

"What do you mean?" But I realized I'd been poking at my eggs and my mood was turning glum again.

"You seem out of sorts."

"I am, I guess. It's been a lot to process."

"Focus on getting back to New York. I'll plan something fun for Friday night."

As soon as he pulled out of the parking lot, however, I could feel myself sinking back into a nasty funk.

One of the things gnawing at me was the mistakes I'd made. As I'd confessed to Killian, it was dumb of me to buy

Cody's disclosure about Alice's call to him. I should have been suspicious of *anyone* Alice had spoken to that day.

And then there was my stupid decision to kick the hornet's nest at Baker Beverage. Once I'd read Cody's comment about his army pal and realized that the implications could be serious, I should have shut the fuck up and, as Alice would have said, skedaddled out of there, instead of pricking and pushing in order to see where it could lead. Was Beau right last summer when he'd said I put myself in unnecessary danger?

Doubts and regrets often surfaced for me after a story was done—over details I'd missed, comments I hadn't considered hard enough. And nearly every crime story I covered served up its own emotional hangover—the result of contemplating senseless deaths, children's lives overturned, and on and on. But this funk just seemed to be, well, funkier than some of the others I'd experienced.

Had I begun to have misgivings about my job, I wondered, and what I wanted out of life? Were those misgivings even at the heart of my hesitancy about marrying again?

Back in the hotel, I wandered to a table in the café, one with a view of the lake, and ordered a cappuccino. No, I told myself, gazing at that dazzling blue, I loved what I did. And I loved Beau. My current morose mood could surely be explained by the fact that this was the first time while on assignment that I'd lost someone I considered a friend.

Watching a boat zip across the lake, I thought back to what Alice had said over dinner when I'd asked her if the job ever got to her. Yes, sometimes, she'd replied. But when that happened, she fished, and by relishing the spaces between each catch—as my father had the spaces between each bird sighting—she regained her equanimity.

That's what I'd do then. Not fish. Never. But back in New York this weekend, after I'd dumped my dirty clothes in the wash and Skyped with my mom, I'd take my father's old binoculars to Central Park and tramp through the wooded areas, scouting for cedar waxwings and yellow-bellied sapsuckers. Sometimes I'd simply drop onto a rock and do nothing but relish the spaces between birds.

Then I'd go home and work on my next book and wait for *Crime Beat* to call again and ask me to take an assignment that hopefully, in Dodson Crowe's words, would have "a few nice layers." And I'd say yes. Because no matter how sad those stories could be, there was always the pulse-pounding rush that came from peeling all the layers away.

ACKNOWLEDGMENTS

F OR THE MOST PART, BEING AN AUTHOR IS AN INCREDIBLY solitary activity, and yet at some point, in order for a book to succeed, you have to bring others into the mix—for research, editing, designing, promotion, and selling the final product. This is my chance to tell those people how grateful I am for their efforts.

First and foremost, I want to thank everyone who helped me with the research on *Such a Perfect Wife*, including Tim Dees, retired police officer and occasional writer and trainer; Will Valenza, Glens Falls Police Department, retired; Lauren Anderson, retired FBI executive; Barbara Butcher, consultant for forensic and medicolegal investigations; Nick Murphy; Kathleen Plalen Tomaselli, investigative reporter and author.

I also want to thank my brothers Mike White, Rick White, and Steve White for helping me with fact-checking in the Lake George area (a nice excuse to spend time with you, too!). And a shout-out to friend Beverly Place, whom I forgot to thank for helping me come up with the title for the *last* Bailey Weggins mystery, *Even If It Kills Her*.

Next, I want to express my incredible gratitude to not one editor but two: Laura Brown, for shepherding this book through its early stages (before she moved to another division at HarperCollins), and my incredible *new* editor, Emily Griffin, who took over and offered such fantastic guidance.

Thank you, too, to others at Harper Perennial, who are such a joy to work with: Amy Baker, VP and associate publisher; Mary Sasso, marketing director; Theresa Dooley, senior publicist; Robin Bilardello, art director; and to James Iacobelli for designing the cover, which I couldn't be happier with.

I'd like to thank my wonderful agent, Sandy Dijkstra, and her team for all their efforts. We've been together from the beginning, and I feel very, very lucky to have the Dijkstra Agency in my life.

Finally, my gratitude goes out to my terrific home team: Isabel DaSilva, social media director; and Laura Nicolassy, my web editor. You ladies are my rock.

Oh wait, I can't sign off without thanking all the Bailey Weggins fans who write me regularly and share their enthusiasm for this series. I so appreciate your support. It means the world to me.

ALSO BY KATE WHITE

EVEN IF IT KILLS HER • A Bailey Weggins Mystery
Available in Paperback, Large Print, and eBook
"Bailey is a smart, sexy sleuth, and her exploits make for thoroughly entertaining reading." —*Booklist*

THE SECRETS YOU KEEP • A Novel
Available in Paperback, Large Print, Digital Audio, and eBook
"Kept me up way past my bedtime, anxiously turning the pages."
—Jessica Knoll, *New York Times* Bestselling Author

THE WRONG MAN • A Novel
Available in Paperback, Large Print, and eBook
"White manages to pull off writing another edge-of-your seat thriller, which keeps the reader enthralled to the very end." —*RT Book Reviews*

EYES ON YOU • A Novel
Available in Paperback, Large Print, Digital Audio, and eBook
"White's most compelling and snappiest stand-alone yet." —*Booklist*

SO PRETTY IT HURTS • A Bailey Weggins Mystery
Available in Paperback, Large Print, Digital Audio, and eBook
"Lives up to the precedent that Kate White has set with her previous Bailey Weggins mysteries and doesn't fail to delight." —*Bookreporter*

THE SIXES • A Novel
Available in Paperback, Large Print, Digital Audio, and eBook
"A terrifying psychological thriller that takes 'mean girls' to a whole new level of creepy." —Harlan Coben, *New York Times* bestselling author

HUSH • A Novel
Available in Paperback, Digital Audio, and eBook
"Dark, sexy, and smart.... A stunningly good read."
—Linda Fairstein, *New York Times* Bestselling Author

www.KateWhite.com

f /KateWhiteAuthor

🐦 @katemwhite

📷 @katewhite_author